AT THE DYING OF THE YEAR

The Richard Nottingham Historical Series
by Chris Nickson

THE BROKEN TOKEN
COLD CRUEL WINTER *
THE CONSTANT LOVERS *
COME THE FEAR *
AT THE DYING OF THE YEAR *

* available from Severn House

AT THE DYING
OF THE YEAR

A Richard Nottingham Book

Chris Nickson

This first world edition published 2013
in Great Britain and the USA by
Crème de la Crime, an imprint of
SEVERN HOUSE PUBLISHERS LTD of
9–15 High Street, Sutton, Surrey, England, SM1 1DF..

Copyright © 2013 by Chris Nickson.

British Library Cataloguing in Publication Data

Nickson, Chris.
At the dying of the year. – (The Richard Nottingham
historical series)
1. Nottingham, Richard (Fictitious character)–Fiction.
2. Murder–Investigation–England–Leeds–Fiction.
3. Leeds (England)–History–18th century–Fiction.
4. Detective and mystery stories.
I. Title II. Series
823.9'2-dc23

ISBN-13: 978-1-78029-042-3 (cased)

All Severn House titles are printed on acid-free paper.

Severn House Publishers support The Forest Stewardship Council [FSC],
the leading international forest certification organisation. All our titles that
are printed on Greenpeace-approved FSC-certified paper carry the FSC logo.

| MIX |
| Paper from |
| responsible sources |
| FSC® C018575 |

Typeset by Palimpsest Book Production Ltd.,
Falkirk, Stirlingshire, Scotland.
Printed and bound in Great Britain by
MPG Books Ltd., Bodmin, Cornwall.

For August, the best cat

Oh my soul, my soul, I'm bound for to rest
In the arms of the angel Gabriel

Traditional campmeeting song

'For storms will rage and oceans roar, when Gabriel stands on
sea and shore, and as he blows his wondrous horn, old worlds
die and new be born.'

Prophecy of Mother Shipton

'Gabriel, thou hadst in Heaven the esteem of wise;
And such I held thee; but this question asked
Puts me in doubt. Lives there who loves his pain?'

John Milton, Paradise Lost

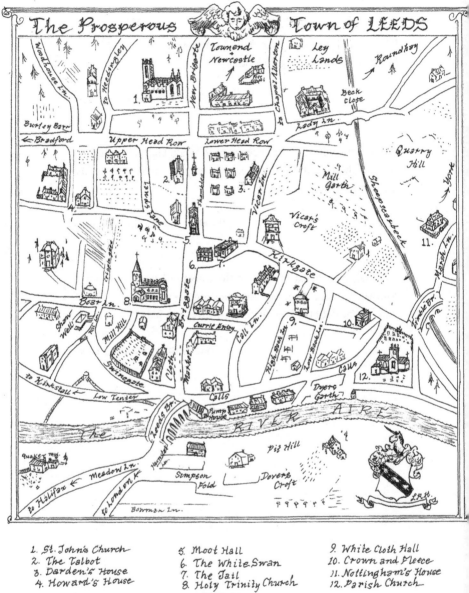

The Prosperous Town of LEEDS

1. St. John's Church
2. The Talbot
3. Darden's House
4. Howard's House
5. Moot Hall
6. The White Swan
7. The Jail
8. Holy Trinity Church
   ∗ Bell Pits
9. White Cloth Hall
10. Crown and Fleece
11. Nottingham's House
12. Parish Church

ONE

R ichard Nottingham exhaled slowly as his boot heels clattered over Timble Bridge, feeling the wool of his breeches rasp against his thighs as he moved. Partway across he stopped to rest for a moment, leaning heavily on the silver-topped stick and listening to the birds singing for the dawn. His breath bloomed in the November air and he pulled the greatcoat collar higher.

Five months had passed since he'd last walked this way to work. Five months since the knife sliced into his belly. For a week he'd drifted in and out of the world, living in a place made of furious heat and bitter chills, the pain always there, powerful enough to fill every thought, every moment. Few believed he'd survive.

Finally the fever burned out of his system and he woke, the daylight so bright it hurt his eyes, his wife Mary sitting by the bed, holding his hand. He'd live, the apothecary announced after examining him, although the healing would take a long time.

The summer of 1733 was warm, sticky, full of the drowsy scent of wildflowers in the fields as he began to walk again, shuffling like an old man. At first he could only manage a few yards before he was exhausted, forced to stop, frustrated by his body and its weakness. Strength returned gradually, at its own dismal pace. He went further, first to the bridge, then into the city, a little more distance each day.

And now he was back to work. Richard Nottingham was Constable of the City of Leeds once more.

He stood at the bottom of Kirkgate, relishing the sight of early smoke rising from chimneys. The thick smells of the place, the shit and piss, the smoke and the stink, rushed into him like perfume, hearing the sounds of voices and the rumble of early carts along the street. His gaze crossed to the Parish Church, eyes picking out the grave of his older daughter, Rose and resting there for a moment, thinking how close he'd come to joining her in the earth.

He pushed the door open and walked into the jail, feeling fear and relief in equal measures. Simply being here seemed like a victory over all the doubts and fears he'd had in the last months. He gazed around the room, as familiar to him as home, and smiled.

John Sedgwick sat at the desk, looking as if he belonged there. Then he glanced up and his face broke into a wide grin. 'Welcome back, boss,' he said, standing quickly and moving aside. For almost half a year he'd been the deputy who'd worked as Constable, with all the responsibility of the job and none of the pay. Now he'd be back where he'd been before. Nottingham tried to read the expression in his eyes.

'Hello, John,' he said, pleasure filling his voice. 'I see it hasn't changed at all.'

'We kept it just this way for you.'

He winced as he lowered himself on to the chair, feeling the sharp twinge of pain shooting from the scar right through his stomach. All because of a stupid, simple mistake; he'd known better for so many years. He'd let down his guard and for one second forgotten everything he'd been taught. That was all it had taken for the man to draw the knife from his boot and cut him open.

A noise came from the cells and he raised his eyebrows questioningly.

'Rob's sweeping them out,' the deputy explained. 'No one in there at the moment.'

Soon enough Rob Lister appeared with a broom, standing straight as he saw the Constable.

'Good to see you back, boss.' He was a young man, his red hair flying wild no matter what he tried to do with it, eyes bright, eager and ready to work. His was a familiar face; he seemed to spend all his free time at Nottingham's house courting the Constable's younger daughter, Emily.

'So what do we have, John?'

'Not too much at the moment. Two men died fighting each other a couple of nights back.'

'At the Talbot?' he asked, sure he knew the answer.

'Aye, where else?' Sedgwick answered with a dark grimace. 'Apart from that there's just a few small thefts, someone shot himself.' He poured a cup of ale from the mug on the desk and passed it over. 'You look like you need it.'

The Constable drank gratefully. He was thirsty, his body ached, and even the small effort of walking from home had drained him. He sat back and brushed the fringe off his forehead.

'You take the thefts,' he said. 'Rob, go and ask around about the fight, see what you can find out before you go home.'

'Yes, boss.' Lister leant the besom against the wall, stretched and yawned exaggeratedly.

'Get on with you,' the deputy laughed. 'Anyone would think you were shy to meet a little honest work.'

'He'd probably rather meet Emily,' Nottingham said with a sly smile. Rob shook his head at the two of them and left.

'He's turning out well,' Sedgwick said thoughtfully. 'Twice during the summer he solved things that I couldn't see.'

'He's bright,' the Constable agreed. 'Don't worry, though, he can't replace you. Have you finished the daily report?'

The deputy pulled it from the top of a pile of papers. The writing was childlike and uneven, but he'd laid everything out clearly enough and Nottingham nodded his approval. 'Good. Now you get busy on those thefts.'

'Yes, boss.' Sedgwick grinned again. He paused, then added, 'It feels right to have you back.'

'It feels right to be back,' Nottingham said with satisfaction. 'Where I should be.'

He belonged in this place; it was part of him. During the endless summer Mary had begged him to retire. She wanted him whole, and with her. After so long when work had come first she wanted her own good years with him; she'd never put it like that, but he knew. And the city had been fair. They'd offered him a small pension and the house on Marsh Lane that had come with the job. But he'd known he could never give her the thing she craved more than all else. He'd seen the fear fly across Mary's face as he'd left the house that morning, the worry he might never return.

He wasn't ready yet to do nothing, though, to watch the days blur endlessly one into the other, to sit and see the seasons change until he died. He needed this. John had come often enough to ask for his opinion and advice on things, and Rob had told him everything that was happening. But it wasn't the same as being involved himself. He'd chafed for the spark of the hunt.

He pushed himself up from the desk, feeling every single one of his years and folded the report into the pocket of his coat. Leaning on the stick he walked up Briggate, exchanging greetings with people, stopping to talk, to smile at the well-wishers and welcome the opportunity to rest.

The Moot Hall stood firm and tall in the middle of the street, a carefully impressive symbol of power, an island that forced people and carts to either side of the road. The Constable took the stairs slowly, then felt his old boots sink deep into the thick Turkey carpet of the polished wood corridor. The smell was different, cleaner and sharper, the warm, protective scent of money.

It would be the first time he'd met William Fenton since the man had become mayor in September. He'd sent a note out to the house a few weeks before with wishes for a speedy recovery, but hadn't visited himself.

A desk sat outside the office, blocking the way like a guard; a clerk glanced up as he approached. He was a young man, neatly groomed in a dark coat and brilliant white stock, with an inquiring smile that showed clean, even teeth.

'Yes, sir?' he asked.

'I have the daily report from the jail for the mayor.'

'If you leave it with me I'll pass it to him.'

Nottingham looked down at him, smiled and said mildly, 'You don't know who I am, do you, lad?'

The clerk shook his head.

'I'm the Constable here. I'm just back to work. I've always met with the mayors every morning.'

The man shifted on his seat and looked embarrassed. 'I'm sorry, sir, I didn't know. Mr Fenton's changed things. He only sees people by appointment.'

'I see,' Nottingham said slowly.

'Mr Sedgwick just gave me the report every day.'

'What's your name?'

'Martin Cobb, sir.'

He took the paper from his pocket and unfolded it. 'Well, Martin, if you'd see this reaches the mayor, with my compliments.'

'I will. And I'm sorry for not knowing who you were, sir.'

He left, feeling the long sting of humiliation. In all his years as Constable, none of the mayors had refused to see him. It didn't bode for a good return. He set his mouth and walked out on to Briggate.

The street was busy, people squeezing and pushing their way past each other with the dark scent of unwashed bodies, carters urging their horses on, wagon wheels creaking under the heavy loads, the fierce smell of horse sweat, then the hard blood tang from the meat hanging in the butchers' shops on the Shambles. He stood, taking it all in. This was the Leeds he loved.

Rob knew the Talbot well. He'd been here too many times in the last year, breaking up fights or pursuing felons. He pushed open the door of the inn and entered, the scent of stale beer and tobacco on the air. The conversation of the few morning drinkers halted as they saw him.

The door leading to the whores' rooms upstairs was closed, the other door to the cockfighting pit bolted and barred. Bell the landlord was kneeling to tap a new barrel of ale; he glanced up, spat on to the stone floor and looked away again.

'The two men who died the other night,' Rob began.

'It were outside.' The man didn't even bother to turn his head, keeping his back to Lister. 'Nowt to do wi' me.'

'Had they been drinking in here?'

''Appen,' he answered. 'We were busy.'

'They'd been seen in here,' Rob told him.

'If you know, why's tha' asking me?' Bell stood up slowly, broader and taller than the Constable's man, his arms thick with muscle, a worn leather apron tight over the hard bulge of his belly. Several days' growth of stubble covered his cheeks. He rested large, scarred hands on the trestle and stared. 'I've said all I'm going to say to you. So you can piss off now, and next time your master can come himself and not send his lapdog.'

Rob eyed him, showing nothing, then slowly turned on his heel and left. Bell had meant to humiliate him; he wasn't the first and he wouldn't be the last. But the words wounded a little less each time. He knew he was young, that they saw him as easy prey, untested and with no power. That was changing. He loved this work and he knew he had a talent for it. He'd learned from Sedgwick and from the boss, and the lessons would continue for a long time yet. He sighed slowly and tried not to yawn.

His job was looking after the nights, supervising the men who kept Leeds safe during the darkness. For all the months the Constable had been gone, he and the deputy had been stretched tight, working long hours, every day of God's week, always exhausted.

He'd ask a few more questions then he'd go to his room and sleep. Later, before work, he'd meet Emily and walk out to the house on Marsh Lane to eat his supper. It was more than a free meal, it was chance to spend time with her. For too long it had felt as if they'd been snatching at moments and minutes together.

Along the Calls he searched for the right house. One of the dead men had lived here, leaving a widow and three children behind him; with luck, the woman would be able to tell him something. He was still looking for the place when he heard a shout and turned. A man was running quickly towards him, stripped to shirt and breeches, his face and hands covered in dirt, the bright light of fear in his eyes.

'You the lad who works with the Constable?' he asked. Rob nodded. 'You'd better come, then. It's the bell pits.' The man jerked his thumb vaguely in the direction of the White Cloth Hall then moved away, his stride fast and jerky.

Lister was pushed to keep pace with the man as they headed along Low Back Passage. 'What is it?' he asked. 'What's in the pit?'

But the man just shook his head. 'Tha'll see soon enough.'

Rob knew about the bell pits; everyone in Leeds did. They were holes that extended just a few feet into the ground, opening into chambers ten or twelve feet across and shaped liked the bells that gave them their names; places where folk gathered scraps of coal for their fires. They'd existed for generations, all over the city, for so long that no one really knew who'd first dug them. He'd never been in one, although the schoolboys often dared each other to go down into the dry warmth. Three of them lay close together, no more than twenty feet apart, each separate from the other, along the path that led from Kirkgate to the White Cloth Hall, mounds of dark earth next to each one. A group of workmen were passing a flagon of ale around, all of them silent, their faces serious.

'Down there.' The man pointed at one of the pits, where a ladder protruded above the lip. Rob glanced at him questioningly, but the man looked away, unwilling to meet his eyes. He gazed at the other men, but none of them would offer him more than a sad stare.

Curious, he placed his boots on the wooden rungs, testing the weight, and began to climb down. He'd barely descended a yard before he stopped, swallowing hard as he smelled it. Something was dead down here, the thick, cloying smell of decay heavy in the heat all around him. He drew a breath through his mouth and went deeper into the pit.

At the bottom, no more than ten feet below the surface, he felt the rough, dry earth under his soles. He was already sweating from the still heat. A thin tunnel of light came down the hole, spilling into a small circle on the ground, deep shadows and pitch darkness reaching beyond. He retched hard, unable to keep the bile down, pulled a handkerchief from his breeches and clamped it over his face and mouth.

It didn't help. He bent over, vomiting again and coughing until there was only a thin trickle of spittle trailing from his lips. The stench of death was so strong he felt he could touch it.

Just at the edge of the gloom he could make out the shape of feet. Six of them, bare, dirty soles showing, three different sizes. He moved two paces closer, his eyes watering. The legs were small, thin. They were children.

TWO

He hurried back up the ladder, falling on his knees at the top and gulping down the fresh air. His legs buckled at he tried to stand, and for a moment he was forced to hold on to someone's arm. The man handed him the jug and he drank deep, swilling the ale around his mouth before spitting out the taste of the pit.

'Bad,' was the only thing the man said.

Rob didn't reply. He didn't own the words for what he'd seen. 'Send someone for Mr Brogden, the coroner,' he said, his voice little more than a hoarse croak. 'I'll bring some men to take the bodies out.'

He marched purposefully up Kirkgate, trying to clear the thoughts and images from his head. For all he knew there were more children down there, hidden by the darkness. He ran a hand through his hair, the stink of the dead clinging fast to his clothes.

The Constable looked up from the desk when the door opened, suddenly alert as he saw Lister's expression.

'Christ, lad, what is it? I thought you'd gone home.' He poured a cup of ale and passed it over. 'Drink that.'

Rob sat, trying to steady the mug in his hand, framing how to tell what he'd witnessed.

'The bell pits by the Cloth Hall,' he began slowly, watching Nottingham's eyes intent on his face. 'There are bodies in one of them.'

'Bodies?' he asked sharply. 'More than one?'

Lister nodded. 'Three that I saw.' He paused. 'They were just children, boss,' he said hopelessly. 'One of the men who died at the Talbot had three children.'

The Constable sat up straight. 'You think it's them?'

'I don't know, boss.' Rob swilled a little more ale around his mouth then swallowed, trying to wash the dank taste away.

'Who found them?' Nottingham asked urgently.

'One of the workmen.'

'You've sent for the coroner?'

'Yes.'

'I'll come straight down. Go and find some of the men to help you get the corpses out.'

'Yes, boss.' He stood, ready to leave.

'Rob?' The lad turned. 'If it helps, this is probably as bad as the job will ever be.'

Lister tried to smile, but it was weak and empty.

The Constable remembered the face of every dead child he'd seen since he'd begun the job. They were impossible to forget, each one clear and sharp in his head. Many had gone from hunger, little more than ghosts even before their hearts gave up the battle to keep beating, some from accidents, crushed by carts or lost to the river. Precious few had been murdered, and he thanked God for that, at least.

Some of the workmen were sitting on the grass when he arrived, others stood in a small group. He nodded and asked, 'Has the coroner arrived yet?'

'Gone down there with a candle,' one of the men answered.

When Brogden climbed back out there was dirt on his immaculate coat and he'd vomited on his shoes with their expensive silver buckles. He brought a flask from his waistcoat, fingers shaking so hard he could barely unscrew the top. He took a long drink and saw the Constable.

'What's down there?' Nottingham asked.

The coroner shook his head, as if he couldn't believe what he'd seen. He raised his eyes. 'Three of them,' he replied quietly. 'Someone's killed them. None of them look older than eight.' Tears began to roll down his cheeks and he pawed at them angrily before walking away.

The Constable ran a hand across his mouth. His thoughts raced away from him. Three? It seemed impossible. Unless they did belong to the dead man, how could so many children vanish without anyone noticing? For the love of God, why would anyone want to murder them and leave them that way? He was still standing there thinking when Lister returned with four others, a ragtaggle group who looked more like beggars than Constable's men.

'You'll have to be my eyes down there,' he told Rob. 'I can't use a ladder. Not yet.'

'I'll tell you what I see, boss.'

'Tie linen around your faces,' Nottingham advised them all, 'and try to breathe as little as you can when you're down there.' He looked at them. 'They're children, it's going to be difficult. There are three of them.' He noticed their eyes widen. 'I'm sorry.'

There was nothing more he could do until they started to bring out the bodies. The workmen had left hurriedly, not wanting to see, and he couldn't blame them. They didn't need this haunting their dreams for years.

The first, a boy perhaps six years old, was placed gently and lovingly on the grass by men who kept their faces deliberately expressionless. Then a girl of maybe eight and finally another boy, small and emaciated, who couldn't have been more than three.

They were all naked, covered in coal dust from the pit, grime all across their faces. Their small corpses had bloated and an army of maggots crawled over them, around their wounds, in their mouths and ears and eye sockets. They'd been dead a few days, maybe even longer; nothing to do with the dead man, the Constable decided. He walked between them, studying each one intently before softly saying, 'Cover them up and take them to the jail, please.'

Rob hung back, his face ashen. Nottingham placed a hand lightly on his shoulder.

'Go and find Mr Sedgwick, then get some sleep.' He glanced back at the children. 'We're going to find the bastard who did this.'

They placed the bodies in the cold cell the city used as a mortuary. The Constable cleaned the worst of the pit dirt off them with a cloth and cold water and washed the maggots and blood from their wounds on to the floor. Now they lay on the bunks and the floor, so tiny, beyond help. The warmth of the pit had left their bellies distended. Rats and the Lord knew what had stolen their eyes, so they were sightless in death; chunks of hair were torn away by vermin, skin bitten and torn. Bruises blossomed dull purple all over their legs, arms, chests and faces, and knife cuts marked every part of their bodies. Each one had been stabbed in the heart. They'd suffered before they were given release.

Nottingham left them there and went back to the desk to pour himself a mug of ale. He swilled the liquid around in his mouth, trying to take away the lonely, bitter taste of death before swallowing. He stood, gazing out of the window at the people who passed, their thoughts on business or worries, a pair of women laughing brightly, all of them a world away from what he'd just seen.

Pain rumbled through his belly. He kept still until it passed, then breathed slowly and drank a little more before returning to the cells.

He'd lost count of the bodies he'd seen in this job. Young, old, male, female, the ones who died as he held them and those who'd gone weeks before, with barely any traces left to show they'd ever been alive. He believed he'd seen every evil man could do. But he hadn't.

Very carefully he lifted the girl's arm, as thin and light as a twig, so tiny and fragile in his hand. He could feel the break in the bone and saw the little finger twisted away from the hand. On the smaller boy, so frail he seemed to be more air than flesh, he could see the imprint of fingers around the neck, the child's tiny fists clenched tight in death. The older boy had a broken nose, his face a swollen mass where he'd been hit over and over.

Gazing around the three of them, at the bodies where the ribs showed clear against the skin, the arms and thighs so scrawny he could close his hands around them, he began to understand. He realized who they'd once been and why no one had reported them gone. He closed his eyes and said a short prayer for their souls.

'Boss?'

He hadn't even heard the deputy enter. Nottingham turned slowly to face him.

'Rob told you?'

Sedgwick nodded, his eyes wide. His son James was six, recently started at the charity school, and he had another young baby at home. For a long time he stood silently and the Constable saw a tear begin to trickle down his cheek. He wiped it away in a swift movement. 'How?' he asked.

'Because they're the ones no one cares about.'

'Were they . . .?

'Yes,' he answered simply.

'The boys too?'

'Yes,' he repeated, scared of what might come out if he said more. He knew the signs and they'd been there on all three of the children. Nottingham returned to the office and sat at the desk, steepling his hands under his chin. He closed his eyes but the faces with their empty, lost eyes remained in his mind.

'Fuck,' the deputy said.

'I doubt it mattered to him what sex they were. He probably just wanted to hurt and use and kill.'

Sedgwick kept gazing at the battered faces. 'I'm sure I've seen one of them before.'

'Scavenging at the market?'

'Aye,' he agreed with a nod. 'The bigger lad. He was trying to steal some meat, or something like that. Ran off when I came around. Just another little vagabond.'

'That's what they all were, John,' the Constable said with a long sigh. 'No families, no homes. That's why no one ever noticed they were gone.'

THREE

The Constable drained the cup and went back in to study the bodies in the cells. He'd been like them once, in a life he'd long put away; he understood what their existence had been like. When he was eight his father had discovered that his wife had a lover. He'd thrown her and his son from the house, leaving them with nothing.

With no money and no skills, Nottingham's mother had become a whore, the lady who'd fallen all the way to earth. The boy had been forced to forage, learned to steal, to survive in a new, hard life. After his mother died he'd been alone, with no one in the world. Living meant simply surviving until the next day.

He'd known other children who lived off their wits and their hope. Some would go to sleep at night with empty bellies, and never wake. Others would just vanish, never heard from or seen again. It was the way things were, they all understood that. Time on earth was brief and it was dangerous.

But murder . . .

Why? he wondered. Why would anyone want to do that? And why *three* children?

The deputy was still standing there, unable to avert his eyes.

'All we can do for them now is find their killer,' Nottingham said.

'When we do you'd better keep me away from him,' Sedgwick told him, teeth clenched.

'You can watch him hang, John,' he promised. He sighed and shook his head. 'Go and see the undertaker. We'll get these poor souls in the ground.'

The deputy walked along Vicar Lane, barely noticing anything. His hands were pushed firmly into the pockets of his greatcoat, flexing into hard fists. Inside, anger rose. He wanted to hit something, someone, anything to douse the fire within.

He thought about James, learning so quickly at school, and Isabell, safe at home with Lizzie. What would happen to them if he died? There'd be nothing for them. No house, no food, and any charity would be precious scarce. There was so little that kept them from falling away.

The sign over the door read Thomas Cooper, Undertaker. Inside, the shop was dark and sober, a full, reverent silence pressed between its walls. The owner came out from behind his desk. He was dressed neatly in a freshly sponged black coat, his face shaved that morning by the barber. He relaxed as he recognized the deputy.

'Someone for us, John?' he asked, then as he saw the other man's face his voice became serious. 'What is it?'

'Three,' Sedgwick told him, feeling the word choke in his throat. 'They're all children.'

'Dear God.' Cooper closed his eyes for a moment. 'Where were they?'

'In one of those bell pits by the Cloth Hall.'

'How long?' the undertaker asked thoughtfully.

'Long enough. A week, mebbe a bit more,' the deputy said.

'Make it tonight when there's no one around, Tom. We don't need folk seeing them.' He raised his eyes. 'Please.'

'I promise.'

The deputy offered a small, weak smile. 'Thank you.'

'Leave it with me, John,' Cooper assured him. 'I'll look after them properly.'

The Constable was still thinking when Sedgwick returned. He cocked his head.

'He'll be here after dark.'

'People are going to know about this, John,' Nottingham said thoughtfully. 'Those workers at the pits won't keep quiet.'

'The mayor won't, either.' Sedgwick noted wryly. 'Happen he'll trust you more than me, boss.'

'No, he won't.' He paused. 'All he'll want is someone on the gallows for this. We'd better find whoever did it quickly.'

'How, boss?'

'We need to talk to the children who are out there.' He waved beyond the window. 'They're the ones who might know.' He paused. 'Jesus.' He slammed his fist down on the desk. 'It's a market day tomorrow, there'll be children all over looking for scraps.'

The Constable was silent for a long time. 'I'll go and talk to them,' he said finally. 'I've been away for months, half of them won't even know my face.' He gave a sour grin. 'And like this, walking with a stick, I'm not going to scare them.'

The deputy nodded. He knew how Nottingham had lived when he was young. The boss understood, he'd be able to talk to the children who hovered like spectres around Leeds, the ones who kept their own counsel and their own company. Perhaps he'd be able to gain their trust, to draw out the words from them and learn what they needed.

'We'll find him, boss.'

'I hope so,' he replied with a sigh. 'It's too late for those in there, though.' He let the words hang for a moment. 'And any before them. Have they looked in the other bell pits?'

'I don't know.'

'Find the workmen who were at the Cloth Hall and ask them,' Nottingham ordered briskly. 'I want to know why they were working

on this pit. Anything you can find out. And have them check
the other pits. If there are more children we need to find them.'
   'I will.'
   'I'm going back to tell the mayor before he hears it from
anyone else.'

After an hour Lister gave up on sleep. From the start he'd known
it would be pointless, a fight against fate. Every single one of
the faces burned fiercely in his mind. As soon as he closed his
eyes he was back in the bell pit, seeing the legs and the darkness,
the smell pressing against his face as if it would suffocate him.
   He pushed off the blanket. There were still hours before he could
meet Emily at the dame school where she taught. If he couldn't
rest he might as well do something worthwhile.
   The Constable had just returned to the jail, easing himself
down into the chair behind the desk as Rob arrived.
   'I thought you'd be back, lad,' he said. 'Couldn't sleep?'
   'No.'
   'Keep seeing them, don't you?'
   'Yes,' Rob answered simply, and poured some of the ale. 'What
can I do, boss?'
   Nottingham sat back and thought. 'Mr Sedgwick's gone to the
Cloth Hall to see if there's anyone in the other pits. Go and join
him, then I want the pair of you out asking questions. Talk to
all your sources,' he said, his voice dark and weary. 'I daresay
the whole city knows about this by now. We find the killer
quickly.' He raised an eyebrow. 'The mayor's orders, as if we
bloody needed them.'

The workmen were lowering ladders into two more of the pits. The
deputy stood with his hands on his hips, waiting as the first of
the labourers climbed down, candles in their hands.
   'Nothing yet?' Lister asked.
   'No,' he answered without turning his head. 'Better hope there
isn't, either.' They stood in silence until the first man emerged.
Rob felt his body tense until the man shook his head, then realized
he'd been holding his breath.
   The other pit was empty, too. Sedgwick worked his jaw slowly
and started to walk away.

'What are you thinking?' Lister asked as he caught up to him.

'Nothing. Everything,' he replied in frustration. 'I was scared we'd find more of them.' He turned and Rob could see the fear in his eyes. 'All I could think was it could have been James down there.' His face hardened. 'I'm going to make that bastard scream when we find him.'

'He'll have a trial.'

Sedgwick spat. 'Why waste the money?'

'But—'

'But what?' he said angrily. 'You really believe we're going to be the only ones out there looking? People hate child killers. Even if they don't care about the children themselves. And if they find him . . .' He let the thought twist in the air. Rob understood; he knew how dangerous a mob could be.

'What were the workmen doing at the pits, anyway?'

'They're filling them in. It's going to be a big bloody job and all. But that new mayor thinks the city should look better, especially around the Cloth Hall. We're so important that we have to impress visitors these days,' he said in disgust. 'Those pits have been open since Adam was a lad. You know people still go down there looking for coal in the winter? When it's bitter out there'll be folk scavenging in the pits.' He paused, but before he could say more, the sharp clatter of a drum made him turn his head.

'What's that?' Rob asked.

'I don't know.' They began to walk briskly along the Calls in the direction of the sound. A small, curious crowd had gathered close to the bridge, drawn in by the crisp, urgent beats, eager for any brief excitement in their day.

'Gather round, lads,' boomed a deep voice. 'Aye, and you lasses, too, we like a pretty face.'

Sedgwick relaxed and started to laugh. 'You know who that is?'

'No.'

'It's the recruiting sergeant.' He winked and nudged Lister in the ribs. 'If you've an urge to escape that Emily, now's your chance, lad. Plenty of adventure. You can come back with a fortune, if you believe what they say.'

Rob snorted. 'I think I'll stay here. More chance of staying alive.'

'There'll be some who'll fall for it,' the deputy told him. 'He'll march off in a day or two with a few in tow, you can wager on that. There's no shortage of fools in the world. I was halfway tempted myself once till I came to my senses.'

The audience had quickly thinned. He looked at the soldier with his worn, smiling face, scarlet coat neatly sponged clean and bright, breeches mostly white, boots worn and travel dusty. Next to him the drummer boy, a lad maybe ten years old, had put up his sticks and was glancing idly around. 'Come on,' the deputy continued, 'we're right by the Old King's Head. I don't know about you, but I need to drink the taste of this morning away.'

The Constable watched Tom and his apprentice wrap the bodies in their winding sheets. They'd carry them away once the streets were quiet and few would see, and take them to the pauper's grave out beyond Sheepscar Beck. The children would lie as forgotten in death as they'd been in life.

The murderer had taken his time with them. He'd relished every pain he'd inflicted, drawn it out to make them hurt even more. And they'd be no match for a grown man.

All over Leeds, people would know that three children had been killed. Now he just had to hope no details came out about the way the bodies had been broken, battered and used. If that happened there'd be fury all over the city. That had been the mayor's fear, Leeds out of control. Not that he'd needed to say anything. The Constable had already seen the resolve and the hatred on Sedgwick's face, the hurt in Rob's eyes, and he knew what was in his own heart. They all wanted this man.

He'd hoped for time to ease back into the job, not working so hard or so long at first, but it wasn't going to be that way.

FOUR

Rob leaned against the wall vainly trying to rub the weariness from his eyes. Evening was drawing in, the weather turning colder. He pulled up his collar, wishing he'd worn his greatcoat. The bell rang exactly on the half hour and the girls trooped meekly out of the dame school, each in her blue dress, carrying a bag. Mrs Rains stood in the doorway, making sure they behaved as they walked down the street.

Five more minutes passed before Emily emerged, the old cloak fastened at the neck, her cap slightly askew, letting a few strands of hair fall to her cheek. He smiled and moved forward as he saw her, reaching out to take the basket she was holding.

'How were they?' he asked.

'The same as ever.' She laughed. 'Lovely. Tiring. Frustrating.' Her hand lingered on his, her eyes merry until she noticed his expression. 'What's wrong?' she asked quickly, panic flashing across her face. 'Has something happened to Papa?'

'No, it's nothing like that,' he assured her swiftly. 'It's what we found this morning.'

'What? What was it?'

He explained as they walked, seeing the horror grow on her face. She clutched at his arm, glancing up at him when he went silent, lost in the dark country of his thoughts. 'They were so helpless,' he said finally, seeing them once again in his mind. 'So small.'

'You'll find whoever did it,' Emily averred. 'I know you will. You and Papa and Mr Sedgwick.'

But what if we don't? he wondered. He'd spent the last three hours talking to everyone he could think of, anyone who might be able to help. From Mark the cobbler to the whores on Briggate, no one had known anything useful. He sighed.

They crossed Timble Bridge, strolling up Marsh Lane and into the house.

'Mama?' Emily called, hanging her cloak on a peg by the

door then pulling off the cap and shaking her hair free. When there was no reply she went and looked through to the kitchen. 'That's strange. She's not here.' Her expression brightened and she opened her arms. 'But it means we have the house to ourselves for a while.'

Nottingham didn't even know how long he'd been sitting there thinking, the ghosts of the dead lingering in the cells as darkness started to fall. He could feel them there, pushing against him for attention, tugging at the memories he'd kept locked away in the corners of his mind. The faces he'd known back when he slept in the woods outside the city, wrapping himself in a stolen blanket for any kind of warmth, the hunger in his belly always there, as natural as breathing. Alice, her blue eyes so big and sad she could charm a coin from the women without saying a word. Peter and Martin, a pair of brothers a year or so older than him, who left one night and were never seen again. Or sickly little Thomas, coughing himself to sleep every night, growing thinner and thinner until he seemed fade into death before their eyes. They all came back to visit him, and he heard their voices as if they'd just spoken soft, broken words in his ear.

The door to the jail opened and roused him. Mary was there, gently smiling. The sight took him aback and he wondered if he was dreaming it. She never visited him at the jail.

'I had to come and buy some things,' she explained, lifting the basket on her arm. 'I was worried about you.'

He stood slowly, his face softening as he put his arms around her. The feel of her, solid under his hands, her hair tickling his neck, banished the phantoms from his head.

'You heard?'

He felt the nod of her head against his chest.

'Three of them,' he told her.

Mary pulled back and studied his face. She didn't need to say anything; he knew the question in her eyes.

'I'm weary and heartsick,' he said eventually and gave a small smile. 'Come on, let's go home.'

'Emily and Rob will be in the house by themselves if he met her after school,' she warned.

'He will have done.' The lad met her every afternoon when

she'd finished teaching. 'We'd better make sure we're noisy and slow as we go in.' He winked at her, picked up the stick and they left together, arm in arm.

'How have you managed today?' she asked as they walked down Kirkgate.

'I've been careful,' he promised her. 'The most I've done is walk to the Moot Hall and back.'

'Was the mayor glad to see you?'

'Not as you'd notice,' he replied quietly. 'When I took the daily report I had to give it to the new clerk he has. And when I told him about the children his only concern was how it might affect the city.' He paused. 'Do you mind if we stop by the churchyard?'

He could have found his way to the grave with his eyes closed. As soon as he'd been able to walk far enough it had been the first place he'd visited. Rose, their older daughter. Soon it would be two years since she'd died, taken in that awful, killing winter. He stood, threading his fingers through Mary's. The grass had grown tall, the inscription on the headstone still clear but starting to wear, the edges of the letters no longer so sharp as lichen grew around the words.

They didn't need words to remember the girl who'd been so loving and eager to please, barely married and with child herself when death came.

Finally he stirred, startled to see that full evening had come while his mind wandered.

'I'm sorry,' he said.

'It doesn't matter,' she told him tenderly. 'I feel peaceful here.'

At the house he was careful to rattle the latch noisily before they entered. It would give Emily and Rob time to make themselves respectable. He'd be disappointed if they hadn't taken advantage of the time alone.

The girl had built a fire and the pair of them sat close to it, careful not to look at each other. The Constable smiled inside. Emily might not want to marry but that didn't mean she wasn't interested in other things with her young man.

'Did you find anything?' he asked Lister.

'Nothing, boss. No one knows anything. But there's a recruiting sergeant in town.'

Nottingham rolled his eyes. 'Find out where he's staying. I'll wager there'll be trouble there tonight; there always is when they're here. Prepare the men for it.'

'Yes, boss.'

'Go and talk to the people down at the camp, too. Someone down there might have known the children. Even names for them would be something.'

'Mr Sedgwick suggested that.'

'Good.' The Constable brightened. 'And I suppose we should feed you before you start work.'

Rob grinned. 'Yes, boss.'

As dusk became night Sedgwick completed his last round and returned to the jail. The undertaker had taken the children, and he imagined them laid gently into the ground in the darkness before the gravediggers sprinkled a thick layer of quicklime on them.

The boss might have come back, but the work day had been as long as before, stretching from before dawn to well into the evening. It felt odd to have someone else making the decisions again and telling him what to do. He'd grown used to being in charge. Maybe he would be again; he could see the Constable wasn't the man he'd once been. The smile was there and his mind seemed sharp enough, but he moved slowly and cautiously, like someone much older than his years.

The deputy locked the jail door, tested it briefly, then made his way home up Briggate and along Lands Lane. Inside the house a fire burned bright and warm in the hearth; Isabell was awake and smiling in the crib he'd made from old scraps of wood.

Sedgwick picked her up and held her at arm's length before bringing her close, burying her face against her and smelling the freshness and the milk on her skin.

'James is upstairs,' Lizzie said. 'He's finishing the work he has to do for school.' She was sitting close to the blaze, using its light to finish mending a shirt. He bent to kiss her and stroke her hair lightly, then tickled the baby until she began to gurgle happily. This was what he lived for, the thing that drove him through every day, knowing he'd come back to his family when it was all over.

He laid the girl back in her bed and climbed to the cramped upper storey of the house. The room was filled with a bed and a paillasse where the boy sat thoughtfully, staring at the slate in front of him, a stub of chalk clutched tight between his small fingers.

'What do you have to do?'

'Sums,' James replied glumly, looking up. 'It's hard.'

The deputy chuckled and ruffled the lad's hair. 'It's worth knowing,' he said. 'Remember, if you know how to count properly no bugger can cheat you.' He'd talked to his son's teacher at the charity school and knew he was learning quickly, already able to read and write spidery letters.

The boy's blue coat hung neatly from a peg. Each afternoon, when James came home, Lizzie sponged it carefully. It was too large but that was good; it would need to last a few years before they'd be able to afford a new one. The first morning he'd walked the boy to school and seen him vanish into the place he'd thought his heart would burst from pride.

'Sleep as soon as you've finished.' He tried to kiss the lad but James wriggled away, never taking his eyes from the numbers in front of him, then scribbling an answer. 'You hear me?'

'Yes, Da.'

He settled by the fire, letting the warmth surround him. Isabell had fallen asleep and he pulled the blanket up around her chin. Lizzie had cut bread and cheese and poured a mug of ale. He drank slowly, gazing into the flames.

'Bad?' she asked. He nodded in reply. He'd knew she'd have heard; the word would have flown around Leeds.

'Very,' he said with a weary sigh. 'It made me think about our two.'

Lizzie reached out and took his hand. 'You can't look after all of them, you know.'

'We don't even know their names,' he told her bleakly. 'Let alone who did it.'

She squeezed his fingers gently. 'You'll find him, John Sedgwick.'

He hoped that was true.

*   *   *

Rob made the rounds with two of the men then headed out along the Aire to the camp. He'd gone to his lodgings for the greatcoat and was glad of it now; with night the sky had cleared, stars shining and the air stinging against his face.

The clock on the Parish Church had struck nine by the time Rob walked along the riverbank. Small fires burned in the darkness, figures in silhouette gathered around them.

There'd be a thick frost tonight, he thought; already the grass crunched beneath his boots and the earth felt hard and rutted. He looked up to see a woman standing in front of him, her arms folded.

'Evening, Mr Lister,' she said, her voice wary. 'What brings you this way? We've not seen you for a while.' Her face broke into a small grin. 'I was starting to think maybe you didn't love us any more.'

He chuckled. 'Hello, Bessie. It's good to see you, too.'

'Must be summat important to bring you down this way.'

'I'm looking for information.'

For much of the year the strays and waifs of the riverbank gathered here every night. Being together gave them safety, somewhere to call home, if only for a few hours. Simon Gordonson had started the camp, but in the late summer he'd left, taking to the roads, and Bessie Sharp had assumed iron control. She was a hefty woman, almost as tall as Lister, with a fearsome gaze and a shrewd mind. Her curls were tucked under her cap, and she wore clothes others had cast off as if they were a queen's robes. She looked after all the lost souls like they were her family, keeping them in line and protecting every one.

'It's about them children, in't it?'

'Yes.'

She glanced at the faces gathered around the fires, pulling a worn shawl tighter around her shoulders. 'There's enough to look after here. Once winter comes proper I'll have plenty to do keeping these alive.' Bessie stared at him. 'So what information are you looking for?'

'About the children. If any of them had lived here, maybe. If anyone might know a name or two.'

She shook her head. 'You know what it's like here. Some folk stay a day or two then move on. What were they like?'

He described the faces still lodged in his mind.

'I'll ask,' Bessie said. 'But don't hold your breath. Any bastard who'll do that deserves more than the rope.'

'Thank you.' If any of them knew anything, he knew she'd badger them until they told her. He brought a pie from the pocket of his coat and handed it to her. She accepted it as if it was her due, not charity.

'It won't go far,' Lister said apologetically, looking at the faces gathered around the flames. There were more than the night before, their faces all pinched and hungry in the flickering light. There were men with the vacant look of the lost, as if they were slowly walking towards death, mothers with young children clutched against their breasts, families in rags and tatters huddled together for the comfort as much as the warmth.

'It'll feed a few. That's a start, Mr Lister, that's a start. You come back tomorrow and I'll tell you if they know owt.'

If he was fortunate there'd be a word or two of help from the camp, he thought as he took the steps by the bridge and began to walk up Briggate. Light shone through gaps in the shutters at the *Leeds Mercury* and for a moment he hesitated, tempted to go over there and try to make some peace with his father. But each time before it had ended in an argument; why would this be any different?

He was almost at the jail when he heard someone running hard up the street. Hand on his cudgel, he waited. The man slowed as he came close, breath steaming wildly in the air.

'You the Constable's man?' he gasped. Lister nodded. 'Fight down at the Crown and Fleece.'

Rob hurried along Kirkgate, careful not to go too fast. It was always best to give them a little time, to let them hit each other for a while before he arrived. That way they had their pride from the fight, but most of them would be ready to end things. That's what the deputy had taught him and he'd seen it was true. After a few minutes the fighters would have had their fill and their blood. But he still kept a tight hold on the cudgel, ready to break some heads.

The Crown and Fleece was set back from the street, close to the Cloth Hall, at the back of a small yard. It was usually an orderly house, just a small inn, neatly kept, and with a clean stable for horses. Lister pushed at the door and walked in. One man lay on the floor, his eyes closed, and another was yelling at the recruiting sergeant who stood in a corner, the battle lust red on his face, heavy fists ready.

'Come on, then,' he challenged the man in front of him, spittle flying from his mouth. 'You were happy enough to take the King's shilling earlier. You're not going to back out now.' He glanced at the man sprawled limply on the ground. 'I'll have you like him and I'll march you both away.'

Lister rapped the cudgel on a bench, the sound sharp and harsh, making them stop and turn. 'Enough,' he shouted. 'You,' he said, pointing at the sergeant, 'sit down. And you,' he said to the other man, 'over there.'

He waited until they'd obeyed, feeling the tension in the room beginning to fall. The man on the floor stirred, moaning and then turning on his side to vomit noisily.

'Give me a good reason not to throw you all in the cells,' Rob told the soldier coldly.

The man glared at him, brushed some dirt from the bright red uniform coat and took a long drink of ale before answering.

'They wanted to join up.' He nodded at the pair. 'Look in their pockets, you'll find the shilling they took. Then they changed their minds.'

'Is that true?' He glanced at the youth, sitting on a bench with his head in his hands.

The young man bobbed his head slowly, never looking up.

'Then you're a soldier now,' Lister told him. 'Same goes for your friend.' He looked around the inn. 'Anyone want to complain about that?'

Men shook their heads and contemplated their ale in silence. Lister caught the eye of the landlord, grinning as the man nodded his relief and appreciation. Usually it was visiting clerics and farmers who stayed at this place, men with quiet lives who didn't raise their voices or their fists in anger.

The sergeant sat alone in the corner, grazes on his large knuckles, hat placed carefully on the bench beside him.

'A word with you,' Rob said, sliding across from him.

The soldier looked up, a sly smile on his face showing a row of rotten teeth. 'Come to join up, have you? Better than being a Constable's man.'

He ignored the comment. 'How long are you staying in Leeds?' he asked. There was no sign of the young drummer boy – long gone to sleep, he expected.

The man shrugged. 'Another day, maybe two. Depends how many want to join the regiment.' He picked carefully at a thread on his uniform coat. It was worn, but carefully looked after, each small rent sewn by skilled fingers. 'It's a good life, we're stationed out in Gibraltar. All sun and warm weather.' He stared at Rob. 'And the girls there would love you.'

'You might want to think about another inn,' Rob advised him. He glanced at the men on the floor. 'Somewhere they don't mind a little rowdiness.'

The sergeant bristled. 'I like the bed here.'

'Then no repeats of tonight,' Lister warned.

'I didn't start that. But once they begin, I finish it.' The soldier clenched his fist.

'No more,' Rob ordered as he stood. 'What's your name?'

'Grady,' the man answered proudly. 'Daniel Grady.

'Then while you're here, make sure you obey the law, Sergeant Grady. The cells can hold soldiers, too.'

He left the inn and walked back up to jail. There'd never be a shortage of those who thought home was too small for their dreams of glory. All they'd become was fodder for the cannons and the guns and the bayonet. The lucky few would come back intact. He'd seen them, sitting quiet in the inns, staring absently at some point beyond the gaze of others.

He made his midnight rounds, checking in with the men. Everything was quiet. Down by the bridge he heard the water rushing, and rested his elbows on the parapets. For a moment he closed his eyes and saw the faces of the dead children.

They needed to find the killer before others did. All through the evening he'd heard whispers and mutterings in the alehouses and on the corners, anger and outrage, men boasting of the things they'd do if they caught the murderer.

He cut along the Calls, going all the way to the church and coming back by the Crown. Everything was quiet there, the shutters tight, the gates to the yard locked. Lister smiled and carried on, the only sound his heels on the street.

FIVE

I t was still dark when he woke suddenly, as if someone had taken his hand and dragged him from the dream. The images in his head tattered to nothing so all that remained was the pain that had been with him ever since the knife entered his body. Outside, a cold world had arrived. The ground was hard under his boots, the late moonlight showing a rime of frost on the fields. He used the stick to steady himself as he walked along the road and over Timble Bridge.

The return to work had exhausted him but he'd still lain awake long into the night, drifting between past and present as if no years separated them. He'd seen the faces of the dead in his mind, studied them until he knew the questions he needed to ask the children at the market. All he needed was to make them stop and listen to him. He remembered how adults always meant danger, how it was safer to avoid them as much as possible. He'd seen his face in the glass; he knew how he'd look to them and it wasn't a handsome picture. He'd turned gaunt in his recovery, the years hanging heavy on his face. The hair he'd once been so proud of was more grey than blond now, and wiry to the touch. Still, he hoped wryly, perhaps they'd see the same fear in him that they felt themselves: that each night could be their last.

The band of light on the eastern horizon was starting to broaden as he reached the jail. He listened as Rob gave the night report, then said, 'Check the inn again this evening. If that sergeant's still there, move him on to the Talbot.' He grinned. 'They'll know how to deal with him there.'

'He'll be out with his drummer today,' Sedgwick pointed out. 'All those country boys coming in for market day.'

'We can't stop him, John, you know that. Just keep your eye on him.'

'Yes, boss.'

'Bessie didn't have anything?' he asked Lister.

'She's going to ask the people at the camp.'

'Go down there again tonight. Nobody else knew anything?'
Lister shook his head. Nottingham looked over at the deputy.
'How about you?'

'Nothing,' Sedgwick answered despondently. 'I've put the word
out but I didn't really need to; they'd be coming to us if they
knew anything. Everyone wants this one, boss. The only good
thing is that they've found no more bodies.'

Nottingham nodded solemnly. In the distance the church bell
rang the half hour. 'Right,' he said, 'I'd better walk around the
cloth market. Let them see I'm back.'

It was exactly as he remembered it, the way he knew it would
be, as it had been for years before his time. The weavers set up
their trestles on either side of Briggate, stretching up from the
bridge, and laid out the cloth they'd finished. The merchants
circulated, making their deals with clothiers in whispers, the
exchanges as muted and reverent as a church service. But it was
the worship of profit, the Constable knew that. Wool was the
religion of Leeds; everyone bowed his head to it and the money
it brought.

He walked down towards the river, taking his time, making
sure everyone noticed that he was back. Some yelled out their
greetings, others nodded and smiled. Tom Williamson, one of
the few friends Nottingham had among the merchants, came over,
a smile wide on his face.

'About time you were working again, Richard,' he said as they
shook hands. 'How do you feel?'

'Better than when I had a knife in me,' he answered wryly.

'You're looking prosperous.' Williamson wore a new coat and
breeches, the wool so dark the colour moved between blue and
black. A neatly cut waistcoat flowed almost to his knees, the silk
as yellow as pale sun with designs in blue and green.

'Business is good,' he replied, sounding almost embarrassed.
'My wife insists I have to look like a success. I said the money
would be better saved, but . . .' He shrugged helplessly. 'I tell
you, Richard, I don't understand women any more now than I
did when I was twenty.' Williamson's face clouded. 'I heard
about the children.'

'We'll find whoever did it,' Nottingham assured him.

'It's a bad thing to come back to,' he said, and the Constable added his solemn agreement. 'Some of us were talking before the market. We thought we could put up a reward to help catch the murderer. It might help.'

Nottingham gave a long sigh as he tried to frame a reply. After a moment he said, 'Don't. I know you want him brought to justice as much as I do, but once you offer money, everyone starts peaching on his neighbour, just hoping to get rich. Do you see the problem, Tom?'

'Of course,' the merchant said quickly. 'We don't want to make your job harder than it is. Is there anything we can do?'

'I don't know.' It was the simple truth. He couldn't recall the last time there'd been an offer of help. It was generous, it showed the outrage in the city, but although money was what the merchants understood, it wasn't the answer here. He smiled. 'I'll need to think about that.'

Williamson clasped his hand again. 'Just let me know. And it's good to see you again, Richard. It truly is.'

The Constable watched him wander away. To most of the merchants he was simply someone to be tolerated, someone to protect them and their wealth from the poor. Williamson had more about him than that. He saw the person, not the position. He'd probably been the one to suggest the reward, thinking of his own young children.

The cloth market wound down, most of the lengths sold, the weavers packing their things away, ready to lead their packhorses back out to the Pennine villages where they lived.

At the other end of Briggate, beyond the Moot Hall and the Shambles, traders were setting up for the Tuesday market, laughing and joking as they worked. Nottingham strolled up to the market cross by the Head Row. Wives and servants were already moving around, searching out the early bargains, picking through stalls of old clothes, bargaining with farmers for the poultry in wooden cages.

He loved the liveliness and noise, but his concentration was elsewhere, looking around to try to spot the children who stayed on the fringes of everything. They survived by barely being noticed, scavenging and stealing what they could and vanishing again.

Finally he saw two boys dart between stalls. His eyes followed them as they disappeared into the entrance of one of the many courts between the houses that lined the street. Back there, in the shadows, they'd feel safer.

He made his way down the street, carefully watching the ginnel, his stick tapping lightly on the flagstones. He had a warm pie in his coat, and small coins in the pocket of his breeches.

The buildings rose around the court, keeping the place in deep shade. Rubbish was piled against the corners and rats scattered as he approached. The stench of decay was strong around the old, dilapidated buildings. Half the windows were missing their glass, the cold and light kept at bay with pieces of rotting cloth. He cleared a space against a wall and sat, feeling pain push through his belly as he lowered himself. Then he took out the pie and laid it on the ground before breaking off a piece and chewing it slowly.

It would take time for their curiosity and fear to get the better of them. But time was something he had. He thought back to when he was very young, when he had both a father and a mother, when the world seemed safe, a magical place of hope and wonder. All that had vanished quickly enough and left him out here.

The bustle of the market seemed a world away, the noise baffled by brick and stone. Back here there was only silent desperation. He kept his eyes on the ground in front of him, listening closely for the smallest sound.

'Are you all right?'

The Constable raised his head slowly. 'Aye, lad, I'll be fine,' he said with a smile. 'I just needed somewhere quiet. Come on out if you want. I've got some food.'

He waited patiently, careful to say nothing more. Too much and he could scare the boy away. This way he seemed harmless, just another old man. He took a little more of the pie and chewed it slowly.

When he looked up again the boy was standing in front of him, leaving enough distance to run. He was small and thin as twigs, his shirt ragged at the cuffs and neck, worn through at the elbows. Tattered breeches hung off skinny legs, hose gathered loosely on his calves, the shoes at least three sizes too large for his feet.

He looked about twelve, but Nottingham knew that was just

a guess. Whatever his age, his face had seen far too much for his years. His eyes were sad, filled now with hunger as he looked at the pie, and he clenched a knife tight in one fist.

'Help yourself. Take it all if you want.'

The boy glanced around quickly, then slipped forward, grabbing the food. Nottingham thought he saw a small form move deep in the shadows, a fleeting impression of a girl who vanished somewhere.

'It's good,' the Constable said as the lad took a bite. 'What's your name?'

'Caleb,' the boy answered as he began to chew. He stared suspiciously at Nottingham. 'Why are you back here, anyway?'

'To learn something.'

Caleb cocked his head, taken by surprise. 'What? There's nowt back here.'

'There's you. And your friends. I see you're keeping some of the food for them.'

'We share.'

The Constable smiled gently. 'We used to do that, too.'

'Oh aye?' He looked doubtful. 'When was that, then?'

'Back when I lived like you.' He said the words evenly, as if they meant nothing, watching the boy's eyes widen in disbelief.

'You? You never did.'

'It was a long time ago.'

'What do you do now?' Caleb took another bite of the pie before carefully stuffing the rest in his pocket.

'I'm the Constable of Leeds.'

'No you're not,' the boy said confidently. 'I've seen him. He's younger than you and taller.'

Nottingham laughed loud. 'That's Mr Sedgwick. He's my deputy. I've been ill for a long time.'

'Oh aye? What was wrong with you?' Caleb asked warily.

'Someone tried to kill me.'

'Really?'

He knew he had the lad's attention now. All he had to do was keep it, and make him believe. 'Someone knifed me. It took a long time to heal. Look.' He pulled up his shirt to display the wound. Much of the redness had vanished, but the scar still stood livid against his flesh.

Caleb stared, staying quiet for a long time.

'Did you really live out here, then? You're not just saying?'

The Constable answered slowly. 'I did. I know what it's like. More years than anyone needs.' He cleared his throat. 'We found three bodies yesterday.'

'Aye, we know,' the boy told him, his voice as weary and aching as an old man's.

'I want whoever killed them,' Nottingham said. 'I'm hoping you and the others out here can help me.'

SIX

C aleb stared coldly at him. 'Why should we?'

'Because I saw what someone did to those three and I want to make sure he can't do it to anyone else.' He looked at the boy. 'Is that enough for you?'

Caleb lowered his head.

'Do the others look up to you?' the Constable asked. 'The lads and lasses?'

'Some,' the boy acknowledged.

'You look after them?'

'If I can.' He shrugged and shook his head. 'I can't always.'

Nottingham understood. There was only so much one person could do. 'How long have you been out here?'

Caleb squatted on his heels. The fear had left his face, bringing an innocence that made him seem younger. 'Five year, near as owt.'

'The ones who died, were they with you?'

The boy closed his eyes and nodded. 'Until they went.'

'What were their names?'

'The lass was called Alison, and the lads were Mark and Luke.' He picked at a large scab on the back of his hand. 'Luke was the little one.'

'When did they go?'

'More than a week.' The boy shrugged. 'They didn't come back one night.'

'Did you look for them?'

Caleb raised empty eyes. 'Why?' he asked. 'I knew what had happened.'

'What was that?'

'They'd gone with him.'

Nottingham glanced up sharply. 'Him?' He could feel his heart thumping hard. He breathed slowly.

'He comes round offering money and food.' The boy turned his head and spat. 'Even somewhere to live sometimes.'

He knew. There had been men like that when he was young. He'd seen the desperate go with them and come back silent, the tears dried on their faces.

'Tell me about him.'

'He started coming back in summer,' Caleb remembered bleakly. 'I warned them all. No one gives owt for nowt. Not to us.'

'Do you know his name?'

'Allus called himself Gabriel.'

The Constable had never heard the name in Leeds before. 'What did he look like?' He tried to keep the urgency out of his voice.

'Like he had money, the way they always do,' the boy said angrily.

'That doesn't help me find him,' he prodded gently.

'You come looking now,' Caleb spat. 'You didn't do owt when Jane went with him and never came back. Or David.'

'I didn't know,' Nottingham told him humbly.

'Aye, and would you have cared?' The boy stood and paced to the other side of the yard.

'I'd have cared,' the Constable answered quietly. 'I'd have done exactly what I'm doing now.'

Caleb turned and sneered. 'Aye, right.'

'Mark, Alison and Luke?'

'Yes.'

'I want to find the man who did all that to them and to Jane and David and I want to see him hang. I'm sorry about the others, but when I don't know something's happened, I can't do anything about it.' He paused. 'Now, are you going to help me?'

*   *   *

'The lad says this Gabriel is big. Taller than me and broader.'
He looked at the deputy.

'It's not much help, is it, boss?' Sedgwick asked. 'What sort
of age?'

'Old is as close as he could come,' Nottingham replied. The
word could mean anything. 'Always wears a good wig, dresses
in a clean grey coat and breeches every time. Offers money or
food. Even a place to stay, as if he was taking them in. Does
that mean anything to you?'

The deputy shook his head. The Constable shifted awkwardly
on the chair. His bones were still chilled from sitting so long on
the cold stone and he tried to find a comfortable position.

'Gabriel's been around since the summer. These aren't the first
he's taken, either. There are two others that Caleb mentioned.'

'Fuck!' Sedgwick slammed his fist down on the desk in frustration. 'I'm sorry, boss. I never heard anything.'

'I know,' Nottingham said sympathetically. 'No one's blaming
you. This bastard's sly, John. And he's deadly.'

'Sounds like he has money.'

The Constable nodded. 'I thought that, too.'

'It's not much to go on, though, is it?'

'It's more than we had before,' Nottingham pointed out. 'I'm
just glad the lad said as much as he did. Caleb doesn't trust us,
John. He knows more, I'm sure of that. He's just keeping it
close.'

'Why?' Sedgwick frowned. 'Doesn't he want this Gabriel
found?'

'He wants that, right enough,' the Constable added without
hesitation. 'He's just waiting to see if we'll do something or
we're all talk.' He leaned back and sighed. 'So now we'd better
find Gabriel.'

'How?'

'The boy's given us a place to start. We work from there. We
know Gabriel's not poor; that cuts out a lot of folk.'

'Aye,' the deputy agreed hesitantly. 'But then we're looking
at the rich. You know what that means. They look after their
own.'

'They won't this time,' Nottingham answered with certainty.
'Put the word out. See if the name Gabriel means anything, or

anyone's noticed a man in a good grey suit and full bottom wig.
Tell them why, too.'

'Yes, boss.'

'We're going to make sure he has nowhere to hide.' He looked
up as the deputy stood. 'I want everyone in Leeds to know by
tomorrow. Let's make the bastard sweat.'

Sedgwick grinned, jammed the old tricorn hat on his head and
left. Alone, the Constable pushed himself out of the chair, feeling
the pain across his belly and the dull ache in his hips. They'd pass
soon enough, and in the meantime there was work to be done.

He started at the Rose and Crown, wandering past the inn and
through to the yard and stables. Hercules was there, grooming one
of the horses and softly whispering to the animal. It was what he did
during the day, his real joy, and in the evenings he'd collect the
mugs and clean up around the drinkers. In return he had a bed in
one of the stalls and his food, all the scraps the others left. As long
as Nottingham could recall Hercules had been around, a small, slight
man, his head growing balder each year. Few paid him attention,
but his ears were sharp and his eyes still saw things most folk missed.

The man turned at the sound of footsteps and nodded his
welcome.

'Does the name Gabriel mean anything?'

Hercules kept stroking the animal's mane. 'Not to me. Should it?'

'How about a man who dresses in grey and wears a wig?'

'Plenty of them around,' he replied shortly.

'Whoever killed those little ones calls himself Gabriel and
dresses that way.' He saw Hercules give a small nod. That was
all he needed. The Constable pulled two coins from his breeches
and put them on the shelf in the stall.

The river roared loud as he crossed the bridge, white water
tumbling and roiling around the stone, in full spate down from
the hills. The sound faded as he walked out along the London
Road. As he passed Simpson Fold, where he'd been knifed, a
chill rushed through him and he turned his head away.

The house he wanted was one of many hidden among a warren
of streets. Unlike its neighbours it was kept with care and pride,
the glass of the windows sparkling, the front step scrubbed free
of the smallest speck of dirt. He knocked on the door and waited

until it opened and the space was filled by a large black man
with a small wig on his head.

'Constable!' he said with a wide grin. 'I heard tha' was back.'

'Hello, Henry. Mr Buck around?'

'Aye, he's in't back. Come on in.' He moved aside, leaving
just enough space for Nottingham to squeeze past. 'Go through.
He'll be that pleased to see thee.'

The parlour was warm, the fire crackling brightly in the hearth.
Joe Buck sat at his desk, immaculately dressed as ever in a coat
and breeches of burgundy velvet, the stock and shirt some expensive shade between cream and white. The room smelled of
beeswax; Henry would have been up early, starting the blaze
then polishing every piece of furniture, the way he did each day.

Buck turned and a warm smile spread across his face. 'Mr
Nottingham,' he said and stood, extending his hand. 'It's good
to see you again.'

Joe Buck made a good living fencing stolen goods. But he
was careful; he kept all his business at a long arm's length; no
matter how he tried, the Constable had never managed to charge
him with anything.

'Come and sit where it's warm, man. Can I pour you a glass
of wine? Ale?'

'Nothing for me,' Nottingham answered, settling gently on the
delicate chair.

'You're looking well,' Buck told him.

The Constable laughed. 'I'm not and we both know it, Joe.
But thank you. At least I'm back.'

'And you've come to see me? I'm flattered.' Buck spread his
hands wide, the skin scrubbed clean and respectable, nails clipped
short.

'Don't be. I'm here because you're going to help me.'

'Oh?' The fence asked with interest.

'The children we found yesterday.'

'That was awful,' Buck said sadly. 'There's no hell bad enough
for whoever did it. What do you want from me, Constable?'

'I'm not going to bugger around, Joe. I want you to tell all
those thieves you deal with to watch for someone in a grey suit
and wig who calls himself Gabriel. And have them tell others.'

'Gabriel?'

'That's the name he uses.'

Buck studied him shrewdly then nodded his assent. 'I'll let everyone know,' he promised. 'We need to kill scum like that.'

'He'll have his trial, Joe, the same as everyone else.' The Constable gave a slow smile. 'Just like you will some day.'

'You'll have to catch me breaking the law first,' Buck grinned.

'Of course.' Nottingham stood slowly, leaning on the stick and wincing.

'Not fully healed?' the other man asked with concern.

'Enough to do my job. Don't worry about that.'

The deputy knew folk all over the city, and he went from one to another passing on the message. The morning passed quickly and hunger rumbled in his belly as he walked up Briggate, lost in his thoughts.

'Spare a farthing, Mr Sedgwick?'

He stopped and looked down to see soldier Sam grinning up at him through a set of broken teeth. He begged on the streets, pushing himself around on a small wooden cart someone had made for him years before. He'd left his legs on a battlefield and now he displayed the stumps, daring people to pass him by without handing him a coin. Summer and winter he was out, and the deputy knew he made good money, enough to keep a room all to himself in one of the courts.

'Got a family to feed, Sam.'

'Aye, you do,' he agreed. 'How's that little babby of yours?'

He grinned. 'She's grand. Nine months now and prettier than her mam.'

'You'd better hope your Lizzie doesn't hear you say that,' he warned.

'She'd be the first to say it.'

'What about your lad? Haven't seen much of him lately.'

'He's at the charity school now and doing well,' the deputy told him with pride.

'You watch, he'll end up on the corporation.'

'As long as he does better than his father, I'll be happy.' A thought struck him. 'You heard about those little ones?'

'Course I did, Mr Sedgwick. Terrible that someone could do that to them. You know what I'd do if I found him?'

'Same as half of Leeds, Sam. You ever heard of anyone named Gabriel?'

The beggar thought for a moment. 'No, I haven't. Why?'

'We think he's the one who killed those children. Dresses in a grey coat and breeches and wears a wig.'

'There's too many dress plain round here, you know that.'

'Keep your eyes open,' he said. 'If you see anything, let us know.'

'I hear Mr Nottingham's back.'

'He is that.'

'That'll be a change for you after being top dog these few months.'

The deputy smiled. 'Aye, and a welcome one. As far as I'm concerned he can keep all that responsibility. Look out for Gabriel, will you? And tell everyone else, too.'

He left, knowing that Sam would pass the word, and walked up to the White Swan at the corner of Kirkgate. The Constable was already seated at a bench, cradling a mug of ale, a bowl of stew in front of him.

'Found anything yet?' he asked as Sedgwick slid in across from him.

'No one knows him.' He ordered a pie and ale from the potboy, then said, 'I talked to soldier Sam. He'll talk to all the other beggars.'

Nottingham nodded his approval. 'Joe Buck's going to let all the thieves know, too. Gabriel's not going to be able to fly far without someone spotting him.'

'Still too late for five of them, though.'

'And however many have gone before,' the Constable said, letting the meaning hang in the air. He sat back, wiping his mouth with the back of his hand. 'Think about it, John. I know Caleb said he's only been coming around since summer, but I doubt this is the first instance. It might have been going on for years. He could have just been very careful.'

'How do you mean, boss?'

'I don't expect he let the ones in the past go. He just hid the bodies well, the way he did with Jane and David.'

SEVEN

The deputy pushed the food away, his appetite gone. 'Oh Christ,' he muttered.

'If they hadn't been working on the bell pits we might never have known.' Nottingham's voice was tight in his throat. 'I don't think he's growing careless. We were just lucky – if you can call it that.' He gave a grim smile. 'At least now we know he's out there and we can catch him.' His fists clenched tight under the table, nails digging hard into the palms. 'Right, let's go back to work. By tonight I want everyone in Leeds to know about Gabriel.' The Constable rose and took hold of the silver-topped stick.

'Did that belong to Amos?' Sedgwick asked. Amos Worthy had been the city's biggest pimp, never convicted of anything as half the Corporation used his girls. He and Nottingham had enjoyed a strange relationship, part hatred, part friendship, until Worthy had died of cancer the year before.

'The old bugger left it to me in his will. I never thought I'd use it.' The Constable laughed. 'I'm never going to be rid of him.'

They both worked through the afternoon, talking to more people, hoping for any indication of who Gabriel might be, and finding nothing. Towards evening a low, cruel wind blew out of the north, cutting like knives against the skin, and the deputy pulled his coat tighter about him as he finished his rounds.

The house on Lands Lane was warm, filled with the smell of cooking, a pot suspended over the fire in the kitchen. Isabell was awake, sitting on the floor, her eyes widening to see her papa come in on a wave of cold air.

'Shut that door,' Lizzie told him sharply, but with a welcoming smile on her face. He pulled her close, rubbing his chilled face against hers. She laughed and shrieked, 'Give over, John Sedgwick, you're perished.' The baby joined the laughter, throwing her head back and giggling. He scooped her up and danced round the room holding her in his arms.

'Where's James?' he asked and Lizzie raised her head towards the ceiling. Still holding Isabell he climbed the stairs to the bedroom they all shared and found the boy at his school work. He settled on the small pallet, tickling the girl lightly on the chest. 'What is it tonight?'

'Spelling.' He looked up, frowning. 'The master said he'd beat anyone who didn't do well.'

The deputy raised his eyebrows. 'Aye, I suppose that would make you study. You know it all yet?' He glanced at the long list of words.

'I hope so, Da,' James replied in a heartfelt voice. 'Can you test me?'

They ran through ten of the words together. Sedgwick was impressed by his son's confidence; he reeled the letters off quickly, right each time.

'Very good,' he said finally. 'You'll make him happy.' He ruffled the boy's hair. 'I'm proud of you. And so is she,' he added with a laugh as the baby gurgled. 'You like school, don't you?'

'Yes, Da.' He slid the slate into his bag. 'I like to know things.'

'You'll do well.' He smiled. 'But you'd better get yourself to bed or your mam won't be happy.'

Rob made his way along the Calls before turning up High Back Lane and coming out on Kirkgate by the White Cloth Hall. The pale stone of the building shone eerily in the moonlight, standing broad and tall, as intimidating as a cathedral.

The Crown and Fleece was quiet. He opened the door to see a few drinkers gathered close to the fire, the landlord leaning on the trestle bar to talk to a customer. He straightened as Rob entered.

'The sergeant moved on?'

The landlord shook his head. 'Upstairs asleep. Didn't find any more recruits so he started drinking. He'll be on his way tomorrow.'

'What about those two lads who signed up?'

'Locked them in the stable. They'll be warm enough in there while morning.'

He accepted the ale he was offered, grateful to have a few minutes out of the chill, edging closer to the hearth until he felt the heat on his face and hands.

Back on the street he could have sworn it was even colder than before. His breath clouded as he walked, the only sound the clatter of his boots on the cobbles. Everyone was indoors and he wished he was among them. It was still only November.

As he made his rounds he thought about Emily. He could understand that she didn't want to marry, didn't want to be the property of any man. Over the months he'd even come to accept it after a fashion. But deep inside he held tight to a knot of hope that she'd change as she grew older. There was plenty of time yet; she'd just turned seventeen over the summer.

The curse was that he loved her. Contrary as she could be, Emily was the only girl he'd ever cared about. But James Lister desired something different for his son, a suitable wife, someone with the right standing and a handsome dowry, not a girl who was the granddaughter of a prostitute. That had caused the rift between them; it was the reason he lived in lodgings now. He hadn't spoken a word to his father since he left, fully six months before. The lights were all out in the house on Briggate when he passed, his parents tucked under the blankets for the night, shutters closed over the offices of the *Leeds Mercury*, the newspaper his father published.

He made his way down to the riverbank, picking out the small fires flickering in the distance. As he came closer, Bessie emerged from the darkness, coming to meet him before he reached the camp.

'Getting brisk out here, Mr Lister.'

'If it keeps on like this we'll have another hard winter,' he agreed. 'Do you have anything for me?'

In the moonlight he saw her shake her head. 'One of the lasses took ill and I was looking after her all night. I didn't have time for owt else.'

'How is she?'

There was a pause, a fill of silence, before she answered.

'She died.'

'I'm sorry.'

She tried to smile but there was no heart in it. 'Aye, well, it happens. There wasn't anything we could do. And there was someone else to look after her little girl.' She shook her head. 'I'll ask them tonight, I promise.'

'I know a little more now.' He told her about Gabriel, seeing the anger rise in her eyes.

'Leave it with me,' Bessie said. 'If anyone knows anything I'll tell you tomorrow.'

The hours passed slowly. By the time the clock struck five he was glad to return to the jail, put more coal on the fire and start writing his report. He could still feel the cold in his bones, as if he might never be completely warm again.

There was a strong blaze in the grate by the time the deputy arrived, hands pushed deep in the pockets of his ancient greatcoat, closing the door swiftly to keep out the bitter dawn air.

'At least you've made it cosy in here,' he said with a grin. 'I knew there was a reason we took you on.'

'Planning on staying here most of the day?'

'Chance would be a fine thing. The boss will have me hither and yon. That recruiting sergeant still at the Crown and Fleece?'

'Leaving today. And he was in his bed early as a Christian last night. No trouble at all.'

'Many take the King's shilling?' Sedgwick asked idly.

Lister shrugged. 'Just two, from what the landlord said. They're locked in the stables.'

'Daft buggers.'

The Constable arrived a few minutes later, breathing deep and warming his hands in front of the blaze before he shrugged off his coat.

'Anything much during the night?'

'All quiet, boss,' Rob told him.

'Were Bessie's people able to help with Gabriel?'

'She's going to ask them. Someone died there, she didn't have the chance.'

Nottingham sat at the desk and glanced at the night report. 'Somebody knows him,' he said firmly.

'We've already talked to everyone,' the deputy observed.

'Then we'll go back and talk to them again. People have passed the word. I don't care if it's a rumour or a whisper, we need something.' He looked at the others. 'John, just speak to everyone you can.'

'Yes, boss.'

'If you walk down to Timble Bridge you'll have more time with Emily,' he advised Lister. 'I daresay she'll need some warming up.' He winked and saw Rob blush as Sedgwick laughed.

He finished his daily report and walked up to the Moot Hall. People were tightly wrapped against the weather, hats jammed down hard on heads so only their eyes were visible. A few cattle lowed plaintively at the Shambles, as if they knew what awaited them.

It was all different upstairs, among the Turkey carpets and the polish of the wood panelling. Servants had come in early to lay the fires, then disappeared as if it had all happened by God's will.

Martin Cobb sat at his desk, sorting through a pile of papers. He smiled broadly to see the Constable.

'Mr Nottingham, your timing's excellent,' he said genially. 'The mayor just asked to see you. Go on in.'

'Sit yourself down.' The mayor nodded at the expensive chair, its legs so spindly and delicate they looked as though they'd never hold a man's weight. The Constable lowered himself carefully.

Fenton was dressed in rich wool, a merchant who spent money on his tailoring, wearing his suit easily. The coat and waistcoat were cut to flatter, and his face was smooth and pink from a recent shave, but the skin under his eyes dark and puffy.

He was thumbing through the newest edition of the *Mercury*. On the desk there was a dish of coffee, carried down hot from Garroway's on the Head Row, the aroma rich in the air of the office.

'Have you found him yet?' he asked, barely raising his eyes.

Nottingham placed his report on the pile of papers awaiting the mayor's attention. 'Not yet, your Worship.'

'I heard you turned down the offer of a reward from the merchants.' He folded the newspaper slowly and sat back. 'Why?'

Nottingham considered his answer for a moment. 'Because I want to find the man who hurt and killed those children, not

someone whose neighbour has a grudge against him and thinks
he can earn some quick money,' he said calmly.

Fenton shook his head. 'I disagree, Constable. Folk will see
the city takes this seriously.'

'We've been talking to people. We know more about him. He
calls himself Gabriel, and he wears a full wig and a grey suit.
By now most of the people in Leeds know that, too.' His voice
was earnest. 'They'll do what they can to help, and they'll do it
without the promise of money.'

'We need to show people we're concerned.'

The Constable sighed and ran a hand through his hair, trying
to stop himself from shouting. 'They already know that. Put up
a reward and you're only going to make our job much harder.
We'll have to follow up every hint or tip, and they'll all be
wrong.'

'And what if one of them's right?' the mayor countered with
a smug smile.

'It's unlikely.' Experience had taught him that. 'And I'd wager
we'd get it without the money.'

'It doesn't really matter, anyway,' Fenton told him flatly. 'The
Corporation's agreed. I'm having the posters printed today.'

'Yes, your Worship.' It was a battle he'd already lost. Now he
had to think how to make the most of the defeat.

'Anything else, Nottingham?'

'No.'

His face was grim as he walked down the corridor. He wanted
to bang his fist against the rich wood and smash a hole in the
wall. At least once he was outside the cold of the wind and
the blood stink from the Shambles seemed real.

As soon as the notices were up people would start coming
forward, hoping to snatch at the wealth. And he knew they'd
need to check each word and suggestion, just in case. It was all
they'd have time to do. He made his way back to the jail, and
pushed the iron deep into the coal to let the blaze rise.

He knew he'd done all he could. He'd find the bastard.

The door flew open. The recruiting sergeant entered, his
uniform neatly buttoned, the scarlet of the coat brilliant in the
dull colour of the jail. The drummer boy slipped in behind him.

'You're the Constable?' the sergeant asked. Nottingham nodded, pulled from his thoughts. The soldier looked fearful. 'My recruits have disappeared.'

'Disappeared?' He didn't understand. 'What do you mean? They've run off?'

'No,' he replied and then shook his head in confusion, pushing his lips together. 'I don't know. They were in the stable and the door was locked. When I went in for them this morning they'd gone.'

'And the door was still locked?'

'Aye, good and tight. I turned the key myself last night and opened it a few minutes ago.' He voice was wary. 'There's a devil in there.'

'Let's go and take a look, Sergeant . . .'

'Grady. Daniel Grady.' The man straightened his back.

'And what's your name?' the Constable asked the drummer.

'Andrew, sir.'

The lad wore old clothes that had been made for a bigger boy, and a pair of drumsticks was thrust through a worn leather belt. His face and hands had been roughly cleaned, the skin shining and red. But his boots were good, almost new and highly polished.

Nottingham rose, gathered his stick and smiled. 'Crown and Fleece, isn't it?' he asked.

The sergeant had locked the stable door and lowered the wooden bar.

'This is how you left it last night?'

'Yes, sir,' Grady said. 'I went to me bed early. The two lads had been drinking, and I knew they'd be warm enough in here with the beasts.'

'Let's see inside.'

The horses whinnied as the door was drawn back to let light into the stable. The air was warm and moist, full with the smell of horse shit and hay. The Constable stood and glanced around the building. There were no windows, and the animals were confined in their stalls. A ladder led up to the hayloft.

'Have you checked up there?'

'I sent the boy up,' Grady answered and Nottingham turned to Andrew.

'There was just hay, sir,' the boy said shyly. 'No sign of anyone.'

He walked around the outside of the stable, searching for another door or any place the recruits could have escaped. There was nothing. The place was only a few years old, the Yorkshire stone still a soft golden colour, the roof on tight with no gaps.

The sergeant looked haunted, confronted by something far beyond his understanding. He moved awkwardly from foot to foot, turning his head from side to side as if he might spot the recruits hiding somewhere in the yard.

'Andrew,' the Constable said, 'go up to the loft again and look in the hay.'

'Yes sir.' The lad moved quickly, used to obeying orders as soon as they were given.

'Kick around in the straw,' he added. Nottingham doubted the boy would find anything, but he wanted to be thorough, and he knew he couldn't climb up there and back down himself.

'Nothing here, sir.'

Grady was still in the yard. He glanced up expectantly.

'Well, Sergeant,' Nottingham said with a sigh. 'You were right, they've disappeared.'

'I told you there were devils here.' The soldier stalked off. The drummer boy looked blankly over his shoulder at the Constable for a moment, then followed.

There were no devils in Leeds, least of all at an inn like this, Nottingham thought. Something had happened. The recruits had managed to escape. The drummer boy could have unlocked the stable door for them, or even a serving girl. He'd need to talk to the landlord and try to pull Andrew aside before the sergeant left. There'd be an answer, he was certain of that, something simple and straightforward. The young men might have gone, but they hadn't simply vanished into the air. No one did that.

It was the last thing he needed. Finding Gabriel was all that mattered, not hunting down a pair who'd likely thought better of their futures after taking the King's shilling. He spent another five minutes searching inside and outside the stable, the horses snorting uncomfortably as he prowled around the building. Finally he stood thoughtfully in the doorway, leaning against the jamb, before striding into the inn.

The sergeant sat at a table, idly moving a mug of ale across the wood.

'The two who've gone, what were their names?'

Grady needed to think for a moment before answering. 'Thomas Lamb and Nathaniel Sharp.' He shrugged. 'That's what they told me, anyway.'

He understood. Young men joined the army for more reasons than adventure. Escaping a wife, debt or the law could all send men to arms, and the names they gave often weren't their own.

'Where's Andrew?'

'I sent him down by the river to practise. We're going down to Wakefield later.' He shook his head as if he was trying to clear it. 'What happened to them? I don't understand.'

'I don't either,' the Constable admitted. He smiled. 'But I will.'

He walked down towards the Aire, passing through a ginnel then cutting over Call Brows and Low Holland, following the sharp tattoo of drumbeats. The boy was marching by the water, the drum hanging from his neck by a thick leather strap, large against his tiny body. He put up the sticks as Nottingham approached.

'You're very good on that.' The boy eyed him warily but said nothing. The Constable gazed out at the water. 'What do you know about the two who disappeared, Andrew?'

'Nothing, sir.' The boy looked up with guileless eyes. 'Just that Sergeant Grady signed them up, sir.'

'How long have you been with the regiment?'

'Almost two years, sir.'

'Do you like it?'

'Yes, sir,' Andrew said, but his words had no conviction.

'Where do you come from, lad?'

'York, sir.'

'You miss it?'

'Sometimes.' He brightened for a moment. 'But Gibraltar is warm.'

'Tell me, what do you think happened to those two, Andrew?'

The boy didn't answer at first, still staring at the Constable. 'Don't know, sir. Really, I don't.'

'Thank you. I wish you well in your travels.'

He walked back to the jail, still not sure if the lad was telling him the truth. He'd probably never know. The deputy was sitting by the desk, laboriously writing out a note.

'Any luck, John?' he asked hopefully.

'Nothing,' Sedgwick responded, his mouth tight with frustration. 'He's nowhere. No one knows him.'

'He's not the only one, it seems.' He explained about the recruits, and a grin spread across the deputy's face.

'Devils?' he laughed. 'Someone felt sorry for them and let them out, more like.'

'Go on down there and talk to the serving girls and the landlord.'

'What about Gabriel?'

'The Corporation's offering a reward,' he said flatly. 'The posters are going up today.'

Sedgwick frowned and let out his breath loudly.

'I warned the mayor,' Nottingham continued.

'Couldn't he give us another day or two?'

'The city needs to show it's concerned,' he said disgustedly, then picked up the quill pen and tossed it across the desk. 'They don't care about the children, you know that. They're only bothered because people are angry.'

'So what are we going to do, boss?'

'There's no choice. We'll have to go through everything that comes in. It doesn't even matter if we know it's wrong.'

'Every bastard in the city's going to come through that door.'

'I know that, John. But there's nothing we can do about it. You'd better get down to the inn and see what you can discover. We'll be busy enough later.'

Alone again, he sat back in frustration. He was no closer to finding Gabriel and he didn't know how the two recruits had escaped. It wasn't a good return to work. He ached all day and by evening he was exhausted, drained by what he'd done. And that had been precious little, he knew.

Perhaps Mary had been right when she'd suggested that he leave the job. It was in the slowest time of his recovery, when the days all seemed dark and clouded and she believed he'd never have good health again. But he'd been certain he needed this; he'd clung to it. Now, mired down this way, he wondered if he should have listened more closely to her.

He picked up the stick, the silver cold against his palm. A hot pie at the Swan would revive his spirits. Before he could reach the door it opened and a man glanced around nervously before ducking quickly into the jail.

He was tall, a worn old bicorn hat on his head, with the diffident, furtive look of a servant on his face.

'You need the law?' the Constable asked.

The man snatched off his hat awkwardly, holding it in front of him and kneading it nervously between his fingers. He opened his mouth to speak and closed it again. The words would need to be teased out of him, Nottingham thought.

'Has something happened?'

'This Gabriel,' the man said finally, his voice husky and barely there. 'It's real, what they say?'

'It is,' the Constable confirmed. 'Do you know anything about him?'

The man bit his lip, as if unsure whether to continue. Finally he blurted out, 'Aye. I think it might be my master.'

EIGHT

He looked sharply at the man, but the anguish on his face made it clear he was serious, torn inside. It had cost him a great deal to come here and say those words.

'Who's your master?' He waited patiently, knowing the answer wouldn't come easily.

'Mr Darden,' the servant said finally.

The Constable groaned inside. Darden was one of the city's richest merchants, a man who'd served on the corporation. If he'd been killing children . . .

'Why do you think he might be Gabriel?' he asked, trying to keep his voice even and steady.

'He has a grey suit and a wig.'

'Plenty of men own those,' Nottingham countered.

'And he came home last week with some blood on his clothes,' the man blurted out. 'On the grey coat.'

'Did he say anything about it?'

'Claimed he'd been at a cockfight at the Talbot.'

That was quite possible. If Darden had been at the front of
the crowd he could easily have been spattered in blood.

'Why don't you believe him?'

'He's never been to one before, and I been with him years
now. 'Sides, he's been different since.'

'How?' He sat again, listening closely.

'He's been quiet. He can't seem to settle to owt. It's not like
him.'

'Have there been any other times in the last few months when
he's seemed strange?' The Constable thought of Jane and David,
the two other children Caleb had told him about.

The man scratched at his head. 'Nay. Not that I can remember
right now.'

'I know it's not easy but you did the right thing in coming to
tell me,' Nottingham thanked him.

The man raised his eyes and gave a tight, wan smile that
betrayed his pain. 'I keep thinking of those little ones.'

'Do you really believe it's Mr Darden?'

'I don't know.' He gazed at the floor. 'That's the truth. But he's
not been hissen for more than a week now, and that's a fact. He
gets up in the night and walks about the house. It just made me
wonder.' He moved the hat between his fingers again. 'You'll
not say it were me, will you?'

'I won't say anything,' the Constable promised. 'I'll look into
it. And if it's him I'll arrest him.'

The man seemed satisfied with that. He gave a quick nod then
jammed the hat low on his head and slipped out of the jail.

Jeremiah Darden. The man had money; he'd made a grander
fortune than most out of the wool trade. For years he'd been an
alderman until he'd resigned, paying a fine to leave office. There
had even been vague talk about Darden becoming mayor,
Nottingham recalled, but it had never happened.

His wife had died two or three years before, he remembered.
The couple had three daughters, bonny girls, all respectably married
off around the county, none of the sons-in-law eager to involve
themselves in anything as dirty as trade. Darden still sometimes
attended the markets at the Cloth Hall and on Briggate. He bought
the occasional length of cloth, but most of the business these days
was done by his factor and his coffers stayed full.

For all that he'd retreated from public life, even Darden's softest words spoke loudly in Leeds. The people with power paid close attention to all he said. He was friend to them all and banker to a few when they needed it, if the rumours were true. And that meant the Constable needed to move very carefully. An accusation against Jeremiah Darden, especially one like this, was very dangerous.

Hot food at the White Swan would have to wait. Instead, he marched down Briggate to the Talbot.

'You didn't slip down and let them out in the night, did you, love?' Sedgwick asked with a sly smile.

The maid at the Crown and Fleece stared squarely at him. She was in her late thirties, hands red and raw from washing pots and sheets, face pinched from years of hard work, strands of grey in the hair that escaped from her cap.

'No, I bloody well did not,' she told him. 'And if you call me love again you're going to walk out of here with a slapped face.'

He held up his hands in apology. 'Well, someone must have let them out. They didn't just fly away.' She glared at him. 'I just thought you might have felt sorry for them.'

The maid snorted and pushed the sleeves higher on her fleshy arms. 'If they were daft enough to believe that sod they can go and be a soldier for all I care.'

'Could someone else have done it?' he asked. She seemed the type to harbour a suspicion. 'The potboy, a serving girl.'

'Happen,' she conceded, then her eyes flashed in triumph and she sniffed. 'But the serving girl sleeps in the same room as me. She wasn't up in the night, I can tell you that. And that stable lad could sleep through the day of judgement. It wasn't him.'

It hadn't been the landlord or his wife, either; after talking to them the deputy was certain of that. They were a couple who simply wanted a quiet, uneventful life, a road that ran straight before them all the way to the churchyard.

He'd walked around the stable, gone inside and climbed up to the loft where the hay stood at least almost as tall as a man, ready for winter. But he couldn't see how the two recruits could have vanished without help, and it hadn't come from the inn, he was certain of that. He didn't know the answer and maybe he never would. As he left the inn he saw the sergeant and the drummer boy ahead of him, starting on their way to Wakefield. The soldier walked with his shoulders slumped, all the confidence gone from his stride.

The Talbot was crowded. Men filled the tables, bent over their dinners; the smell of stew filled the air, heavily spiced to hide the rancid taste of meat long past its best. But the food was cheap and hot and it filled the belly.

He walked up to the long trestle where the landlord was drawing ale and carefully avoiding his glance. The Constable waited half a minute then brought the silver tip of the stick down sharply on the wood. Every head jerked towards him.

'Mr Nottingham,' the man said with a forced smile. 'I didn't see you standing there.' He wiped his hands slowly on his leather apron.

'I'm sure you didn't, Mr Bell. You worked hard enough not to. I want a word with you.'

'We're busy and the girl's off ill,' the landlord protested.

'Then the quicker you give me answers, the sooner you'll be serving again, won't you? Down that end where it's quiet.'

Bell kept glancing back, making sure everything remained orderly. The noise in the tavern slowly grew again.

'Is this about them two who died?' he asked. 'I told that lad of yours, they were outside.'

The Constable didn't reply. He kept staring at the landlord, making him uneasy. That way there was the chance of dragging a little truth from him.

'They started fighting in here but I kicked them out, and that was an end to it as far as I was concerned.'

'When did you last hold a cockfight?'

The question took Bell by surprise. 'A week ago Saturday,' he answered after a moment's thought. 'Why? Nowt wrong with that.'

'Do you know Jeremiah Darden?'

'The merchant?' Bell asked warily. Nottingham nodded. 'Aye, by sight, same as most in the city.' He was on edge, uncertainty in his eyes as he refused to hold the Constable's gaze.

'Does he come to the cockfights?'

'Him?'

'Yes.'

Bell shook his head. 'Never seen him at one in my time. Why?'

'Was he at the last one you had?'

'I just said—'

'Yes or no,' Nottingham asked. His voice was quiet but firm.

'No.'

'Then I thank you.' He looked over the press of people wanting drink. 'You can go back to your work now.' As the landlord turned away, he added, 'I'll be back to talk about those two deaths another time.'

So Darden had lied, he thought as he returned to the jail. It could mean that the servant's suspicions were right and the man was Gabriel. Or it could mean any number of other things. He stoked up the fire and sat for a while, drawing in the heat and trying to think.

He needed to talk to Darden; that was beyond any doubt. And he knew he had to inform the mayor first. It would be better to wait until tomorrow, after the reward had been announced. Fenton could bluster all he liked then, but he wouldn't be able to stop the Constable following up on a tip.

By late afternoon men were pasting the posters on boards and buildings. The ink was still fresh enough to run, blurring the words, but no one could miss the amount the corporation was offering for the arrest of Gabriel. Twenty pounds. It would take most of the working men in Leeds more than half a year to earn that much. Some wit had pasted one of the posters to the door of the jail and he tore it off as he left, crumpling the paper and letting it fall to the ground.

There were more of the notices on the pillars leading to the White Cloth Hall. A man stood and read the words aloud to a crowd that broke into loud murmurs when he announced the reward. It would be like that all over the city, greed quickly clouding men's eyes and minds.

They didn't even notice Nottingham walk past as he headed out past the Parish Church towards Timble Bridge and home. The men with power could open their purses and offer enough to turn heads, enough to make it seem as if they cared, but they'd do nothing to help the children like Caleb or the people who saw Bessie's camp as their only home.

'What's wrong?' Mary asked as he walked through to the kitchen and held her close. He kept his arms around her, her cheek next to his, until he felt the anger inside begin to ebb and he could open his eyes again.

'The Corporation's put up a reward for the man who killed the children. Twenty pounds.'

'Do they honestly believe that will help?' she asked in horror.

'They do,' he answered sadly.

She shook her head in disgust. 'Just leave them to it, Richard,' she said. 'Tell them you're still not well enough. We'll manage.'

He stroked her hair gently. 'I can't. You know I can't walk out and leave John and Rob to deal with it all. I saw those children. I saw what Gabriel had done.' He stepped back to look deep into her eyes. 'I can't walk away from them, either.'

'I know,' she said with a sigh of resignation. 'I know you too well. But sometimes I wish you didn't have duty in your veins. The city takes advantage of you.'

Rob saw the notices as he waited outside the dame school for Emily. People were talking eagerly about the reward on offer as they passed, how they'd spend it, imagining who they knew who might be Gabriel.

He leaned against the wall, hands pushed deep in the pockets of his greatcoat. Evening was starting to fall, the air bitter and damp against his face. No doubt folk would be out tonight, eager to name names and hope for the money. It was stupid.

She came through the door and he stood upright, smiling, his heart lighter. Emily put her arm through his and they began to walk down the street. Rob pointed out the poster and she stopped to read it.

'A reward?' she asked.

'Yes,' he answered with a sigh. 'A big one, too. It shows how concerned they are.'

'But everyone . . .' She paused for a moment. 'It's not going to help what you do at all, is it?'

'No,' he told her, 'it's not.'

She took tighter hold of his arm and said, 'Let's take a walk by the river.'

'Now?' Rob asked in astonishment. 'In this weather?'

'Then there won't be many people around,' she answered with a smile, and he knew he wouldn't be able to refuse her.

Emily led and he was content to follow. She strode past the warehouses and the stink of the dye works as if they barely existed, pulling him along by the hand, before clambering up the bank into a stand of trees, all the leaves gone from their branches. The track ran to a dip in the ground, sheltered from the wind and out of sight. She turned around, gazing up at the sky, a smile on her lips that he couldn't read.

'You look like you know this place.'

'When I was little my sister and I used to come here.' She paced around slowly, reaching out to touch a tree or bending to make out something he couldn't see. 'It was our special place. Even Mama and Papa didn't know about it. I haven't been back here since Rose died.' She gathered her cloak and sat on an old, weathered tree trunk that lay on the ground. 'We'd sit here and she'd tell me stories. Or sometimes we'd play.' She patted the log and he settled next to her.

'So why did you want to bring me here?' He stroked her neck, the skin soft and warm under his fingertip. She turned and kissed him quickly.

'Because I wanted you to know about it, too,' she explained. 'I wanted us to have somewhere that was ours, where no one else can find us. And in summer . . .' Her eyes twinkled; he imagined the hollow hidden by bushes and leaves and grinned. Emily took his hand and began to slide her fingers between his. 'Papa told me some things while he was recovering,' she began, her glance flickering to him, then away and back again, and he knew they'd reached the true reason for coming here. He waited; she'd continue when she was ready. 'Do you remember Amos Worthy?'

'Of course,' he replied, taken aback by her question.

'He knew my grandmama. He loved her. That's what Papa told me. I think it surprised him when he learned that.' Lister was certain that it had. 'He left me some money in his will.'

'What?' The word flew out of him.

'He told Papa that he wanted to give me freedom. I'll receive it when I come of age.'

When she came of age, he thought. That was still four years away, a lifetime, one he wanted to spend with her. But he knew Emily; if she was talking about it, she needed to make a decision about this now, otherwise it would rub at her every day and leave her raw.

'It would be my money.' Her eyes widened. '*My* money. Enough to live on.' She paused. 'For us both to live on.'

'You know what he was, don't you?'

She nodded, her lips pushed together.

'What do you want to do?'

'What would you do?' she countered.

It was a long time before he answered, allowing his thoughts to form and the words to take shape. He held her hand as she watched him.

'I think I'd say no. But I'd wish I'd been able to say yes.'

She sighed and rested her head on his shoulder. 'That's what I told Papa I'd do. He said I should wait, that I might change my mind by the time I'm twenty-one.'

But she wouldn't. He knew her well enough by now to be certain of that, and he loved her deeply enough to be grateful for it.

'I love you,' he said quietly. They sat for a few more minutes as the darkness grew around them, then made their way back to the house on Marsh Lane.

'We were wondering where you two had been,' Mary Nottingham said brightly, and Rob saw her glance swiftly at Emily's clothes to make certain she was properly dressed.

'Sit down, lad,' the Constable told him. 'I need to talk to you before we eat.'

Lister lowered himself on to an old joint stool. The warmth from the fire started to soak through his clothes and into his skin. 'What is it, boss?'

'What do you know about Jeremiah Darden?'

Rob pursed his lips and tried to recall things he'd heard. 'Nothing, really. No more than anyone else.'

Nottingham nodded slowly. 'What about your father?'

Lister let out a long breath and held his hands out to the blaze as if he wanted to cup its heat between them. 'I'm sure he'd know chapter and verse,' he replied. 'Why?'

'One of Darden's servants thinks he might be Gabriel.'

Rob raised an eyebrow. 'Did he think that before or after the reward was posted?'

'Before.' The Constable waited a moment before continuing. 'I'd like to you talk to your father and find out what he knows about Darden.'

'Boss . . .' Rob said warily. 'You know he might not want to speak to me.'

'He will,' Nottingham told him with a confident smile.

The shutters were closed at the office of the *Leeds Mercury*, no light leaking through. He knocked on the heavy door that stood to the side and heard the sound of footsteps on the stair. The servant held up a candle, eyes widening to see him.

'Mr Robert!'

'Hello, Sarah,' he said with a smile. 'I've come to see my father. Is he upstairs?'

'He is. Come on in.'

He passed by, the smells of the house, of cooked cabbage and wax, as familiar as if he'd never left. James Lister was in the parlour, sitting before the fire in his favourite chair, a volume of Defoe page-down on his lap. He looked up as Rob entered, cocking his head questioningly.

'I'd not looked to see you here again,' he said. There was no warmth in his words.

'Hello, Father,' Rob said. He looked around the room. It was exactly as he remembered it, books filling the shelves along the walls, candles lighting the place.

'Given up on the lass, have you?'

Rob shook his head. 'I'm here on business, nothing more.'

'Oh?' James Lister sat upright, his face suddenly alive and interested. 'What do you need?'

'Information on Jeremiah Darden.'

The older man rubbed his chin. 'Why do you need to know about him?'

Rob gave a small smile. 'I can't tell you, and there's nothing you can print, Father. Just as if you were dealing with Mr Nottingham.'

Lister chuckled. 'You've a long way to go yet before you're Constable, lad.' He paused and narrowed his eyes. 'Is this to do with the reward?'

'What would make you think that?'

'Timing. I take it you don't need the common knowledge?' He waited a moment for an answer then plunged on. 'The Corporation wanted Darden to be mayor a few years ago. He'd been an alderman since he was a young man. He turned it down and resigned. Paid the fine to be allowed to leave and that was it. Hasn't done much since.'

'Why?' Rob asked.

The older man mulled over his reply. 'He's never said, although plenty of people had their ideas. Honestly, I don't know.' He offered a small shrug. 'It's a mystery. I do know he pulled back from business around the same time.'

'How is he as a man?'

Lister removed his spectacles and wiped them carefully on the elaborate silk of his waistcoat. 'Not especially social. He never was, I suppose. More so when his wife was alive, perhaps. I remember they'd go to assemblies and balls sometimes. He married young and doted on those daughters of his. Now they're all married off he doesn't seem to have much in his life.'

'And his temperament?'

Lister gave a smile. 'Jeremiah Darden's never been one to suffer fools.'

Rob laughed. 'You mean he's an awkward bastard.'

His father pursed his mouth. 'Your words, not mine.' He cleared his throat. 'How are your lodgings?'

'Good enough for what I need. You've no idea why Mr Darden stepped away from public life? That's unlike you.'

'There's nothing queerer than folk. That's what they say and it's true enough. You should have learnt that in your job by now. There were a few rumours about him and a girl.'

'A girl? Who was she?'

'A very young girl,' Lister said pointedly. 'No one really believed it, but he left the Corporation.

'What were the rumours?'

The older man waved them away with his hand. 'Tittle-tattle. Whispers behind hands.' He made a face. 'It seemed ridiculous.

Just folk making trouble. I didn't believe it then and I won't believe it now. Jeremiah Darden's an upright man, always has been. He's given plenty of his wealth to charity over the years.' He paused. 'You didn't know that, did you?'

'I don't know anything about him,' Rob pointed out. 'That's why I came to ask you.'

'And I've told you.'

'Then thank you, Father.' He gave a small bow and turned.

'Come for your dinner some Sunday,' Lister said quietly to his son's back. 'Your mother would love to see you again.' Rob took two paces down the stairs. 'Bring that girl if you like.' Rob nodded and left the house.

The cold air felt clean against his skin. His father had taken him by surprise, ambushed him. What was behind that offer? Did he really want to reconcile or was he hoping for a chance to humiliate Emily? God alone knew. But he needed to put it out of his mind for the moment.

Maybe his father had been wrong to discount all the gossip about Darden and the girl. They'd need to investigate that.

He strode down Briggate and along the path by the Aire. Bessie was helping a girl feed her small child when he found her, spooning something into the infant's mouth, encouraging and cajoling her to eat more. He waited silently until she'd finished and wiped her hand on her dress, gathering a shawl tight around her shoulders.

'Babies making babies,' she said with a slow shake of her head. 'They don't know.'

'How are you, Bessie?'

'I'll live. More than some of these will if it gets any colder. We could use more food,' she said pointedly.

'I'll talk to the baker. He should have some old loaves.'

'It'll all help, love.' She nodded her approval. 'I've asked around about those children.'

'Anything?' Rob asked hopefully.

'They tend to keep to themselves. They don't trust anyone else. I'm sorry, Mr Lister.'

'What about Gabriel?'

'I don't think people have talked about owt else since the posters went up.' She snorted. 'Truth is, no one here's seen him. They might think they have, but it's just hoping for the money.'

'Thank you, Bessie.'

'Nay, lad. I just wish I could do more. You find him, though.'

'We will.'

'And kill him. It's no more than he deserves.'

NINE

John Sedgwick woke with a start, sitting up with his eyes wide and heart racing as the dream dissolved in his head.

'What is it?' Lizzie asked, her voice full of sleep.

He breathed slowly and wiped the night sweat off his face. 'Nothing. Don't worry about it, love.' He stroked her hair and neck until he felt her drift away. It was still full dark but there would be no more rest, not after the images he'd seen, of James and Isabell tortured, used and bloody, and left for dead at the side of the road. He could hear them both sleeping, the baby in her crib, the boy on his small bed.

Quietly, he rose and dressed, took some bread from the kitchen and slipped out of the door. He knew that moving, doing something, was the only way to make the pictures go away.

Still an hour to dawn, he judged, the time when the blackness was blackest and the thoughts were always bleak. The air had turned even colder and a low fog clung tight to the ground, creeping like an army over the land.

Rob was at the jail, the scrape of his nib on paper loud as he wrote out the night report. The deputy settled close by the fire, took the bread from his pocket and began to eat.

'Many come in for the reward?' he asked.

Lister frowned. 'Ten of them last night, and that's just the ones who found me here.'

'Anything likely?'

'What do you think? Some of them would peach on their dog if it would bring in sixpence. Anyway, someone came and gave the boss a name yesterday.'

'Oh?' Sedgwick asked with interest.

'You're going to love this. It's Jeremiah Darden.'

The deputy laughed. 'That old bastard? You can't be serious.'

'I am. The boss asked me to find out about him from my father.'

'And did you?' he asked slowly. 'You went to see him?'

Rob nodded. 'Last night.'

'What did he have to say?'

'About Darden?'

'Aye.'

'Seems there was a rumour about him and a very young girl. He was supposed to become mayor but instead he resigned from the Corporation. No one who mattered believed it, but . . .'

'You told the boss yet?'

'No.'

'And what else did your father say to you?'

'Invited me for Sunday dinner.' He paused. 'With Emily.'

The deputy raised his eyebrows in surprise. 'What are you going to do?'

He sighed. 'I don't know. I'll have to talk to her.'

The door opened and the Constable walked in. 'That fog's getting thicker,' he said, shrugging off his coat. 'If it keeps up you won't be able to see the Moot Hall soon.'

'I'd not call that a bad thing,' Sedgwick laughed.

'You might be right there.' He gave a small smile and sat in the chair. 'Right, what do we have?' He listened closely as Rob related what he'd learned and the deputy aired his frustration. 'We'll have more people giving us names today. Look into them, John. We need to follow up on everything. I'm going to talk to the mayor and then see Mr Darden.'

'Yes, boss.'

'Go back to everyone you've talked to, see if they've remembered anything.' He glanced at Rob. 'And the same for you tonight.'

Martin Cobb sat behind his desk, the scrape of his quill the only noise in the corridor. Nottingham placed the report on the desk.

'I need to see the mayor.'

'Constable . . .' the clerk began but Nottingham cut him off, his tone brooking no protest.

'Now.'

Cobb looked down for a moment, then back up. 'If it's important you'd better go in.'

Fenton was standing at the window, looking out at a city lost in the fog. He turned as the door opened.

'Any results from the poster?'

'Someone came to see me yesterday with a name.'

'And?' the mayor asked brusquely.

'The name was Jeremiah Darden.'

'You believe it?' Fenton almost shouted the words, his face reddening. 'Are you a fool? Has being off work addled your brains?'

'He lied about how some blood ended up on his grey coat,' the Constable told him flatly. 'The same colour Gabriel wears. That's enough to warrant talking to him.'

'If you accuse him you'll end up looking ridiculous,' the mayor warned.

'I haven't accused anyone yet. I just want to ask him some questions.'

'Then make sure you keep it to that. Even if you should find something to properly incriminate Mr Darden, you will not arrest him without my authority.' He paused. 'Do you understand that, Nottingham?'

The Constable stared at him. 'I'll do my job, your Worship. The one the city pays me to do.' He gave a small bow and left.

He needed to calm his temper before seeing Darden. After seeing the mayor his blood was hot, and it needed to be cold as January for the encounter. He let the fog swallow him, drifting down Briggate to Leeds Bridge. Sounds were muffled, even the creak of carts as they approached, and people came and vanished like ghosts in a dream.

The water rushed by, a few yards below him, with a noise as deep as the devil's laughter. He leaned on the parapet and watched it, roiling and curling around the stanchions, until the anger had passed. Then he cut through to Vicar Lane to the house that had been in Darden's family for generations.

The limewash had been renewed recently, still a bright, glowing white against the dark timbers. The windows were small and old, the door heavy, worn oak. At the side of the building a cobbled path led to the warehouse where Darden had his business.

He'd had few dealings with the man over the years; he'd maybe met him three or four times, and they'd never spoken long enough for him to gain a solid impression beyond the sense of wealth and power that surrounded him like perfume.

Nottingham let his fist fall on the door three times and waited. Soon he could hear a rush of footsteps and then he was looking at the harried face of the servant who'd appeared at the jail.

'Yes, sir?' the man asked as if they'd never seen each other before.

Nottingham smiled. 'I'm the Constable of Leeds. I'd like to see Mr Darden.'

He entered the hall and waited while the servant went into a room, hearing the small murmur of voices. Then he was shown into a parlour where Jeremiah Darden sat in his chair, a copy of the *Mercury* spread over his lap. He took off his spectacles, a quizzical look on his face. There was an air of cleanliness about him, but the rich always looked clean and smelt of sanctity, Nottingham thought. Dirt never clung to them.

'Constable?'

'Yes, sir,' Nottingham answered.

'You wanted to see me?'

'Yes. You've heard what happened to the children?'

'The ones in the bell pit? Of course.' He folded the newspaper and dropped it on the floor. Even seated he was a big, powerful man, his hands large, thighs thick in a pair of pale blue breeches, his hose pure white, shoes polished, silver buckles sparkling in the light from a hot fire. 'What's that to do with me?'

'Where were you a week ago Saturday?' the Constable asked, keeping his eyes on Darden's face.

The man sat and thought. 'Was that when they had the cock-fight at the Talbot?' he said after a few moments.

'Yes.'

'Then that's where I was.' He gave a small, bemused chuckle and rubbed his chin. 'The first time I've ever been, if you can believe that.' There was no sign of worry or hesitation.

'Did you enjoy it?'

'Not especially. I only went because my factor's been saying for years that I should see it. I finally gave in.' He snorted. 'I lost a guinea and came home with blood on my coat from the damn bird. Anyway, what does that have to do with those children?'

'You've seen the posters the city put up?'

'Of course. I've given a pound towards the reward myself. Fenton came calling on me for money.'

The man had complete confidence, Nottingham thought. Pride seemed to seep from every pore. Most people would be nervous if the law came asking questions, but Darden acted as if it was the most normal conversation in the world, with nothing at all to hide.

'It's brought out plenty of people wanting the reward and giving us names.'

'I still don't see how that brings you here, Constable.'

'Yours was one of the names.'

For a second the man's face darkened, as if his temper was about to explode. Then he gave a long, deep laugh. 'Me? And you believed them?'

'We're following up on everything,' Nottingham said genially.

'Well, there's nothing here for you. If you don't believe I was at the cockfight, ask my factor, Mr Howard, or whoever it is that owns the Talbot. They'll tell you.'

'I will,' the Constable promised and smiled. 'After all, I have to do my job.'

Darden stared at him as if trying to see a deeper meaning in the words, then gave a curt nod. 'Next time try using a little intelligence, though. You should know better than to suspect a man like me. Good day, Constable. I don't imagine you'll need to return here.'

Outside, the fog wreathed around him as he walked. Darden had attempted to be polite, but there had been something beneath that, a deep disregard, arrogance, as if the man had believed himself above everything. He'd never asked about the children, never mentioned them, as if their deaths were nothing at all to him.

And he'd lied about being at the cockfight, the Constable was certain of that, just as he was sure that if he returned to the Talbot tomorrow, Bell would remember that the merchant had been there after all. And Solomon Howard was Darden's factor, the man closest to him. He'd worked for and with the man for years now; he'd say whatever he was bidden to say.

In his gut he now believed that Darden was Gabriel. Proving it – even being allowed to try – would be another matter altogether. And the man knew that full well. He believed he was untouchable.

'John, I want Holden watching Darden every day. He's the best we have. Tell Rob to assign another of the men to cover nights.'

'Yes, boss.' He hesitated. 'Are you sure it's him?'

'I am,' Nottingham replied with certainty. He frowned. 'He's clever, though. Didn't even blink at the questions, answered everything perfectly naturally. And at the end warned me not to come back.'

'What? He threatened?'

The Constable shook his head. 'Nothing as obvious as that. He just gave me a very strong hint that I should consider him above suspicion.'

'So how are we going to prove any of this, boss?'

'I'm going to find Caleb and have the lad take a look at him. He's seen Gabriel, he can tell me if it's Darden.'

'And if it isn't?'

'It is,' Nottingham said.

'What about all these people giving us names? If I've had one this morning, I've had twenty of them.'

'Do what you can and pass the rest to the men to look into. They'll all come to nothing, anyway.'

'What about the mayor?'

'I'll tell him we're looking at everything.' He gave a sly grin. 'It'll be the truth. We will be, just not quite the way he wants.'

Sedgwick glanced out of the window. 'With this fog Holden will have problems following Darden. It's not going to clear today.'

'I don't care if he knows we have someone on him. He won't be doing anything stupid.' The Constable pushed the fringe off his forehead. 'I want him to know we're there.'

'He'll go to the mayor, boss.'

'Let him.' He rummaged through a small pile of papers on the desk. 'Do you have anything more on those recruits who vanished?'

'Bugger all.' He gave a deep sigh. 'I went back again. No one will admit to letting them go and they didn't leave without help. It doesn't make any sense to me. I don't think we're going to get anywhere on it.'

The bell at the Parish Church sounded for noon, the noise deadened by the fog.

'Come on,' the Constable said, 'let's go next door to the Swan and have dinner. See if the world looks any better with a full belly.'

TEN

Nottingham walked down Briggate, the chill of the fog seeping through to his bones. His greatcoat felt damp to the touch, tiny drops forming on the wool. In the distance he could hear shouting; he moved faster, following the sounds down towards Swinegate. As he turned the corner the noise grew louder, a babble of voices yelling obscenities and threats. He charged forward, shouldering men aside until he reached the middle of the mob.

'Stop!' he shouted, using his stick to push people away. A man was on the ground, curled in on himself, his hat a few yards away, dark wig close to his head. Someone raised his foot to kick and the Constable hit him sharply on the knee. 'What's going on here?' When no one answered, he said, 'You know who I am. You can give me some answers or spend tonight in the jail.' He pointed at a fat man wearing a threadbare coat and sweating as if he'd worked half a day 'You. Tell me.'

'It's him,' he answered, trying to catch his breath. 'It's that Gabriel. He killed them children.'

The Constable glanced down. He knew the man's face. He was Mr Sorensen, one of three Swedish merchants who'd arrived in Leeds ten years before. They'd set up in business and slowly established themselves, marrying local women and becoming part of the fabric of Leeds.

'Why would you think that?'

'Just look at him,' the fat man answered with a smirk, and a few others nodded and murmured. 'He's got a grey coat and breeches and a wig. Listen to him, you can tell by the way he speaks. He dun't sound right.'

He moved forward a pace and Nottingham raised the stick as a warning, smelling the heaviness of ale on the man's breath. He knew all too well how the mood of a mob could shift in an instant. He needed to control them or there'd be more violence.

He picked out a spindly man with a long face at the front of the crowd. 'You, what's your name?'

Taken aback, the man answered without thinking, 'Tom, sir.'

'You think you can attack a man on the street?' the Constable asked.

The man looked around the gathered faces and shifted uneasily. 'We were arresting him,' he said. 'To get the reward.'

Somewhere, Nottingham could hear running feet. But the fog was too thick to see anything or even judge how far away they were.

'No, you weren't. If you'd carried on you'd have killed him. Do you want to hang for murder, Tom?' He said the words evenly and let them have their impact. None of the crowd had moved back. They weren't willing to listen, the blood lust had risen. The fat man was leering at him, ready to pounce forwards. He balanced the stick, ready to use it, holding it so the silver top would hurt whoever it hit.

'Right, break this up.' Two of his men came through the mist, swinging their cudgels ready for a fight. Now the odds had changed the swagger vanished from the small group, like air going out of a bladder.

'Take this one to the jail,' the Constable ordered. He looked around. 'Any of you still here when I count to three will go with him.'

'You can't do that,' the fat man protested.

Nottingham turned to him. 'I just did it. You're going to be charged with assault.' He put his face close to the man. 'This

isn't a city where you can take the law into your own hands.
You're going to learn that.'

His men took the fat man's arms. Everyone else had vanished.
Carefully, he knelt by the merchant. The man was conscious.
His nose had been broken and there was blood all around his face.
'Can you stand?'

'I think so,' Sorensen answered, his voice so thick with pain
and fear the Constable could barely make out the words. He
hawked, spitting out some blood and two teeth, moving himself
gingerly on to his hands and knees and staying there as he gathered his strength.

The Constable held him by the arm to steady him, giving
Sorensen something to grab as he raised himself with a long
groan. Nottingham bent and picked up the man's wig and hat.

'Why?' The merchant moved his head slowly to clear it. 'Why
they do that?'

'They thought you were Gabriel. The child killer.'

'Me?' Sorensen's eyes widened in disbelief. 'But why?'

'Because you're wearing grey. Because you sound different.
Because they all want the reward.'

'So.' He nodded and began to dust himself down.'

'Do you want me to fetch the apothecary?'

'No,' Sorensen answered. 'But help me home if you will, Mr
Nottingham.' He spoke in a curious accent, the native singsong
of his words overlaid with the stony roughness of Leeds. He
limped a few steps, grimacing, then set his mouth and tried to
walk normally, still favouring his left leg.

'I know Leeds,' Sorensen said thoughtfully. 'I been here ten
years. I know people not so stupid always.'

'Not always,' the Constable agreed. 'But twenty pounds is a
fortune to many of them. And some of them don't trust outsiders.'

The merchant shook his head sadly. They walked slowly up
Briggate towards Sorensen's new house at Town End, just beyond
the Head Row. 'Idiots,' he muttered quietly.

'You're right,' Nottingham agreed. 'But remember they're poor,
they don't know much.' He gave a sad smile. 'It's not an excuse.'

'Mr Fenton asked me to contribute to the reward. I said no.'
He turned to the Constable and raised an eyebrow. 'Maybe this
is what I get instead,' he said wryly.

'Tell the mayor. He might listen to you.'

They parted at the merchant's door. The man had a large home with a clean, spare front.

'Thank you for coming when you did,' Sorensen told him.

'Send for the apothecary,' Nottingham advised. 'He can give you something so you won't hurt so much later.'

'You know?' The man rubbed his jaw. Bruises were beginning to bloom on his face.

'I do.' He had too much experience of all that. He hesitated, then added, 'It might be best if you didn't wear anything grey or a wig. At least for now.'

The attack hadn't surprised him. It was bound to happen sooner or later, for exactly the reasons he'd given Sorensen. It probably wouldn't be the only one, either. All it needed was a single spark and there'd be other blazes like this, with no one around to stamp them out.

The mayor had offered the reward and he wouldn't withdraw it now. Even an attack on a merchant like the Swede wouldn't make him change his mind. Fenton wasn't the kind of man who could admit he was wrong.

The fat man sat in the cell, eyes furious, face florid, the veins broken all around his nose. He stood as he saw the Constable.

'You can't do this to me.' His voice was ragged and raw.

'Sit down and shut up.' He stared until the man reluctantly obeyed.

'We was just trying to stop Gabriel,' the man said, but all his power had gone.

'Instead you set on an innocent man.'

The man said nothing.

'You'll be at the Petty Sessions tomorrow. No one's going to give rough justice in Leeds.'

Sedgwick had a list of names and addresses of people someone thought could be Gabriel. He spent the afternoon going from one to the next. None of them was the man, and he knew they wouldn't be.

Over the years he'd learned to trust the boss. If he said Darden was Gabriel, then he was. What he couldn't see was how they were going to prove it and take him to the gallows. Even if they could find evidence, the mayor and the Corporation would protect him. They'd never let one of their own be found guilty of a crime like this.

How could they find out more? He wondered about Darden's factor, Solomon Howard. He didn't know the man but he'd seen him often enough at the cloth markets. He was prim, close to priggish. He always dressed well, more like a merchant than an employee, carrying an air of superiority with him.

In his late forties, he was Darden's man through and through, and had been for years. No one knew the merchant better. He'd be privy to many of the man's secrets. But Howard had always struck him as a brittle man, with little backbone under the thin veneer. How would he react if they began questioning him?

He played with the idea, keeping it at the back of his mind as he worked. By the time evening gathered he'd talked to almost twenty men, none of them remotely like Gabriel, rag pickers and labourers, clerks, shopkeepers on Briggate. But however much he hated it and saw it as a waste of his good time, he knew it had to be done. There were more names for Rob later, and this would go on for days yet.

He completed his final round, the fog still thick as a blanket around him. His feet ached, his mind was weary, and all he wanted was the quiet love of his family at the house on Lands Lane.

The fire was burning low and no one was downstairs when he entered. Surprised, he climbed the stairs. Lizzie was bent over Isabell's crib, while James stood close by. The fear in the room was so powerful he could have touched it.

'What is it?' he asked, his voice hushed. Lizzie turned and he saw terror on her face.

'She's burning up, John.' Lizzie sounded on the edge of desperation. 'She's been getting hotter all day. I've tried everything.' There were tracks on her cheeks where she'd been crying, haunted smudges under her eyes. James just stared at his little sister. The baby's face was red, but she was quiet. 'Do something, John, please,' Lizzie begged.

He ran.

He pounded through the fog, hearing the wet slap of his feet on the ground, all the way to Kirshaw the apothecary's house. He kept hammering on the door until a servant came, and asked breathlessly for the master.

As soon as he saw the man the tumble of thoughts and horrors cleared in his brain. 'I need you at my house,' he said firmly. The apothecary knew him, he did enough work for the city.

'Who is it?'

'My little girl. She's been on fire all day.'

The man frowned. 'All day?'

'Aye. You have to come now.'

Kirshaw nodded. 'I'll get my bag. Go home, Mr Sedgwick, I'll be there as soon as I can.'

The deputy took a deep breath, caught between the need to be with his family and dragging the man along.

'As soon as I can,' the apothecary repeated gently. 'I promise you.'

He nodded, turned on his heel and ran again until his lungs burned in his chest. He saw Isabell, dying, dead, felt the hole that would consume his life if she was no longer there.

'He's coming,' he told Lizzie and held her close, his other arm around James's shoulders. He wanted to tell them that everything would be fine, that Isabell would soon be crying and laughing as if nothing had happened. But even as he tried, the words caught in his throat and he knew he couldn't speak them. He couldn't feed those lies to the people he loved. He knew the truth, he'd seen the anguish on too many faces as tiny coffins were buried in the churchyard.

Lizzie felt stiff, rigid under his touch, as if she was scared to move. He heard the knock at the door, and pushed James away to answer it. Then the apothecary was there with his calm manner, easing them aside and bending over the cradle. The deputy watched Kirshaw's fingers stroke the baby's face and look into her eyes. Lizzie reached out and gripped his hand tightly. He looked at her and gave a tight smile that she couldn't return.

The apothecary took his time, wetting a cloth and wiping Isabell's forehead. Sedgwick held his breath, willing the seconds to pass quickly, for the man to say something, to offer some comfort.

Then Kirshaw stood, wiping his hands slowly on the cloth. He was a tall man, withered and stooped with age, his beard grey and bushy, his mouth pursed and thoughtful.

'How long has she been like this?' he asked.

'It started this morning,' Lizzie answered in a bare, fractured croak.

'Before that?'

The deputy tightened his fingers around hers.

'She seemed fine yesterday. Maybe . . .'

'What?' said the apothecary.

'A little scratchy in her throat,' Lizzie told him.

He nodded, then began to pace in the cramped room. 'I've seen quite a few cases like hers. She'll live—' Sedgwick felt relief course through him '—but she's going to be like this for another day, maybe two. She'll stay very hot. You must keep wiping her with a cold, wet cloth. You must.' He stared at them to make sure they understood.

'What about after that?' the deputy asked him. 'What then?'

The apothecary brightened. 'The fever will go, very quickly, and she'll start to get spots.'

'Spots?' The tremor had returned to Lizzie's voice.

'They'll last a few days and it will all be over,' he assured her. 'But you have to keep her cool while she's like this,' he repeated. 'It's vital. If anything bad happens, send for me.' He stooped to pick up his bag.

'What could happen?' He needed to know. Kirshaw hesitated before replying.

'Tell me, Mr Sedgwick, have you seen anyone have a fit?'

He had, and the quick madness of it terrified him. 'That could happen to her?'

'It might,' the apothecary answered carefully. 'If it does, send someone for me immediately.'

'Thank you,' Sedgwick said. He followed the man downstairs and stood by the door as Kirshaw pulled the heavy greatcoat over his scrawny body.

'She'll recover, with God's blessing,' he said, clapped the deputy on the shoulder and was gone. One of the few benefits of being a Constable's man was that he didn't have to pay the apothecary; Kirshaw made enough money from the city.

Upstairs, Lizzie was gently bathing Isabell with cold water from a basin. He stroked her hair.

'She'll be fine,' he said. 'You heard what he said.'

Lizzie turned her heard, her face anguished, tortured. 'But what if she's not, John? What if she has one of them fits?'

The thought was full in his mind, too. 'Then we'll send for Kirshaw again.' He sat on the bed and pulled James close. 'Don't worry, lad, she'll be back to herself in a few days. I promise.'

The boy nodded, his eyes more hopeful than convinced.

'You go off to bed,' Sedgwick told him. 'There's school for you in the morning.'

'Yes, Da.'

They kept a single candle burning in the corner, the tallow smell thick and greasy in the room, and took it in turns to wipe down the baby. Finally he said, 'You try and sleep for a while.'

'Sleep?' Lizzie said, as if it was a new word she'd never heard before. 'I can't do that, John. Not now.'

But she did, rolling and restless, muttering words too low to make out while he tended his daughter. He could see the pain on his little girl's face, and when her eyes opened the questions she had for him that she didn't have the words to ask. He soothed her and stroked her with the cloth and sat back as she drifted away for a few minutes.

Outside, he could hear all the small night noises of Leeds, the lonely set of footsteps, the voice that drifted on the air from somewhere. He could identify the hours by their sounds. Another few more of them and he'd be back at work, chasing down more worthless tips while his mind stayed here.

The Constable looked at him and said, 'You look like you haven't slept, John.'

'I haven't,' he answered, rubbing at his gritty eyes with the back of his hands. He explained why. 'Lizzie's looking after her now.'

'Any change?'

'Not yet,' he answered quietly. He ached inside for his daughter, caught in so much fear and distress, with no understanding of what was happening to her.

'You know what to do today.'

'What about Darden?'

Nottingham sat back and pushed the fringe off his forehead just as Rob entered.

'Tomorrow's market day. I'll try to find Caleb again. He knows more than he told me, I'm sure of that. I'd like him to take a look at Darden. If he identifies him . . .'

'Who do you think a magistrate would believe, boss?' Lister asked.

The Constable gave a grim smile. 'I know.'

'What about the factor?' Sedgwick asked. Nottingham stared at him. 'They're close, those two.'

'It's a thought.' He considered the idea. 'But he's been with Darden for years. He'll be loyal, I'll put money on it.'

'Push him a little. See what happens,' the deputy suggested. 'I'll do it if you like.'

The Constable thought for a minute. It wouldn't hurt to exert a little pressure. It would let Darden known that his station and his money wouldn't see him home free.

'No, I'll do it,' he said finally. 'I'll find him at the cloth market.'

'In public?' Sedgwick asked. 'Boss . . .'

'I'll ask him to come here afterwards for a talk,' Nottingham said with a smile.

'I'll wager he shows up with a lawyer.'

The Constable shrugged. 'Let him. I want him worried, even if I don't get anything from him.' He looked at Rob. 'Anything much during the night?'

'No, boss.'

'Come in early tonight if you can.'

'Yes, boss.'

Nottingham grinned. 'I imagine you have somewhere to be soon. Emily should be on her way to school.'

The lad blushed.

'Off you go.'

'Thank you, boss,' Sedgwick said once they were alone again.

'Right, you have work to do and I have the daily report to write.'

Sitting quietly at the desk, he flexed his fingers before picking up the quill and writing. It had been a bad night, the pain in his stomach making it hard to settle and sleep. He felt empty of emotion, carrying on only by the habit of years. Tomorrow he'd need to be sharp, and pray God rested again.

For now, though, he'd do his job, walk over to the Moot Hall with the report, then follow up on some of the tips that had come in. In his bones he knew there was nothing in them but he had to do his duty.

Martin Cobb glanced up as the Constable laid the report on his desk. 'Mr Fenton wants to talk to you.'

He'd been wondering if Darden would talk to the mayor; now he knew.

'Is he in?'

'He is, you can go through,' the clerk said, and returned to his papers.

A warm fire burned in the grate of Fenton's office, hot enough for the man to take off his coat and display a waistcoat with designs of birds and flowers delicately picked out in colourful silk. His shirt was crisp white, the stock carefully tied at his neck.

'Jeremiah Darden came to see me yesterday afternoon,' he began. 'He said you paid him a visit.'

'I told you I planned on it.'

'And I told you to tread very carefully.' The mayor had iron in his voice. 'He told me you as near as dammit accused him of being Gabriel.'

'But I didn't,' the Constable countered. He was standing, hands gripped tight on the back of the chair.

'And you'd bloody well better not.'

'Why?' Nottingham asked simply.

Fury flooded through the mayor's face. 'I've known Jeremiah Darden most of my life, I've done business with him.' He brought his palm down sharply on the desk. 'He's no more capable of something like that than I am.'

The Constable eyed him steadily, saying nothing for a long time. Even if Darden was Gabriel and the truth came screaming at the door, Fenton and the others who ran Leeds would shut their ears. 'What are you ordering me to do, your Worship?' he asked finally.

'I'm not giving you any orders, Nottingham.' Fenton paused, choosing his words with great care. 'But I'll tell you something for nothing. There are some folk on the Corporation who thought you should have retired after you were hurt. They believe Leeds needs a new Constable. Going after Mr Darden won't do anything to change their minds.' He gave a curt nod of dismissal.

Briggate was lively, servants out and gossiping, the apprentices laughing with each other, shops with shutters wide, welcoming trade, an exotic mix of spices as he passed the grocer, leather displayed invitingly at the glover, the slop of bloody guts and innards at the Shambles, stray dogs fighting over the scraps.

So all the good aldermen were gathering around one of their own, Nottingham thought as he walked down the street. But the aldermen hadn't seen the pain and the helplessness on the faces of the dead children. They hadn't stroked the bruises, wiped away the coal dust where the corpses had been thrown away. And however much they offered as a reward, they didn't care.

He turned on his heel and walked back to the Head Row. The first drops of rain hit his face as he opened the door to Garroway's Coffee House. The smell was so thick it caught at the back of his throat, the air steamy and damp, windows misted over with condensation.

There were only a few men in the place, cups and crumbs scattered across the tables in front of them. Tom Williamson sat in his usual place close to the banked fire, two of last week's London papers on the bench in front of him, the pages of the *Mercury* strewn lazily on the floor at this side.

'You must be wanting something if you've come here, Richard,' he said with a smile. 'Come and sit down.'

The merchant was wearing another new coat and breeches, dark green velvet this time, cut to the height of London fashion, and a waistcoat whose design was shot through with silver thread. The clothes of a rich man, Nottingham thought as he settled, one growing richer by the day. Working hard and using his brain he'd taken his father's merchant business and made it into something bigger and more prosperous.

'Were you looking for me?'

'I was,' the Constable admitted. 'You got your way with the reward, I see.'

Williamson had the grace to look shamefaced. 'I'm sorry,

Richard. It had gone too far, too many people believed it was a good idea. Has it been any help?'

'Bugger all.' He laughed.

'Is there anything I can do?'

'You could tell me about Solomon Howard, Darden's factor.'

'Solomon?' The request took him by surprise. 'You don't think he's—'

'I don't think anything, Tom,' he replied quietly. 'I just need to know about him.'

Williamson breathed in deeply, gathering his thoughts.

'Well, he's been Jeremiah's factor for as long as I can remember.' He rubbed his chin. 'He's good at his job, always seems to know what the markets abroad are going to want. And he's vain, he looks more like a merchant than most merchants. Jeremiah pays him well, I know that. He's more or less one of us, even if he doesn't have his own business. And Jeremiah's promised him the business when he dies.'

'It won't go to his daughters?'

'No. Their husbands aren't interested. They'd only sell it, anyway, and they all have money. So Solomon is very loyal.' He gave a short bark of laughter. 'As you can imagine.'

'What's he like as a man?'

'Very dry,' Williamson replied after a moment. 'I don't think I've ever heard him laugh. Never married, I do know that.' He chuckled. 'I doubt he could find a woman who'd put up with him, even for what he earns. I think the man spends most of his waking hours working.'

'Most of us do,' the Constable observed wryly.

'You know what I mean. Solomon doesn't have anything else in his life.'

'Where does he live?'

'I've no idea,' the merchant replied. 'I see him at the market and I've had dealings with him, but that's as far as it goes. I'm not sure he has any friends besides Jeremiah. I'm not certain you'd exactly call them friends, either.'

'There was some cloud over Mr Darden becoming mayor, wasn't there?' Nottingham decided to edge the question into the conversation.

Williamson shrugged. 'I've no idea, Richard. My father was still

running the business then. All anyone told me was that he'd decided
to resign from the Corporation. Why all the interest, anyway?'

'It's just something I'm looking into.'

'How are you managing at your job?' He nodded at the walking
stick. 'Does that help?'

'It's there when I need it.' He smiled and stood. 'Like my job,
I'm better off with it. Thank you, Tom; don't work too hard.'

'Hannah's doing her best to make sure I don't. Now she wants
me to take her to London.'

'You'll look the part of a society man down there, I'm sure.'

ELEVEN

I t had been another bad night, one when sleep came reluctantly,
coaxed and persuaded and then only staying for the briefest
times. Nottingham rose early, dressed and washed, found
bread in the kitchen and ale in the jug to break his fast.

The evening before Mary had watched as he undressed, the
candle flickering on the small table by the bed. She'd pointed
out the scars on his body, all the batterings and bruisings of his
life working to uphold the law. She'd counted seventeen, some
so old he only had faint memories of how he'd acquired them,
the most recent still livid and painful.

'How many more, Richard?' she asked sadly, running his
fingers lightly over an ancient knife wound on his arm. She
looked up at him, eyes filled with love and gentleness. 'How
many? And how bad will the next one be?'

He didn't even try to answer. Each one of them had come with
his job, each had its story, forgotten or not. He understood what
she was asking, but he couldn't tell her what she wanted to hear
and they both knew it.

It had rained during the night, leaving the roads muddy before
turning into a misting drizzle which lightly dampened his face as
he walked to the jail. It was still dark, just the birds in the trees,
their songs answering each other, the music loud and beautiful in
his ears.

Lister was sitting at the desk, completing the night report. 'What do we have?' He held his hands out to the fire, letting the warmth soak into him. He seemed to feel the chill and damp more easily these days.

'Three in the cells, boss. Two of them were drunk and fighting on Briggate, so we used the cudgels on them. They'll be off to the Petty Sessions later. And another one that the men pulled out of the Aire before he drowned. He didn't smell of drink.'

'Trying to kill himself?'

Lister shrugged. 'He was fast asleep last time I looked.'

'You get off home, lad. Catch up on your rest.'

'Is there anything more on those children, boss?' He paused a moment. 'They keep coming back to me.'

The Constable placed a hand on his shoulder. 'That shows you take it seriously. Makes you human. Don't ever lose that. If you do, it's time to get out of this type of work.' He gave a sigh. 'I might have more later. We'll see.'

The deputy's face was strained when he arrived, flesh taut over his bones, eyes sunken in dark smudges of skin. He just shook his head in answer to Nottingham's unspoken query.

'Could be another day or more yet.' He poured himself a mug of ale, drank and slammed the mug down on the desk. 'All we can do is keep bathing her.'

'How's Lizzie?'

'Dead on her feet. Torn apart.' It was all he could bring himself to say of her desperation and the screams in her eyes.

'How many do you have left on that list of names?' the Constable asked.

Sedgwick pulled a folded piece of grubby paper from his pocket. 'Ten,' he answered. 'They'll all be pointless, you know that.'

'Give it to me, I'll look after it. Go home.'

'Are you sure, boss?'

'You did more than enough when I was gone. Come back when Isabell's fever has broken.'

'If.' He knew enough to understand that the worst could happen. It so often did.

'It will,' Nottingham told him with confidence. 'Go.'

*   *   *

The Constable was careful to reach the cloth market on Briggate just before the bell rang for the start of selling. The merchants were already there, waiting and gossiping in the middle of the street while the weavers made their last minute preparations, arranging and draping their cloth to best advantage.

Solomon Howard was off by himself, gazing down the street at all the lengths on display. They'd never met; none of the hedgerow scandals that flared up and died down around Leeds had ever mentioned him.

'Mr Howard.'

The man turned, taken by surprise. 'Good morning, Constable. A pleasure, sir.' He had a deep, rich voice that was a contrast to his delicate features. His wig was black and carefully curled, falling artfully on to his shoulders and he wore a thick woollen greatcoat that hung open to display an exquisitely cut coat and breeches of wool dyed deep burgundy. The gold buckles on his shoes gleamed and his linen was spotless white. He stood taller than Nottingham, looking down his nose at him, wearing a smile like a worn fist. 'How can I help you?'

'I was hoping for a word with you.'

Howard raised his eyebrows. 'Me?'

Nottingham smiled. 'Perhaps you could come to the jail when the market's finished. It'll only a take a few minutes.'

Worry flickered briefly over the man's face. 'I'm very busy. I have appointments. I'll need to pay the clothiers.'

'I'm sure your clerks can do that, sir. And it won't take long, I promise.'

'Very well, then,' Howard agreed with a sigh.

'Thank you.' He walked away just as the bell began to peal, and didn't look back. The factor would spend the next hour wondering and sweating, distracted from his work. Others would be crowding round, asking their own questions, and the man would have no answers for them.

On the way to the jail he stopped at the Talbot. Bell was clearing the mugs and plates where the clothiers had breakfasted on their Brigg End shots of beef and ale.

'Constable,' the landlord greeted him warily.

'Do you know Mr Howard?'

'Solomon?' Bell's face broke into a grin. 'Course I do. He's been coming to the cockfights for years. Lost a pretty penny on them, too. Can't gamble to save his soul, that one.' He paused. 'You've reminded me now. That time you were asking about . . .'

'Yes?' he asked, although he knew what the man was going to say.

'I recall he brought Mr Darden with him. Does that help you?' he asked with a smirk.

'Thank you.'

It was no more than he'd expected. A few coins had changed hands and something that never happened was suddenly remembered. And that was the end of that tale.

He was sitting at his desk by the time the cloth market ended. All the papers sat in neat piles, the jug filled with ale. Five minutes later Howard arrived, glancing round the room with curiosity.

'Sit down.' The Constable smiled. 'Thank you for coming.'

'What is it you want, Mr Nottingham? I told you, I'm a busy man.' The factor sounded affronted, a bluff of anger.

'Do you go to the cockfights, Mr Howard?'

'The cockfights?' Whatever he'd been expecting, that wasn't it, Nottingham thought. 'Yes, I do. Why?'

'Have you ever taken your employer with you?'

'Once.' Confidence returned to the man's face. 'Just two weeks ago. He didn't care for it. Ended up with blood on his coat. It's ruined, it'll never come out properly.'

'At the Talbot?'

'Yes. Ask Bell the landlord. He knows me, he'll have seen us.'

The Constable smiled at the smoothness of the lie.

'What do you think about Gabriel?'

'Gabriel?'

'The man who killed those children,' Nottingham said. 'That's what he calls himself.'

The factor looked down. 'Terrible. Awful.'

'Why do you think a man does something like that?'

'What?' Howard glanced up sharply and Nottingham saw the tiniest glimmer of fear. 'How would I know? What are you trying to say, Constable? Are you accusing me?'

Nottingham held up his hands, palms outwards. 'I'm not accusing anyone, Mr Howard,' he answered calmly. 'I simply want to know your thoughts, that's all.'

'Then I can't help you. I wouldn't know what to say.' He stood. 'Was there anything more?'

'I appreciate your time. And I'm sure you'll tell me if you believe you know who Gabriel could be.'

Howard slammed the door behind him. Nottingham listened as a cart rumbled slowly up Kirkgate and heard the low sound of voices passing outside the window. He'd been as obvious as he could without an outright accusation. Now he'd have to wait and see what happened with Darden and his factor. But there were other ways to move things along . . .

He stopped at the pie seller, choosing one that almost burned his hand as he carried it. He slipped through the market crowds at the top of Briggate, eyes alert for any sign of Caleb or the other children but seeing nothing. He wandered for a few minutes, quickly caught up in the shouts and bustle, then slipped down the passageway into the empty court.

He pushed away the corpse of a dog, its body already bloating, and sat down. All he could do was wait and hope that Caleb would appear, a ghost seen in the daylight. He closed his eyes and leaned his head back against the cold stone of a building.

'You still don't look like a Constable.'

The boy was standing close. There was a fresh rip in his breeches and his face was grubbier than it had been on Tuesday, his hair a rat's nest of tangles. Nottingham looked into the deep shadows and saw a shape again, highlighted just enough for him to be certain it was a girl. He blinked and she'd gone.

'I am, though,' He held out the pie. 'Something for you and the others.'

Caleb darted forward and took it from him. 'And have you found that Gabriel yet?' There was a note of disbelief in his voice.

'I think I have.' He paused, giving time for the words to sink in and watching the expression on the lad's face. 'But I'm going to need your help to be sure.'

'Oh aye?' The boy sounded doubtful. 'And what can I do?'

'I want you to see him and identify him. Don't worry,' he added swiftly, 'he won't see you.'

'I don't give a bugger if he sees me or not.' Caleb turned his head and spat in defiance. Nottingham smiled. 'Who is it? Rich man, is he?'

'Yes.'

The boy nodded as if that made absolute sense. 'What will you do to him?'

'If he's Gabriel I'll see him hang.'

'Even if he has money?'

'Even then.'

Caleb thought about the words. How many promises had he heard in his life, the Constable wondered, and how many of them had been broken?

'Aye. I'll do it.'

'I have a man watching him. I'll take you to him.' He stood slowly, leaning heavily on the stick.

'You won't be there?'

'I trust my men,' Nottingham told him.

They threaded through the crowds at the market. 'How long have you been Constable, then?' Caleb asked. The boy's eyes darted from side to side trying to take in everything, judging, assessing.

'Since before you were born. Too long, some people think.'

The boy eyed him curiously. 'Why do they say that?'

'This isn't a job for making friends, lad.'

'Are you good at it?'

'I try,' he replied as they turned on to the Head Row. 'How did you end up out here?'

Caleb shrugged. There was pain inside the boy's head, the Constable knew that, but he'd never let anyone see it. To do that would be weakness.

'There was only me mam. She looked after us, but she took ill and died. Then it was me and me sister and me little brother. The cold got them both one winter.'

Them and many others. The ground froze so hard that the city had stored the corpses in every place it could find until the thaw began.

On Vicar Lane he paused, and Caleb stood still. Finally Nottingham saw Holden, half-hidden from view in the dark entrance to a court, his eyes firmly on Darden's house.

'Boss,' Holden said as they eased in past him.

'Has he been out today?'

'Not yet. Darden's usually inside while dinner time. Howard came after the cloth market, left a few minutes back. Darden will likely go down to the warehouse this afternoon. Who's this?' he asked, looking at the boy.

'This is Caleb. He's seen Gabriel. I want him to take a look at Darden to be sure it's the same man.'

The man nodded.

'Stay with Mr Holden,' the Constable instructed. He pulled some coins from his pocket and put them in the lad's hand. 'If you're working, it's only right you get paid for your time.'

Caleb said nothing, but curled his fingers tightly around the money.

'Just be honest. If you know the face, say so. But don't lie about it to please me,' Nottingham warned. 'I just want the truth, you understand that?'

'Yes.'

'Mr Holden will look after you.'

On the way back to the jail he stopped at the Crown and Fleece. The place was empty, with the close, stale morning smell of taverns. A fire burned in the grate and the light through the window showed the dust motes in the air. All the tables and benches had been cleaned, the floor neatly swept.

The landlord was tasting a fresh batch of ale, sipping slowly and looking thoughtful.

'Constable,' he said with a brief nod. 'Care for a mug? It's turned out well. Just ready this morning.'

Nottingham drank gratefully and smiled. 'You're right, there's a good taste to it. Thank you.' He took a little more and placed the cup on the trestle. 'I was wondering if there'd been any more word on those missing soldiers.'

'Nothing.' He paused, scratched his head and lowered his voice. 'Tell you the truth, I'm buggered if I know what happened. The lasses who work here have been wondering if that sergeant was right and there's devils about.'

'You know better than that.'

'Aye, but . . .' He shrugged. 'You tell me what happened to them, then.'

'I don't know. But there'll be an answer somewhere.' The Constable swallowed the rest of the ale. 'I might come back later for more of that.'

Sedgwick had managed to sleep for an hour. Lizzie sat on the edge of the bed, wringing out the cloth over a bowl of cold water then placing it on Isabell's forehead. The baby slept on, burned to exhaustion with fever.

James had gone to school reluctantly, but the deputy knew he was better off there with his mind on other things. He pushed off the blanket, laid a hand lightly on Lizzie's shoulder and padded down the stairs. The bread was old and hard but he tore off a chunk anyway, then trimmed mould from the edge of a piece of cheese, eating without tasting, for something to do, just to fill his belly. Then Lizzie called, 'John, come here! Now!'

He ran back up to the bedroom. Lizzie was smiling and crying.

'It's broken. She's getting cooler. Feel her.'

He put his hand on the baby's cheek. He rested his fingers on her chest and her arm. Isabell's face was peaceful, her breathing easier. He pulled Lizzie close, stroking her hair as she buried her face against him.

'She's going to be fine now,' he whispered. 'Fine.' He kept his arms around her as her tears fell in relief and he thanked the God he didn't believe in for saving his daughter.

'I don't know what I'd have done . . .' she began.

He smiled at her. 'It doesn't matter,' he told her, his mouth against her ear. Not this time, he thought grimly. But Isabell was still a baby. How many died before they had a chance to grow? There might yet be a day when they were crying together.

He opened the shutters. The November light was grey and dreary, but at least it felt like life.

'You sleep,' he said. 'I'll meet James from school and give him the news.'

Lizzie squeezed his hand. 'How did I get such a good man, John Sedgwick?'

'You were lucky,' he answered with a grin and tousled her hair. 'You rest now. She probably won't wake up for a while yet.'

Downstairs he placed his hands on the table, feeling out the scars in the wood. They'd been lucky. But how much luck could any family have? He stretched, easing the tension out of his neck then scooped up the crumbs of bread and the tiny pieces of cheese he'd left and ate them.

Nottingham waited. Soon, he told himself. Soon Holden would arrive and tell him. Once he had his evidence even the mayor and the Corporation wouldn't be able to defend Darden. They'd have to give him up, to sacrifice him.

He stirred at every loud footstep out on Kirkgate, a small knot of pain that wouldn't go away nagging around the scar in his belly. He tried to concentrate on other things but his mind kept drifting, seeing the faces of dead children.

The bell at the Parish Church rang four. Outside the afternoon had become twilight. Another hour or two and folk would be going home from work, a new urgency in their stride. And he waited.

He picked up the report on the missing recruits, scanning through it quickly in case he'd missed something before. There was nothing he could see; they'd simply disappeared somehow. It was a good trick, a way to escape the army and leave everyone guessing. They'd probably never know the truth of what really happened.

Finally the door opened and Holden walked in alone.

'Well?' the Constable asked. 'Did you see him?'

'He came out a short while back. That lad was perished after standing so long.'

'What did he say?'

'I'm sorry, boss. He said Darden isn't Gabriel.'

TWELVE

'What?' He'd been so certain.

'We saw him walk out of the door and down Vicar Lane. I was watching the lad's face. He wasn't lying, boss, I'm sure of that.'

'What did Caleb say?' The Constable asked urgently.

'After Darden had gone, I asked him, and he shook his head.

He told me he'd never seen the man before and that Gabriel was taller and not as old as Darden.'

'What else?'

'That was all, boss. He ran off after that.'

Nottingham sighed. 'Thank you.'

'Do you want me to keep following Darden?'

'No, let it lie.'

He made the final round of the day, walking out along Low Holland where the new warehouses blossomed, small ships and barges tied up beside them to carry cloth down to Hull. Smoke rose from the chimney of the dyeworks in the distance, and the rank stink of the place hung in the air.

The Constable turned back. It was dark, and the clouds had vanished, leaving the air cold enough to make his breath bloom in front of his face as he passed the empty tenting fields, the path he'd followed so many times in his life.

How could he have been so wrong? Everything he knew had told him that Jeremiah Darden was Gabriel. Had he lost so much when he was away? He pushed the fringe of his forehead with a short, angry gesture. And if it wasn't Darden, who was Gabriel?

At least the mayor would be happy.

He tried to think. Gabriel was taller and younger than Darden, Caleb claimed. The merchant was close to Nottingham's height, no more than an inch between them. There were plenty in Leeds bigger than that. And younger. Darden was in his middle fifties if he was a day. But he could clearly remember the lad saying that Gabriel was old. What was old to a boy of that age?

He kicked at the dirt in frustration. They were right back where they'd begun.

Rob was at the jail when he returned, dressed in his good woollen greatcoat to go out and check on the night men.

'You don't need anyone watching Mr Darden now,' the Constable told him. 'That boy said he wasn't Gabriel.'

'So who is?'

'I don't know. Someone taller and younger, he says.'

'There's no shortage of them.' Rob chewed his lip for a moment. 'What about the factor?'

'Howard?'

'Yes.'

Oh, sweet Christ. Solomon Howard stood a good four inches above his employer and he was probably close to forty. Old but still younger. All his sharpness must have gone if he hadn't been able to see that. He'd need to find Caleb once more and have him see the factor.

'Put your man on him instead,' he ordered. 'And tell Mr Sedgwick I want Holden to follow Howard in the daytime.'

'Yes, boss.'

The Constable smiled. The lad could go places. 'Just keep the city in order during the night.'

Rob poked and pushed his way through the dark hours, keeping moving to stay awake. Sleep hadn't come during the day; he'd thought over and over about his father's invitation. What baffled him was the reason behind it. James Lister did nothing without a considered reason. Was the man offering his own kind of apology, or was there something darker beneath the words?

He'd said nothing to Emily yet. He wouldn't until he believed he knew why his father wanted them there. The man rarely forgave and never forgot, and Rob had humiliated him when he moved into lodgings after they'd argued over Emily.

Saturday night had passed calmly with the usual number of drunks and fights that left blood on the floor. A few would wake in the cells, others would take time to heal, but no one had died.

Now Leeds was quiet, from Lands Lane to the other side of the bridge. Folk were in their beds, wrapped in darkness. The only footsteps he heard as he walked around were his own. He still clutched the cudgel tightly in his hand. He'd been taken by surprise before and it was never going to happen again.

The moon was close to full, bright in the cold, cloudless sky. He took a final turn down by the river, where the light shone like jewels on the water. Close to the bank, bumping back and forth in a small eddy, he made out a dark object.

He searched around for a thick branch and slid down right to the edge of the Aire, reaching out to poke and turn the bundle. It slipped and slid away from him, turning slowly in the current; then something rose and he could make out a hand.

'Shit,' he said quietly. 'Shit.'

Rob tried to grab the body, and by the time he'd managed to haul it on to land his boots were soaked. He stood back, breathing hard, and saw the corpse was little more than a child. He knew what to do: he ran through the streets until he found one of the night men, and sent him off to fetch Brogden the coroner. And the boss needed to know about another dead boy.

It was another hour before they'd carried the boy back to the jail, covered with a stained old sheet. The Constable was already there, his face still puffy with sleep. He'd thrown on his clothes, not bothering with a stock, his hose mismatched.

He followed them into the cold cell they used as a morgue. 'Where was he?'

'About a hundred yards above the bridge. I haven't had chance to examine him. I didn't recognize his face.'

Nottingham peeled back the top of the sheet. The face looked peaceful, so young and clear, washed clean by the water.

'I do. He was called Caleb.'

THIRTEEN

The Constable took his time looking for wounds. There were small scars on his arms, but nothing from any recent fights, and no stab wound on his chest. Slowly and tenderly he turned the boy, tracing the skin of his back to search for anything. Finally he parted the long hair, still soaked and full of the stench of the river.

'That's it,' he said to Rob. 'A lump. Someone hit him there, then he either fell into the river or he was pushed.'

'Gabriel?'

The Constable looked up. 'I don't know. But Caleb was the only one we know who'd seen him. Did you set a man on Howard?'

'Yes, boss,' Rob replied.

'Go and find him, I want to know what he saw.'

Left alone, Nottingham stared down at the boy, reaching out to close his eyes. He'd stopped believing the platitudes of the church when Rose had died. There'd be no seat at the right hand of God for Caleb, only the burn of lime on dead flesh in the unmarked grave of the poor.

He knew that any number of people could have killed the boy, for more reasons than he could count. But he had no faith in coincidences. This was Gabriel's work, protecting himself; he was certain of that.

Outside, dawn was breaking, the light starting to clear. He rubbed the weariness out of his eyes and poured a mug of ale, sipping slowly as he tried to think.

The door opened and Rob returned, followed by Lake, the man who'd been watching Solomon Howard. Lake was a night creature, small with dark eyes full of secrets.

'Did Howard go anywhere tonight?' Nottingham asked.

'To the Talbot, sir,' Lake answered. His skin was sallow and heavily pock-marked, nose bulbous, the veins red and broken by drink.

'Did you go inside?'

The man shook his head. 'The folk in there know what I do.'

'How long did he stay?'

'An hour. Happen a bit longer.'

There were plenty of ways in and out of the Talbot; the landlord had made sure of that.

'How did he seem when he left?'

Lake shrugged. 'Nowt unusual. He went home and the house went dark a few minutes after that.'

'Thank you.'

There was nothing he could use. And after his error with Darden he'd need to walk very carefully around Howard. No doubt the landlord would testify that the factor had been there and maybe even produce a whore he'd used. And perhaps it would be no more than the truth.

The time he'd spent recovering had dulled his senses. He'd been wrong about Darden, and now he was uncertain whether he dare trust his own feelings. Nottingham ran a hand through his hair and sighed, then began to pace around the room, trying to shake his thoughts into some kind of order.

He was no further along when the deputy arrived, smiling and eager to work.

'Morning, boss.'

'Isabell?' the Constable asked.

'The fever broke yesterday. Now she's coming out in spots, just like the apothecary promised. I never thought I'd be so glad to hear a babby scream and cry.' He gave a wide grin. 'Why are you in on a Sunday, anyway?'

'Someone killed Caleb. Rob pulled him from the river last night.'

'Darden?'

'He's not Gabriel.' He explained all that had happened.

Sedgwick snorted. 'There's three ways out of the Talbot that I know.'

'We've got nothing on the factor, John. Nothing at all. I'll wager you a shilling that the mayor's going to call me in tomorrow and ask why I was questioning him.'

'What now, boss?'

'I want you to start asking around and see what you can find on Solomon Howard. And I'd better go home and get ready for church.' He paused. 'It's good news about Isabell.'

'It is. For a time there . . .'

'I know,' he said. 'I know. Be thankful.'

He walked to church with Mary on one arm and Emily on the other. The morning was crisp, brisk, slate clouds scudding across the sky, the year dying slowly as winter came creeping. He dozed as Reverend Cookson gave his sermon, the words reaching him as a drone until his eyes closed.

Mary nudged him awake in time to stand for the final prayer. Glancing around, he saw other faces that looked as if they'd just been shaken from sleep. Outside, men coughed and cleared the dust from their throats, standing around awkwardly as their wives chattered merrily.

A hand closed tightly around his arm and pulled him away from the throng. Mayor Fenton wore the chain of office proudly over his coat, a polite public smile on his lips but his eyes hateful and furious.

'I want you in my office tomorrow morning, Nottingham.'

'Yes, your Worship,' the Constable answered.

'Have you caught him yet?'

'No.' For now, at least, he'd leave it at that.

Fenton snorted and turned away. 'Tomorrow,' he repeated.

'What did the mayor want?' Mary asked as they strolled home. Emily was talking to her friends before meeting Rob; they'd have the luxury of a house to themselves for a few hours.

'What do they always want? He's not happy with me.' He smiled at her. 'I'll worry about it when I'm going to the Moot Hall.'

All the deputy could find was shreds of gossip and tittle-tattle. Solomon Howard hadn't been born to money. He'd been a child who'd grown up around Briggate, the son of a draper with a shop down by the bridge. Not rich, but not without a penny, either.

Sedgwick had talked to a pair of men who'd known him back in those days. Even then he'd been one to keep to himself, they'd told him, solitary and silent, with a love of money, spending little and keeping his coins hidden.

His father had paid to apprentice him to another draper over in Bradford. It was no more than a handful of miles but the lad had rarely come back to visit his parents. When he did return to Leeds he was twenty and just appointed as Darden's factor. He was young for the job but learned quickly from his employer. The young man had grown into well-cut coats and breeches and long, draped waistcoats shot through with thread that ached to be gold.

From there Sedgwick had chased ghosts of words. Howard had lived a quiet life. He'd never married and if he'd had any dalliances he'd been discreet enough about them.

Then someone had told the deputy about the whore. He found her in a gin shop, old before her time, the flesh of her face sagging as she nursed a small glass. Her chin was soft, the grey showing in her hair. He bought her another dram and she looked up with clouded, tired eyes. 'Aye, there were a few of us he used. Me, Sally, Ann. He paid well enough. But he was a rough bastard for his money.'

'What do you mean?'

'Tha' knows.' She blushed, a flush of surprising innocence. 'He liked to hurt me when he did it.' She held up her right hand;

the little finger was crooked. 'He did that. Broke it.' She swallowed the gin. 'None of us liked it when he came around, we'd not be able to work for a day or two after.'

'Then why did you go with him?' the deputy asked.

'Because he paid as much as we'd make in a week, mister. You think any lass can turn that down?'

He ordered more gin for her, a small jug this time. She smiled, showing brown, broken teeth.

'What does he do these days?'

She shook her head. 'I don't know, love, but good luck to her, whoever she is. He dropped me as soon as I started looking old.' She drank greedily and gave a short, hard laugh. 'Not that anyone else wants to pay for me now, either.'

He left a couple of pennies on the bench for her. Another hour and she'd probably forget she'd ever talked to him.

The day was edging towards twilight, a damp, chilly mist beginning to form as Sedgwick walked along Boar Lane. There were few people about; candlelight shone through gaps in the window shutters as people settled in their homes for the night.

He turned up Cripplegate then trod through the old manor orchard to reach Mill Hill Lane and followed it to the Head Row by Burley Bar. Howard's house stood by itself across the road, close to the corner of the road out to Woodhouse. It was a trim building, square-fronted and even, built in the new style, a short path leading to the door. The garden was neatly kept, a wall taller than a man at the back of the property to keep people out. The closest neighbour was a good thirty yards away. A girl – or a child – could scream in there and no one would hear. It could be worth talking to the servants, he thought as he strolled.

'Evening, Mr Sedgwick.' Holden was in the shadows, leaning against a tree, his eyes fixed on the house.

'Has he been out today?'

'Just to church.'

'How many work for him?'

'Two that I've seen. Do you remember Hugh Smithson?'

The deputy searched through his memory. 'Wasn't he the one we caught digging up railings to sell them?'

Holden grinned. 'That was Dick Sawyer. No, we thought Hugh was beating and robbing folk but we could never prove it.'

'Aye, that's it,' Sedgwick said slowly, the man's face taking shape in his mind.

'He's working for Howard now. By the look of it he lives in.'

'That's worth knowing.' He thought for a moment. 'If you see Hugh going out for a drink, come and find me.'

He was glad to close the door behind him and feel the warmth of the fire. Isabell was sitting on the flagstones playing with the horse he'd awkwardly whittled from a piece of wood. She looked up at him with a wide, innocent smile, a scatter of white spots across her face.

'Hello, beautiful,' he said, scooping her up in his arms and tickling her so she giggled. 'How's she been?'

'You'd think she'd never been poorly at all,' Lizzie answered. She shook her head but there was relief in her voice. 'James is over at Joseph's, that lad from school. I told him to be back by six.'

He replaced the little girl on the floor and put the toy in her tiny hands, then stood a moment to watch her. Lizzie came up behind him and wrapped her arms around his waist.

'Hard to believe you and me made a little miracle like that,' she said.

He turned and held her close. 'Not when she has a mam like you.'

She laughed. 'I bet you say that to all the girls, John Sedgwick.'

'Not for a while now.' He grinned.

'And you'd better keep it that way if you know what's good for you. Come on, there's pottage in the pot. Are you hungry?'

'Bloody starving.'

'Just as well I made plenty then, isn't it?'

The Constable finished the daily report, gave the ink a moment to dry, then folded the paper. He straightened his stock and coat and set out for the Moot Hall.

Martin Cobb was already at his desk, smiling as Nottingham approached.

'The mayor wants to see you.'

'He told me after church yesterday.' He placed the report on the desk and knocked on the door, hearing a murmur then entering.

'Sit down,' Fenton told him. 'I told you to leave Jeremiah Darden be.'

'I did.'

'So instead you've gone after his factor.' The mayor stood and began to pace around the room. 'Mr Darden came to see me on Saturday to complain. What do you have to say about it?'

'I'm doing my job properly. The job the city gave me.'

'The city can take it away, too.' He paused to give weight to the words. 'If that happens there'll be no pension and no house.'

The Constable said nothing.

'I want this Gabriel as much as anyone,' Fenton continued, 'but I'll not have you persecuting Mr Darden or anyone who works for him. Do I make myself clear?'

'Very.' He could feel his voice tight in his throat. 'Was there anything else, your Worship.'

'No. You can go.'

FOURTEEN

Out on Briggate a thin wind pulled at his face. The street was busy but he might as well have been alone. He turned on to Kirkgate, passed the jail and the Parish Church, the tip of his stick tapping lightly on the road as he walked.

He stopped at Timble Bridge to watch the water flow until his temper had cooled. Finally he made his way up to the house on Marsh Lane. A pot of water was steaming over the fire. Mary was working in the kitchen, sleeves pushed up as she washed the linen, her skin a deep, blushing pink from the heat, the air filled with the harsh smell of lye.

He stood still and quiet, watching her for a long moment until some sense made her look around.

'Richard,' she said, the word full of panic and fear. What—'

'I'm fine,' he assured her quickly. 'I needed a few minutes away.'

'Why? What's happened?' She dried her hands on a square of cloth. 'I can tell something's wrong, it's all over your face.'

She'd known him too well, too long. He couldn't hide

anything from her. But in all their years together, he could count on one hand the number of times he'd discussed his work with her. Home was a place away from that, a refuge, and she understood that. Now slowly he laid out every piece as Mary listened closely.

He told her all he knew, everything he believed, the words trickling out gradually, and finishing with the threats the mayor had made, the words still hot in his ear. She was silent for a long time when he was done, the quiet gathering around them.

'Do you really think this man Howard is guilty?' she asked finally.

'I don't know. I thought it was Darden and I was wrong about that. But someone killed Caleb. It might have been Solomon Howard. I don't know enough to say yet.'

'You need to find out.'

'Yes.' He looked around the room. 'But if I do . . .'

'You could retire now.'

'I could,' he agreed softly.

'No one would think the worse of you.'

He said nothing. She reached out and took his hand. 'But you won't, will you?' She smiled softly.

'I will if you really want me to.'

Mary took a deep breath. 'No.' She looked at him with a small, loving smile. 'And you know I can't ask that, don't you, Richard? When this is done, maybe.'

He held her close.

'We've lived with nothing before,' she said. 'I daresay we can again if need be.'

'Thank you.'

The deputy was at the jail when he returned.

'You were a long time with the mayor, boss.'

'I had somewhere else to go. What did you find out about Mr Howard?'

'There's plenty he keeps hidden.' He related what he'd learned, then added, 'He has Hugh Smithson working for him now.'

'Does he now?' The Constable raised his eyebrows. 'There's not many would employ someone like that. Could be worth having a word with Hugh. We haven't talked to him in a while.'

Sedgwick grinned. 'I'm going to, boss. Somewhere quiet.'
'I doubt he'll say much, but it's worth a try.'
He shrugged. 'Get a few drinks in him first, you never know.'
'The mayor won't be happy.'
'If he finds out. Leave him to me.'
Nottingham stood. 'Come on, let's go next door and find something to eat.'

Rob was late, tying his stock as he ran up Briggate. Emily would be walking home after school, wondering why he wasn't there. He spotted her in the distance along Kirkgate, and by the time he reached her he was breathless.
'I slept too long,' he gasped.
She touched a finger to his lips before he could say more. 'Don't.' Her eyes were warm and gentle. 'I grew up with Papa, I know what it's like.'
He walked alongside her, hearing the soft swish of her skirt as she moved. Overhead the clouds had darkened and thickened, smudging the horizon.
'We'd better hurry up,' he told her. 'It's going to rain soon.'
'You'll be soaked tonight.'
Rob shrugged. It came as part of the job. His good greatcoat and a hat would keep him dry enough. At least there'd be little crime if it poured.
A shout made him turn. He saw the landlord of the Crown and Fleece gesturing at him.
'You work for t'Constable, don't you?' the man shouted.
'Yes,' he answered, 'but—'
'I need thee, lad.'
He looked helplessly at Emily.
'Go on,' she said with a smile. 'Come along after if you can. Mama will have made enough for you.'
He watched as she turned away, then he strode towards the inn. 'What is it?' he asked with a sigh.
'In the stable.' The landlord gestured with a thick arm.
As soon as he was inside he could smell it, the thick, awful stench of decay.
'Aye, that's it.' The man folded his arms. 'The boy forked out

some hay a few minutes back and suddenly the stink was everywhere.'

Rob glanced up at the loft, then took a piece of linen from his coat pocket and tied it around his face.

The stable boy had dropped his fork on the straw. Rob picked it up and began to dig slowly. There was much less of it than the last time he'd been here, no more than two feet thick on the platform; he'd never imagined horses ate so much. He tried to breathe through his mouth as he worked, just taking in small gulps of air. In two strokes the tines pushed against something soft, and he started to clear the hay.

All that remained of them were scraps of clothing, clean white bone and some stinking, sickly flesh that the rats had left. He gazed at them for a moment then climbed down, walking out into the yard before gulping in the air. The rain had begun and he lifted his head to feel it clean against his face. They should have dug deeper when they were searching, he thought. They hadn't done their job well.

'You'd better go for the coroner,' he said.

By the time Brogden arrived the rain was a deluge, the ground full of dark puddles.

'Where?' he asked, holding a scented handkerchief against his face.

'Up there.'

It took the man less than a minute to return. 'Dead,' he said quickly and scurried back outside, bending to puke on the cobbles before dabbing delicately at his mouth.

The landlord stood behind the trestle, drinking deep from a mug. He poured another and passed it to Rob without a word. The fire was blazing in the hearth. As soon as word of the corpses passed round this place would be full of men drawn by the gossip.

'I'll bring some men to move the remains. They'll need something to clear their throats after, though.'

'Aye, lad.' The man nodded without looking at him. 'I'll see to it, don't tha' worry there.'

Rob watched the men carry the remains of the recruits away to the paupers' graves beyond Sheepscar Beck. He held on to a pair of small leather satchels. Each contained a change of old clothes and a few hard-saved coins. No letters, not even a pen, and no idea of where they'd come from.

He could easily imagine how they'd died. A cold night, a few drinks, and they'd have burrowed into the hay for warmth. Down there they'd have slept but found no air to breathe. They'd gone deep enough that it had taken this long to discover them as feed had been tossed down to the horses.

There had been no devils, no one setting them free in the night. The answer had been simple in the end. And one they should have found long before.

'Get rid of that hay,' he advised the landlord, 'and scrub down the loft before you put any more in.

They were standing in front of the stable, the doors wide open to air it. The wave of rain had passed, but more was in the air.

'I can't believe it. They were only sleeping there.' The landlord shook his head.

The Crown and Fleece would be famous for a few days. Folk would come to drink and see where the two recruits died. Tragedy was always a good spur to business.

Then the rain returned, a sweeping onslaught from the west that soaked him before he'd even reached the jail. He banked up the fire and hung his coat over a chair to dry before settling to write up the discovery of the bodies.

He stood by the window, watching the drops bounce off the road. With luck there'd be nothing else to drag him out from here. He'd complete his rounds before dawn. The river would be up, pushing hard against the banks. The way the night had gone so far it would be his luck to find another corpse in the river.

He thought back to Sunday afternoon. He'd met Emily after church and they'd walked along the river to Kirkstall Abbey. All the way out they'd prattled idly, about anything, everything, her eyes smiling and happy. They'd walked through the ruins for an hour before strolling back.

'My father asked if we'd like to go over for dinner one Sunday,' he said finally. For days he'd wondered how to tell her, trying to find something in their talks that would lead to it. In the end all he could do was blurt it out.

'He did?' she answered in surprise. 'Was he serious?'

Rob nodded.

'He asked me, too?' She sounded suspicious. 'The whore's granddaughter?'

'That's what he said.'

'Why does he want me there?' she wondered. 'So he can have a chance to humiliate me?'

'I don't know.' He squeezed her hand. 'I wondered if it could be his way of saying sorry.'

They strolled quietly for a while as the shadows began to lengthen.

'What do you think? Do you want to go?' Emily asked.

'I'm not sure,' he admitted with a sigh. 'If we did and he started . . .' She looked at him expectantly. 'If he did we'd leave and never return,' he promised.

He'd eaten supper with Emily and her parents before returning to his lodgings. He stopped in front of the door, then turned and headed up Briggate.

His father was seated at the table scribbling notes in the margin of a book.

'Twice in such a short time,' Lister said wryly, taking off his spectacles and gesturing at a chair. 'Sit down.'

Rob remained standing. 'The last time I was here you invited us over one Sunday. Did you mean it?'

'When have I ever said anything I didn't mean?' he asked with amusement.

'And both of us?'

His father nodded. 'Both of you.'

'Will you be civil?'

Lister smiled. 'I assure you, I shall be the soul of politeness. Does that satisfy you?'

'If you insult her we'll walk out,' Rob warned.

'There'll be none of that at my table.'

'Then we accept.'

He still wasn't certain it had been the right decision. He looked at the rain running like a river down Kirkgate. It was done now. They'd dine with his parents next Sunday.

FIFTEEN

The rain had petered away again with the dawn, but the skies still weighed heavy, the colour of pewter, and the ground was thick with mud. Sedgwick moved through the crowds at the market, sellers crying their wares loudly, buyers haggling over the price. He had his eyes on a man who looked determined not to be noticed, watching him in case he cut a purse and tried to run.

'Do you still want to talk to Smithson?' Holden fell in step beside the deputy. 'He's in the Rose and Crown.'

'I thought you were following Howard.'

Holden smiled. 'He went to the warehouse when the cloth market finished. He'll be there all day so I decided to go back to the house. Smithson's bought a few things and now he's enjoying a quiet drink.'

Sedgwick grinned. 'About time I had a word with him, then.'

'You won't be able to miss him.'

He was right. Smithson was sitting on a bench, elbows resting on the table. He had wide shoulders, no neck and wrists as thick as some men's thighs.

'Hello, Hugh,' the deputy said, settling down across from him. 'It's been a long time. Staying out of trouble?'

The man nodded warily.

'That's a good cut of cloth,' the deputy continued, reaching across and fingering the collar. 'Still, I hear you have a position now.'

Smithson grunted.

'Good employer, is he, Mr Howard?'

The man put down his glass and focused on the deputy. 'Aye, good enough. He pays well. What about it?'

'Doesn't look as if he works you too hard.'

'I do what he wants.'

The deputy had forgotten the way that Smithson's voice sounded as if it had dragged over gravel. 'Much time off?'

'Every Sunday.'

'All the servants?'

'Aye, both of us. Why?'

'I'm just curious.' He smiled. 'You see much of Mr Darden?'

Smithson sat back and folded his arms. 'What do you want to know for, Mr Sedgwick?'

'I want to make sure you're well looked after, Hugh. Can't have anyone taking advantage of you.'

'Mr Howard would never do that.'

'Did you tell him about your past?' the deputy wondered. 'I know we never proved it but we were sure you were guilty.'

'That was a long time ago,' the man demurred.

'You're an honest, hardworking man these days?'

'I am that,' he answered proudly. 'You ask anyone.'

'So if I happened to see Mr Howard and mentioned that we thought his servant had once battered someone to death it wouldn't matter to him?'

Smithson's face set firm. 'That would be slander.'

'It would only be what we thought.' He paused. 'Although perhaps he might let you go after learning that. No more wages or time to slip away for a drink. No more Sundays off.'

The man sighed. 'What do you want?'

'Tell me about your employer. He likes his whores, from what I hear.'

'I wouldn't know.' His mouth set in a tight line.

'There's a lass who works in the house, too.'

Smithson chuckled. 'She's forty if she's a day. Hardly a lass.'

'How is he with her?'

The man shrugged. 'Same as he is with me. We know our place and he treats us fairly.'

'And what does he do when you're not there?'

'I've no idea, Mr Sedgwick. I'm not there.'

'Does he go out much?'

'Aye, he'll go to the cockfights or an assembly sometimes. Most days he's working until after dark.'

'He must be a rich man.'

Smithson drained the mug and stared at him. 'Anything else, Mr Sedgwick?' He started to rise, tall and menacing.

'Nothing. But it's good to know where we can find you, Hugh.'

He watched the servant leave, forced to bend his head slightly to go through the door. Smithson was clever enough not to mention the meeting to his employer; it could only bring questions the man would rather not answer. For all that, he hadn't learned anything other than Howard was generous, giving them every Sunday off. There was plenty a man could do with a whole day in an empty house.

The Constable had seen Rob in the morning, still bedraggled from his rounds, hair hanging in tangles around his face.

'Emily said there was something at the Crown and Fleece.'

'We found our answer.'

Nottingham listened with a frown, then said, 'We should have done more there.' He sighed. 'Go on home and dry off.'

He'd taken the daily report to the Moot Hall and strolled down Briggate for the cloth market. Howard and Darden were standing together, discussing something intently. He raised his hat to them and continued down the street, feeling the anger of their gaze hot on his neck.

At least fewer people were pursuing the reward for Gabriel; the novelty of it had passed. There were just three new names and he could strike one of those immediately. Old Jeffrey Halton could scarcely walk down the street and his hand shook so hard his wife had to feed him. But there'd be other tips coming in. Folk didn't easily forget a sum like twenty pounds.

He bought a pie from the seller at the market, spotting the deputy in the distance, a full head taller than most of the people bobbing along the street. Quietly, he slipped through the opening and into the court where he'd met Caleb.

The ground was thick with mud from the rain, the stink of rubbish stronger than ever. The Constable leaned against a wall that was heavy with slime. The sounds of the market seemed muted and distant, a world apart from here.

He waited, hoping that one of the children would come. It was unlikely, but he had to try. He needed to be able to talk to them, to know if Gabriel returned and if any more of them disappeared.

The church bell tolled the quarter hour, then the half, and he was still alone, the pie growing cold in his hand. Finally he moved away, ready to return to the bustle of Briggate.

'Wait.'

He halted and turned. He stood facing a girl, small and thin, wearing an old gown full of rents and patches, deep blue once, but the colour had faded and worn to nothing. She had a proud little face, dirt smudged across her cheeks, and dark hair that hung matted to her shoulders. In her hand she carried a knife.

'You're t' Constable, aren't you?' There was no fear in her voice and she stared steadily at him.

'I am.'

'Caleb told me about you. He's gone.'

'I know,' Nottingham said.

'He's dead, isn't he?'

'Yes,' he answered simply. 'You're the girl who was in the shadows when I talked to him, aren't you?'

She didn't lower her eyes, just nodded once. 'Who killed him?'

'I think it was Gabriel,' the Constable answered her. He held out the pie. 'What's your name?'

'Lucy.' She took the food from him, small, deft fingers wrapping it carefully in a dirty kerchief.

'Have you seen Gabriel?'

She stood straighter, her mouth moving in disgust. 'Often enough, whenever he's come around. He even tried to get me to go with him once.' She paused. 'Is it right, what Caleb said? That you lived out here.'

'Yes. But it was a long time ago now.'

'And now you have a house and servants?'

He smiled gently. 'A house. No servants.'

Lucy nodded then asked, 'How did he die?'

'He was in the river.'

'He could swim,' she said quietly.

'Someone had hit him on the head.'

The girl stayed silent for a long time. 'He looked after me.'

'I'm sorry.'

'Are you going to catch him?'

'I'm going to try.'

She looked doubtful. 'You were wrong before. Caleb told me that.'

'I know,' he admitted. 'But Caleb helped me. He'd seen Gabriel.'

'So have I.' She paused. 'Helping you got him killed.'

He said nothing but bobbed his head sadly. 'I need to catch this man.' He watched her face. 'Would you know him again?'

'Oh aye,' Lucy said with a snort. 'I'd know that face anywhere.'

'Would you help me? Like Caleb did.'

She eyed him calmly.

'I want Gabriel,' the Constable said. 'For Caleb. And Mark and Luke and Alice and all the others.'

'I'm not afraid,' Lucy told him, although he could see the lie in her eyes.

'I know.'

'What'll happen if you catch him?'

'He'll hang,' Nottingham answered. He waited a few moments.

'I'll help you,' she agreed finally, her face set.

'Thank you. But I need a better way to find you than this.'

Lucy hesitated. 'You know the old manor house? There's part of an old shed there that still has a roof. I sleep out there with some of the others. Knock twice before you come in and I won't kill you.' Her voice was serious and hard.

'I'll come for you in the morning,' he said and moved towards the passageway.

'Mister?' she called. 'You said you didn't have a servant?'

'That's right.'

'Do you want one?'

'What are you going to do?' the deputy asked. He soaked up the juices of the stew with a piece of bread and pushed the bowl away.

'I'll have her take a look at Howard tomorrow,' Nottingham said. They sat at the bench in a corner of the White Swan, the other customers happy to keep their distance.

'What if she says it's him? No one who matters is going to believe her.'

'We will,' he said. 'Then we can dig deeper and find some evidence we can use.'

'You were sure it was Darden, boss, and you were wrong,' Sedgwick reminded him.

'I know.' He'd pored over it often enough since, rubbing it raw.

'I caught up with Hugh Smithson.'

'What did he have to say for himself? Anything useful?'

'Just that the servants receive every Sunday off.'

'Every Sunday?' The Constable raised his eyebrows.

'Aye, that's what I thought, too.'

'Do you think he'll say anything to Howard?'

The deputy shook his head and grinned. 'Seems Hugh hadn't told him about his past and he'd rather it stayed quiet.'

'That's good work, John.'

'What are you going to do if it's not Howard?'

'I don't know. I really don't know.'

SIXTEEN

'**B**efore you finish I want you to come with me.'

'Where, boss?'

Rob had handed over the night report. A frost had hardened the ground and frozen the wheel tracks on the road into deep ruts; the chill had been damp enough to cut through to his bones as he'd completed his rounds. Now he wanted nothing more than a chance to see Emily for a few minutes as she walked to school, and then the warmth of his bed.

'You'll see.'

He followed the Constable up Briggate, stopping for bread at the baker's, and along the Head Row, past Garroway's, its windows covered with steam, the heady, exotic scent of coffee in the air. At Burley Bar, the edge of the city, they turned down Mill Hill Lane and into the tangle of grass and trees that had once been the orchard of the manor house.

Nottingham had to look carefully before he found the building, half of it so thickly covered in ivy that it looked as if nature had claimed it back. Slates covered some of the roof, leaving dark, bare patches that gaped to the morning. He knocked twice on a door eaten away by rot, and waited. Rob opened his mouth to speak but the Constable held up his hand.

'Lucy,' he said. 'I told you I'd come.'

Inside someone dragged at the door, the hinges squealing. The girl walked out of the darkness, blinking in the bare daylight. Pulled tight around her shoulders she had a threadbare shawl someone had thrown away, and the knife was in her hand.

Nottingham handed her the loaf. 'You can use this. You and the others.'

'Aye,' she agreed, bobbing her head. 'Thank you.'

'You said you could help me. Like I told you yesterday, there's someone I'd like you to see, someone I think might be Gabriel.'

Rob saw panic rise in her eyes.

'He won't see you,' the Constable promised her. 'I'll make sure of it.'

The girl gestured back over her shoulder. 'One of the little ones is poorly,' she said. 'I can't leave her.'

'Rob, go and fetch apothecary Kirshaw. Bring him here.'

Surprised, he turned and walked away quickly, making his way down to Briggate and pounding on the apothecary's door until the old servant answered. From there it took another five minutes of fussing before the man was ready to leave, the bag weighing him down on one side.

'Where are we going?' Kirshaw asked, his voice petulant. His coat, old and trailing almost to the ground, was buttoned all the way to his throat against the November chill.

'Mr Nottingham wants you to look at someone.'

The apothecary muttered as he followed, lifting his legs to move through the overgrown grounds of the manor. The Constable was waiting by the building.

'Thank you for coming,' he said. The girl stood at his side, looking down at the ground.

'Where is he?' the apothecary grumbled.

'She,' Nottingham corrected him. 'She's in there.'

'She?' Kirshaw bristled.

'A little girl. Look at her, help her.'

'Who's going to pay me?'

The Constable smiled. 'You'll get your reward in heaven,' he said slowly, his voice firm enough to brook no argument. 'Mr Lister will stay and help you.'

Light filtered through the door. The child was in a corner, a ragged blanket pulled around her. Rob watched as the apothecary lifted one of her hands then ran a hand across her forehead, muttering to himself. He delved into the bag, then turned.

'Don't just stand there,' Kirshaw said sharply. 'Fetch some water.'

'Will he make her well?' Lucy asked as they walked.

'If he can,' Nottingham told her.

'What if he can't?'

'He'll do everything he can.'

She nodded. He knew the world she lived in, where the line between life and death often blurred to nothing, where some never woke in the morning.

He found Holden standing behind a hefty oak tree close to Howard's house.

'Keep her out of sight,' he ordered. 'Howard can't see her.'

'Yes, boss.'

'Mr Holden knows what to do,' he told her. 'Just listen to him.'

She looked scared. 'You did this with Caleb, didn't you?' she asked.

'Yes,' he admitted. She stared at him, her eyes unblinking. 'Mr Holden will make sure no one sees you.'

Finally, with a sad, unbelieving smile, she nodded.

By the time the apothecary left, the little girl was sleeping quietly. Kirshaw had fed her a few drops of liquid in water Rob brought from the spring.

'She needs food,' the apothecary said as he stood. 'There's nothing to her. She needs to be warm and something hot in her.' He looked at Rob. 'She needs looking after. Do that and she'll be fine. If not . . .' He shrugged and gathered his bottles and potions. 'And tell Mr Nottingham I'll be sending my bill to the Corporation.'

'You do that.'

Alone, Rob watched the girl. A few of the other children had come, then scattered like sparrows when they saw him, vanished from view. He couldn't leave her helpless and on her own. He scavenged dead wood from the orchard and lit a small fire in the building then settled back against a wall.

He was dozing when Lucy returned. The blaze had brought a little warmth to the room and the child slept on, a smile on her lips, the blanket pulled around her face.

'How is she?'

'She'll rest for a while. When did she eat last?'

'Yesterday, maybe,' Lucy said. 'Day before.'

Rob pulled some coins from his pocket. 'Buy her some food. Something hot.'

The Constable completed the daily report and left it with Martin Cobb at the Moot Hall. He'd taken three men to the Petty Sessions for their trials: the baker with adulterated bread would find himself in the stocks on Briggate and the two apprentices found drunk would be handed over to the masters for a thrashing.

He listened to the people passing, a murmur of voices outside the window, the creak of carts and the yelling of the drivers. Finally the door opened wide and Holden strode in.

'She says it's him, boss. Howard is Gabriel.'

Inside he felt a surge of satisfaction replacing the anxiety that had been bubbling through him.

'Go and find Mr Sedgwick then keep watching. Where's Howard now?'

'Down at the warehouse. He'll probably be there until dusk.'

'Stick with him.' He paused. 'Let him see you,' he decided. 'I want him to know we're there.'

'Yes, boss.'

The deputy arrived within the quarter hour, breathless and grinning.

'Bob told me. What are we going to do now?'

Nottingham picked up a mug of ale and sipped slowly. 'We're going to find the evidence to put him on the gibbet.'

'What about that lass who recognized him?' Sedgwick asked. 'You know what happened to Caleb.'

'I might have an idea there.' He said no more.

'Are you going to bring Howard in again?'

'Not yet,' the Constable answered slowly. He pushed the fringe off his forehead. 'I want him to understand that we know. It'll stop him trying anything else, too.'

'He'll be down here with a lawyer,' the deputy warned.

'Let him.' Nottingham smiled. 'He'll have to explain things to others then. In the meantime I want you to ask around more. See if there are other little dark secrets you can find.'

'Yes, boss.'

The house was filled with the smell of a stew cooking on the fire. He heard Mary moving around upstairs and the swish of a broom.

'Home in the middle of the day again?' she asked wryly as she saw him standing in the doorway of the bedroom. 'Folk will think you don't like to work any more.'

'You need a serving girl to do that,' he said.

'And become a lady of leisure?' She laughed.

He looked at her hands, red from work, the knuckles becoming gnarled and misshapen. 'You deserve it after all these years. At least not to work as hard.'

'We haven't had anyone since Pamela, and the girls were little then.'

'Maybe it's time we had someone else.'

Mary leaned on the besom and stared at him suspiciously. 'Why now? What is it, Richard?'

He explained it all, watching the emotions cross her face.

'Where would she sleep?' she asked. 'We don't have any room.'

'In the kitchen,' he countered. 'Believe me, it's better than where she is now.'

She swept a little more, pushing the dust closer to him so it settled on his boots. 'If she doesn't obey and work hard I'll dismiss her,' she threatened.

'Of course.'

Mary nodded her agreement, then asked, 'What would you have done if I'd said no?'

'I'd have told John that Lizzie needs some help.'

She laughed. 'You had it all worked out, didn't you? Go on, get out and bring her back here.'

He knocked twice on the door of the building. The walls were solid enough, put together for the ages, but even at its best it had never been intended for man nor beast. Slowly the door was pulled open over the rough ground and Lucy stood there, the knife in her small fist. Late daylight came in through the missing slates of the roof. The little girl had gone.

'Where is she?'

'Some of the others found a place where she'd be warmer. Down in the Ley Lands.'

He knew the way children became family, tending one another, the older caring for the younger as much as they could.

'What about you?'

'I'm safe here.' She shrugged.

'You asked if I wanted a servant.'

He watched the glimmer of hope in her eyes before she spoke warily. 'Aye, and you never answered.'

'Have you done the work before?'

Lucy snorted and gestured at her dress. 'Who do you think I'd know who needs servants, mister?'

'Are you willing to work hard?'

She lifted her chin. 'Give me a chance and see.'

'I will,' he told her.

'What?' She looked at him in disbelief. 'Do you mean it?'

'I do. You'll help my wife, and it'll be easier to keep you safe. Who do you need to tell first?'

'The others, so they know nothing's happened to me.'

'Do that, and meet me at the jail. Bring your things.'

'It's been a long time since you lived out here, hasn't it, mister?' she said. 'What do you think I own?'

'Do you know how to cook and clean?'

'I can clean,' the girl said with a proud nod. 'And I'll cook if you'll show me.'

Nottingham stood, trying not to smile. Lucy was willing enough but she wasn't about to be cowed by anyone.

'I daresay we can cut down an old dress to fit you,' Mary said hopefully, looking at the girl's thin arms. 'And we need to put some meat on you, too. When did you last eat properly?'

'I don't know,' Lucy answered.

'She's no more than a twig, Richard.'

'She'll still do her share,' he answered and winked at Lucy. He knew his wife all too well. The girl would work, that much was true, but no more than her mistress, and in a few days she'd seem like a member of the family, another daughter rather than a servant.

'Sit down,' Mary said, and the girl did as she was ordered, looking uncomfortable perched on the chair at the table. 'Food first, then we'll get all that dirt off you.'

They ate in peaceful silence; the girl watched and copied their manners, then when they'd finished she gathered up the dishes and carried them carefully into the kitchen.

'Give her a scrub and she'll be a pretty young thing,' Mary told him. 'She looks like she'll learn quick enough.'.

'I daresay,' he agreed with a grin. And, he thought, she'd be well away from Gabriel.

SEVENTEEN

The days had passed too quickly. Wednesday had turned into Sunday and he'd barely had time to think. The nights had grown colder, the grass rimed with frost by morning, the earth solid under his boots as he made his rounds.

Rob had managed to enjoy minutes here and there with Emily, staying twice for supper served by Lucy, her clean face serious as she worked, so different from the girl he'd seen in the hut. Holden and the night man stayed close to Howard, and the Constable waited to let the factor make the next move.

The church bells woke him after just a couple of hours of rest, the way they did each week, but his sleep had been broken, troubled by the thoughts of what lay ahead. He rose and washed, then tried to tame his hair with a comb. The landlady had sponged his good suit and laundered his other shirt and stock.

Rob dressed slowly, feeling the tightness in his belly. Once the service was over he'd meet Emily outside the church. They could walk a few minutes and then go to eat dinner with his parents. He doubted he'd eat much; instead he'd listen to every word from his father and weigh them for the barbs they might contain. Maybe the man really did want peace. He hoped that, but he didn't expect it; James Lister was someone who'd bite all the way to his grave. It was his way and he was unlikely to change now. If he chose to snap and snarl they'd leave, and that would be a true end to things.

Before he left he looked in the glass. The suit was the best wool, tailored to fit him well, the cut still in style and the breeches tight over his thighs. He retied the stock and put on the heavy greatcoat.

Emily was already in the churchyard, talking and laughing with some of the other girls. She left them as he hurried through the lych gate, happy to see him, only a fleeting trace of worry on her face.

'How was the service?' he asked.

'Papa fell asleep twice, but at least he didn't snore like Mr Peters. His wife had to keep nudging him to keep him quiet.'

'Are you sure you want to go? We can always cry off.'

Rob saw her hesitate for a fleeting moment, then she drew in a breath and said, 'I'm ready. Let's see if your father has really changed.' He took her hand and they began to stroll. The clouds were high, the outline of a weak sun faint behind them as a chill wind drew down from the north.

They went out along Vicar Lane, past the houses, some grand, some old and tumble-down, then up the Head Row to the Market Cross. Emily's voice was bright in the cold air, repeating something one of her girls at school had said that had forced her to stifle her laughter.

Other couples were parading arm in arm on Briggate. He saw a few faces he recognized, a girl he'd once liked walking with a man almost old enough to be her father. In the distance he made out the lanky figure of the deputy deep in conversation with a man.

As they crossed over Boar Lane he took a deep breath. Emily had stopped talking. At the door he looked at her. She gave a small nod and he knocked.

James Lister and his wife were in the parlour at the top of the stairs. The fire burned hot in the hearth and the room was full of the smell of roasting beef. Lister rose to greet them, beaming, taking his son's hand in his own, while his wife, a bird of a woman long cowed into silence by her husband's opinions and prone to attacks of nerves, stayed seated. The servant brought wine as his father talked, asking with apparent interest after their health and their work. A good host, Rob decided, but he'd seen the man that way before with the rich men of the city, putting them at ease.

Emily sat upright on her chair, her body stiff, her hand clutched tightly around the glass. She'd barely taken a sip, and she'd answered the questions politely but with a minimum of words, her voice soft and low. She'd never been here before, and he saw her glance around curiously, taking in the shelves of books, the thick Turkey rug and dark furniture that spoke quietly of money.

Finally the servant called them through to dinner, and carved the meat once they were seated, juice and blood pooling on the platter. They ate with a few passing compliments on the food, Lister pouring wine for himself three times before he pushed the empty plate away, sighing with satisfaction.

'Nothing better than a good hot meal,' he said. 'Do you get enough of those in your lodgings, Robert?'

'The landlady feeds me well. I don't always have time to eat.'

'You should insist on it. A full belly means a contented mind, an active mind.'

'What about those who can't afford to eat?' Emily asked. 'There are more than enough of those.'

'The poor have always been with us,' Lister said benignly. His wife cut small pieces of meat, chewing and looking around nervously. 'That's what the Bible says, isn't it? And they always will be.'

Emily smiled sweetly. 'But doesn't the Bible also talk about the difficulty of a rich man entering heaven, sir?'

Lister laughed. 'Indeed.' He laughed and drank more, raising his glass to her. 'Very sharp, young lady. But it's the nature of man to have rich and poor. They balance each other; history's shown us that. I don't find any shame in having money. I do understand others aren't as fortunate.'

'There's charity for the poor.'

'There is, and a good thing it can be, too.' He drank once more. 'For those who deserve it, of course.'

'What do you do to help them?' she asked.

Lister opened his arms, palms upward. 'That's not my job, my dear. Plenty of people give – look at Mr Harrison last century with the church and almshouses he gave to the city. The Corporation offers money to those who are without. My job is merely to report it.'

Rob clenched his fists under the table. He could feel the clash rushing closer but there was nothing he could do to stop it.

Emily took a tiny sip of wine, just enough to moisten her lips. 'There but for fortune go all of us. Who can tell what God has in store?'

Lister nodded seriously. 'Of course,' he agreed. 'Your family knows that well.'

'We do,' she agreed. Rob knew his father was baiting her and he felt a small surge of pleasure that she remained so calm. 'But that was hardly fortune, sir, it was law. I'm sure you'll agree with that. Laws made for men, not women.'

'Laws made for all of us,' Lister countered smoothly. 'Your grandmother made her choices and had to pay the consequences by law.'

'Tell me, sir, how much do you know about her?'

'I know all that's needful, my dear.'

Emily kept her voice sweet and even. 'Needful?' she asked. 'Then I'm sure you'll be aware she brought a large dowry that her husband stole from her, as the law allowed.' She waited no more than a heartbeat and added, 'More money than your wife commanded, perhaps.'

She stood, turning briefly to thank Rob's mother for the meal, turned on her heel and left the room. As he stood, Rob saw his mother's expression still blank, and his father's eye hard with anger. Then he strode out behind Emily.

They were halfway down Kirkgate, Timble Bridge in sight, before she spoke.

'I'm sorry.'

'What for?'

'I know you'd hoped for a reconciliation. But he just goaded me so much.' She shook her head. 'And he managed it in so few words.'

'I was proud of you,' he insisted. 'That was the first time I've ever seen anyone better him. You left him speechless.' She gave a sad smile and he pulled her close, her cheek against his. 'And we never have to go back there again.'

*   *   *

'When will she start talking?' James asked. He was kneeling on the floor playing with Isabell. She laughed with clear joy, grabbing for his hands, trying to grab them before he moved them out of reach.

'Soon enough,' his father told him. He leaned forward and added in a loud whisper. 'If she's like most girls, once she starts she'll never shut up again.'

'I heard that, John Sedgwick,' Lizzie warned him. She'd pulled the old pot off the hearth and was dishing the pottage into bowls. 'You'd better watch what you tell that lad if you want to eat here again.'

The deputy winked at his son. It felt good to be home, to sit in the firelight with his family. Most of Isabell's spots had faded, just as the apothecary predicted, and the fear had vanished.

'Of course, your mam's not like that,' he told the boy. 'There's not another one like her.'

She placed the food on the table. 'You'd do well to remember that, too,' she said with a smile. She scooped up the little girl and sat, holding her carefully on her lap.

It had been a long day. A couple had been robbed as they made their way home from service at St John's. Young, dark and poor was all the description the pair could offer. It could have been half the young men in Leeds. He'd set two of his men to go through the beer shops and look for someone spending freely; they'd taken him before the clock struck four. Roaring drunk and joyful, he still had one shilling left of the five that he'd stolen. For that he'd spend the next seven years in the Indies. If he was lucky he'd survive long enough to come home.

He'd followed hint and whisper from person to person trying to learn more about Solomon Howard. At the house of someone who'd once clerked for Darden he'd sat in front of an empty grate and heard the man tell how the factor counted every penny and every pound each day.

'Him and the master, they'd shut the door behind them and plot and scheme for hours.' The clerk pulled his coat tighter around his chest to try and keep out the chill. 'God alone knows what they talked about.'

'What was he like?' the deputy asked.

'A cold bugger.' The man shook his head. 'Loves his money.

I'll give him this, though, he's clever. He knows what'll sell where and how to get the best price for it.'

'What about whores?'

'I only saw him working, and it was nothing but business there.' He thought for a moment. 'There was a woman he had as a servant for a while, though. She might know something.'

'Do you remember her name?'

'Meg something-or-other.' He shrugged and shook his head.

'Meg Robinson?' The deputy searched through his memory for women named Meg.

'I don't know. I'm not sure I ever knew her surname.'

It was enough to start Sedgwick down another road, and two hours later he found the woman named Meg Brennan. She was perhaps twenty, bulky and plain, a baby suckling at her breast, three more children filling the room with noise.

'My man's out,' she said. 'Drinking up his pay, most like. Same as bloody ever.'

'You worked for Solomon Howard?'

'Him,' she snorted. 'Aye, for four year before I met my man and this lot began popping out.' She caught him looking at her. 'I were pretty back then, everyone said, and trim, too. Why'd you want to know about him?'

'We're just asking questions.' He smiled. 'Was he a good employer?'

'You mean was he all over me, don't you, love?'

'Was he?'

'He was, and I let him because my mam needed the money and I didn't know no better. Rough bastard as well.'

'How old were you when it started?'

'Twelve. I'd been there a fortnight.'

'Didn't you say anything?'

Meg Brennan moved the baby to the other breast and stared at him. 'Who to, eh? I thought they were all like that. My mam kept telling me I was lucky to have a position with a man like him. She'd not have listened. I was the oldest, I had to work.'

'Did he bring other girls there?'

'Not as I ever saw, but he wouldn't need to when he had me, would he?'

'What did he do when you said you were leaving?'

'He wa'nt as interested in me then. I'd filled out, hadn't I? I worked out my notice and left. He wa'nt even around the day I went. No goodbye, nowt.'

'Was he having other lasses by then?'

'Aye, I expect so,' she answered with a deep sigh. 'But if he were, it wa'nt at home. Once he lost interest in me, he had me working all the hours God sent. Beat me if he didn't like what I'd done, too.'

'Hard?'

Meg stayed silent for a long time. 'Aye.'

He rose to leave, feeling pained for stirring the dust of memories in her.

'I don't know why you're after him,' she said quietly, 'but whatever it is, I hope you make the bastard pay for it.'

'Penny for them,' Lizzie said. James was in his bed, Isabell asleep on her mother's lap, and they sat in front of the fire, enjoying a few quiet moments.

'They're not worth that,' he told her. 'It's just work.'

'When isn't it?' She reached over and pressed his hand. 'Is it better now that Mr Nottingham's back?'

'He's . . .' He struggled for the words. 'He looks older now. Tired.'

'You would be too if that had happened to you.'

'Mebbe. He's still sharp.'

'It'll be your chance to be Constable in time.'

'If they offer it. This bloody mayor won't, I'll tell you that.'

'There'll be another mayor next year. Happen he'll be better.'

'I'm not sure I want it. When the boss was off . . .'

'When Mr Nottingham was ill you were a man short then and I hardly ever saw you. The Corporation wouldn't pay to take on someone else. But think about it, John, there'd be more money, a bigger house for the children.'

'We get by, don't we?'

'We do. Barely.'

'Anyway, the boss won't be going anywhere soon. Not until we've found Gabriel, anyway. So it doesn't even matter yet.'

'Yet,' Lizzie said. 'You could be Constable for a long time.'

'Is that what you want?'

'I want you to have your due,' she told him firmly. 'When he does go you've earned that position.'

'Mebbe,' he said doubtfully.

The Constable walked up Kirkgate well before dawn. He'd woken early, but Lucy had been up before him, the fire in the kitchen already lit and water boiling to wash the linens. She'd greeted him with a smile, bread and cheese already cut for him to break his fast.

'I heard you moving upstairs,' she said, pushing a strand of hair behind her ear and pouring a mug of ale. 'You'll need that to wash it down.'

The girl wasn't afraid of work, he thought as his boot heels clicked against the stone. She was learning well, too, and taking the hardest of the work from Mary's shoulders. He'd heard his wife with the girl the previous evening, teaching her to make bread, guiding her through the proportions and the kneading until she was satisfied. Show her once and the girl remembered, his wife said happily. Lucy seemed happy enough with her position, too, settling into a routine. He'd swear she was already putting on a little weight, her cheeks fuller and rosier.

Rob was at the desk, scribbling away quickly with the quill. 'Busy night?'

'Not really. They don't seem to like it when it turns cold.' And winter certainly seemed to have arrived. Sleet had fallen during the evening, and the wind from the west brought the threat of worse. 'There was one thing, boss. Harris the draper was walking home with his boy. He was wearing a grey suit, his son's only eight . . .'

'Oh Christ,' the Constable exclaimed.

'Three of them set on him, calling him Gabriel. Two of ours were close enough to crack some heads before it got out of hand.' He nodded at the cells. 'The ones who did it are in there.'

'No damage to Harris or his lad?'

'They're fine.'

Nottingham nodded and walked across the room, stopping to stare out of the window. After a while he said, 'Emily told me what happened yesterday. I'm sorry, lad.'

Lister smiled. 'Did she say she bested him?'

'No,' Nottingham answered in surprise. 'She didn't mention that.'

'It was wonderful, boss. Emily left my father speechless, then she stood up, thanked my mother and we left. There's people who'd have paid good money to see that.'

'I might myself,' the Constable laughed. 'But it still wasn't good for you.'

Rob shrugged and stayed silent.

'You go on home. Stay for your supper tonight if you like. Young Lucy's trying her hand at cooking.'

The deputy arrived a few minutes later, full of the morning, the broad grin making him look like a gleeful child.

'Looks like you learned something interesting about Mr Howard.'

'I did that, boss.'

The Constable listened carefully, letting Sedgwick tell his tale in full.

'Not a pleasant man, by all accounts.'

'But rich enough. And there's always Darden to protect him.'

'We don't know he does that,' Nottingham pointed out.

'Like as not, though. They've worked together for years, he must know.'

Maybe, he thought. Certainly he'd heard nothing to persuade him that Howard wasn't Gabriel.

'Keep Holden close on him.'

'We still need proof, boss.'

'I know.' And finding something they could use would be the trick. For now he'd do all he could to make the factor feel uncomfortable. 'See if you can discover anything more about him today.'

He completed the daily report and carried it over to the Moot Hall. Out on the horizon the clouds looked heavy and menacing. If they blew in there could be an early snow. He dropped the paper on Martin Cobb's desk, half-expecting a demand from the mayor to see him. But in no more than a moment he was back on Briggate.

His body was healing slowly. He felt better than when he'd returned to work, stronger, able to complete a day without weariness. He was still using the silver-topped stick, and by late afternoon, when his muscles ached, it helped, but soon he'd be able to manage without.

Back at the jail he poured a mug of ale and stoked the fire, wondering what else he could do about Solomon Howard. Whatever lingering doubts he'd had about the man being Gabriel had vanished now.

He was still pondering when the door opened and lawyer Benson entered, with the factor right behind him.

EIGHTEEN

'**M**r Benson. Mr Howard.' He greeted them with a short nod. 'Sit down, please.'

'We won't be staying long, Constable.' Benson had a bluff voice to match his appearance, the broad, jowly face of a man who knew how to indulge his income. His belly pushed hard against the thick wool of his greatcoat and he pulled off a pair of expensive leather gloves.

'What can I do for you, gentlemen?'

'Mr Howard tells me you have a man following him. Is that true?'

'It is,' Nottingham said.

For a moment Benson seemed surprised at the admission before recovering. 'You understand that's completely unacceptable. Why are you hounding my client this way?'

Nottingham glanced at Howard. The man's eyes were focused and full of hate. 'Because I have reason to believe that Mr Howard might be Gabriel.'

'What?' The lawyer bellowed the word. 'Are you accusing my client?'

'No,' the Constable replied calmly. 'If I accuse him, he'll know. I'm investigating. That's my job.'

'What you're doing isn't investigation. It's harassment, and it's damaging Mr Howard's reputation.'

'Is it?' Nottingham asked blandly. 'Then my apologies.'

'Call him off, Constable,' Benson told him. 'Or you'll face a lawsuit.' He gave a smile that showed a set of white teeth. 'I'm sure you don't want that. I'll bid you good day.'

He turned, the factor following him. At the door Howard glared before leaving.

Half a minute passed before Holden slipped in. 'Never good news when there's a lawyer involved, boss.'

Nottingham chuckled. 'You've got that right enough. It seems we've upset Mr Howard.'

'Do you want me to leave him be?'

'For now,' the Constable told him after some consideration. He'd rattled the man, that was something. And the factor hadn't gone to his employer or the mayor. Quite what that meant, he didn't know yet. 'Go and find Mr Sedgwick. He'll have a job for you.'

'Yes, boss.'

Alone again, Nottingham drained the dregs of the ale and wondered what to do next. Howard was worried if he was appearing with his lawyer. How could he increase the pressure on the man?

'Any ideas?' he asked next morning, glancing towards Sedgwick and Lister. A thin covering of snow had fallen during the night, just enough to brighten the land for a few hours. Already it felt a little warmer; by noon it would all be gone.

'Can we search his house?' Rob asked.

'He'd never let us, and we don't have enough to justify it.'

'What about that girl's identification? Isn't that enough?'

The Constable shook his head. 'Not this time. Howard's already threatening a lawsuit for being followed.'

'What if we search without him knowing?' the deputy wondered thoughtfully.

Nottingham pushed the fringe off his forehead and looked at him. 'What did you have in mind, John?' he said softly.

'We can't, boss,' Rob protested, but the Constable held up a hand to quiet him.

'See if there's anything in his house that connects him to the children and take it. If that doesn't rattle him, nothing will.'

'How are we going to do that? None of us has the skills.'

Sedgwick smiled. 'I daresay Hugh Smithson could be persuaded to let me in if I kept silent about his past.'

Nottingham was silent for a long time. Then: 'You'd better make sure you're not caught.'

'I will.'

'It's not right, boss,' Rob said after the deputy had left. 'Doing it that way.'

'It's not right to torture and kill children, either.' His voice was firm and his eyes hard. 'I'll do what I have to in order to find out who murdered them.'

'You're certain it's Howard?'

'I'm positive. Lucy identified him. Do you still see the faces at night?'

Lister nodded.

The Constable softened his tone. 'That's why I'm doing this. He's one of the people who thinks he can build walls of money to protect himself. But I'll dig under them.'

He knocked softly on the door. One, a pause, and then two more. Smithson opened it and the deputy slipped in quickly.

'Be quick, please, Mr Sedgwick. The cook will only be an hour at the market.'

'I'll be as fast as I can, Hugh.'

He felt the thud of his heart in his ribs. It had taken a few days to set this up. There was a meeting with Smithson, with hints and threats of letting the man's past slip to his master and a warning of what would happen after. Even when he'd reluctantly agreed, they still needed a time when both Howard and the cook would be gone.

Now it was Saturday morning. The factor had been at the cloth market and he'd spend the rest of the day at the warehouse. The deputy had watched the cook leave for market, a basket over her arm, before climbing over the wall into the back garden of the house.

He took a deep breath and climbed the stairs. Howard would keep anything incriminating well hidden, in a locked desk or chest. The bedroom was well-furnished, the mattress of down, the sheets fine linen. Six suits hung from pegs, more than he'd even seen together before, and all of them costly but none of them grey. Ten long waistcoats, silk embroidered with gold thread in beautiful patterns of peacocks, birds and flowers, the colours dazzlingly bright. He checked the pockets, then the two chests full of shirts and hose. There was nothing.

Moving softly, he checked the rest of the rooms before going back down. The desk in the parlour was open, with a letter half-written. He searched carefully through the drawers, then moved on. In the dining room a dark oak dresser filled one wall, displaying a collection of silver plate, cutlery stored carefully in a chest.

Finally he tried another door. It was locked. He took a small set of picks from the pocket of his breeches and tried one, then another. At the fourth attempt one fitted, and he was in the room. Light came from a barred window that looked out on the garden.

The strongbox was crafted to keep money safe, with three heavy locks; it would take too long to open them all. Ledgers were stacked on the desk, next to a quill and an inkwell. There was little of interest in the drawers, bills from tailors and shoemakers.

Time was running short and so far he'd come up empty-handed. The hearth was empty but he could feel the sweat running down his back. Another chest stood in the corner. He fumbled with the picks, his hands slick, then it was open.

The grey suit was carefully folded, breeches on top of the coat, dark stains on them both. He lifted them out. Underneath was a knife, the blade wiped roughly clean, and a riding crop. A silk pouch lay on the bottom; in it were neatly-tied locks of hair of all colours, more than ten of them, all soft to the touch.

The deputy put it inside his shirt, then the knife in his pocket. The suit was too bulky to carry and he placed it back in the chest before securing it again. It took precious moments of trying before the lock clicked once more on the door to the room.

Smithson was still at the back door, pacing anxiously up and down the room. 'I'll not ask if you found what you wanted,' he said.

'Best not,' Sedgwick advised him.

'You promise you won't say anything to Mr Howard?'

'I told you, Hugh. You ought to know by now that I keep my word.'

With a quick scramble over the wall he was out and breathing deeply. He waited a minute or two, his back against the stone, breath blooming in the cold air, before walking slowly back to the jail.

'What did you find?' the Constable asked urgently as Sedgwick poured himself a glass of ale and downed it in a single gulp. His throat was dry as a summer road and his hands shook slightly. Rob had stayed, eager to see if the deputy had discovered anything. Now he watched as the deputy produced a knife and pulled out a small silk packet. 'Hidden away in a chest in his strong-room.' He paused. 'There's a grey suit there, too.'

Nottingham was opening the pouch, watching as locks of hair tumbled to the desk and counting through them. 'Eleven,' he said dully. 'And we only have the names of five of them. Does anyone know you took these?' the Constable asked.

Sedgwick shook his head. 'Hugh just guarded the back door. I'm certain he doesn't know that his employer is Gabriel.'

Nottingham turned to Lister. 'Howard will look in that chest soon enough. Then we'll see.'

'You said Darden lied about going to the cockfight at the Talbot,' Rob said slowly. 'What if he and Howard are in this together?'

'I suspect they probably are.'

The Constable had considered it often enough in the last few days. Everything had churned in his mind during the long nights when sleep didn't arrive swiftly. Inside, he believed that the merchant and factor were both guilty of killing the children; it would explain so much. He glanced down at the hair again, some straight, some curly, each lock carefully cleaned and tied before being put away.

Knowing was one thing. For all his brave words, Nottingham understood that proving it in court would be impossible against two men with wealth and influence. They'd draw their power around them and the two of them would protect each other. The Corporation would never allow Darden to be convicted, not with the stain that would put on its reputation. His only hope was that the two men would do something, make some error, and they were too clever for that. They'd managed to keep their sins hidden for a long time; they'd be careful no sun shone on them now.

'Can we keep a man on them, boss?' the deputy asked.

'Lawyer Benson's made it very clear there'll be a lawsuit if we do.' He gestured at the knife and hair. 'We can't use this. We don't even have it.'

'So what can we do now?' Lister asked.

'We wait and hope.'

By the end of the day he felt drained. He'd tried to imagine some way to bring the men to justice and he'd come up with nothing. Unless they did something stupid, he was impotent. An icy drizzle had begun during the afternoon and he clattered across Timble Bridge with his head bowed, kicking at a stone and watching it roll into the beck.

A fire was burning in the grate and he stood gratefully before it, the warmth seeping slowly into his bones. He could hear Mary and Lucy chattering in the kitchen. The girl was smiling more, so proud of the dress cut down for her that she kept stopping to glance at herself in the looking glass.

Eleven children dead – twelve with Caleb – and he could name only half of them. They'd never find the other bodies, never learn who they were. And the men who'd killed them could carry on with their business, making money, still alive and flaunting their wealth.

He wanted them to pay. He wanted to be in court when the judge sentenced them. He wanted to see the mayor's face as the two men jounced at the end of a rope on Chapeltown Moor. But he didn't see any road he could follow to make that happen.

'You're miles away, Richard,' Mary said.

He'd never even heard her approach. 'Just thinking,' he answered with a smile.

'You don't look happy.'

'It'll pass. Who's cooking today?'

'Lucy.' She laughed at his expression. 'Don't worry, I showed her what to do.'

'As long as it tastes better than the pottage she made.'

'It will,' she laughed. 'She's coming along quickly. I'll let her go to the market for me on Tuesday.'

'Please don't,' he said. 'One of the reasons she's here is to keep her out of sight.'

'Of course.' She smiled sadly. 'She's just so alive that I keep forgetting about that.'

'Glad she's here?'

She nodded and held him. He laid his arms around her, smelling her hair, her face against his shoulder.

'Emily and Rob will be here soon, she's bringing him for his supper,' she said.

'They've been out walking?'

'They're young and in love,' she reminded him. 'They won't even have noticed the weather. We went out in worse than this.'

'Only because your father wouldn't trust us alone in a room.'

She slapped his arm playfully. 'And you know he was right on that.'

'Maybe he was,' he conceded with a grin.

The door opened and Emily swept in, dragging off her bonnet and shaking out the damp from her cape. Rob entered behind her, the pair of them talking loudly, and the house suddenly felt full and livelier.

'Staying to eat, then, lad?' the Constable asked.

'Yes, boss.'

'We'll give you first bite.' His eyes twinkled and he squeezed Mary's arm lightly. 'Especially as you liked that pottage so much the other night.'

By the time Lucy carried the pot to the table, careful not to spill a drop, they were seated and ready. The girl started to return to the kitchen but Mary said, 'Pull up a stool. Sit down.'

'Ma'am?' Lucy looked at her in confusion.

'You're one of us, you live here. Come and eat with us.'

The girl flashed a look at Nottingham. He gave her a quick nod.

'Thank you.'

She stayed quiet during the meal, watching the others as they talked. The Constable saw her staring hungrily at the pot and said, 'Help yourself to more if you want. There's still some left.'

She still ate greedily, keeping her face close to the plate, scarcely tasting the food. He remembered the first good meal he'd had after living rough. The old Constable had taken him home and put a bowl of stew in front of him. At first he'd thought it was a joke of some kind, that it would be snatched away from him. Then he'd gobbled it all down, not even chewing the meat and gristle, before wiping up every drop of the juice with a piece of bread. It still seemed like the best thing he'd ever tasted.

As the light waned outside the window, he sat back, hearing the bright laughter between Rob and Emily, seeing the tenderness on Mary's face at having her family around her, and he felt glad he was still alive. When the pain of his wound had been its worst, back at the start of the summer, he'd believed death might be better. Now he was grateful to have survived, to enjoy moments like this and see his daughter happy. She might be contrary at times, unwilling to marry her young man, but his love for her was as big as heaven.

Eventually Rob stood. Nottingham knew the lad was reluctant to leave, but Saturday was always the busiest night of the week. Men had been paid and wanted to drink away all the miseries of the week. There'd be arguments and fights, in a bad week even murder.

'Just watch yourself,' he advised.

'Yes, boss.'

Lucy disappeared with the dishes, and the brief moments of joy passed. He sat in front of the fire with Mary. She had a book open, her yearly reading of *Pilgrim's Progress*, and he had the *Leeds Mercury* draped over his knees.

'They're right together, aren't they?' he asked.

'They are,' Mary agreed. 'I suppose we looked like that once. Young and in love.'

'Once.' He chuckled, then sighed. 'Do you think she'll ever give in and marry him?'

'Only if she really wants to, when she's good and ready. I don't even try and talk to her about it any more. She can be as stubborn as you when she wants.'

'Stubborn?'

'You are and you know it,' she said with a gentle smile. 'It's one of your attractions.'

'One of many?'

'Don't fish for compliments, Richard.'

Monday had dawned clear, the stars still bright in the sky as he walked to work. Tomorrow, he thought, he'd leave the stick at home; he felt he'd be fine without it, and would look less of an invalid.

'How was Saturday night?' he asked Rob.

'Busy.' The lad rubbed at his eyes. His face looked drawn, the red hair even wilder than usual. 'We'd no sooner stopped one fight then we'd be called to another. The cells were packed yesterday morning. Mr Sedgwick kicked most of them out when they'd sobered up.'

'Anything serious?'

Rob shrugged. 'A pair of woundings. Nothing fatal. There's two back there for the Petty Sessions later.' He passed over the report.

'You go and get some sleep.'

'I will, boss.'

At the Moot Hall he'd half-expected again to be called into the mayor's office. He was surprised Fenton wasn't putting more pressure on him to find Gabriel. Then again, he thought, the man could always claim that the Corporation had done its part, put up the reward, and any failing was from the Constable and his men.

The day passed quietly enough. He spent the time in thought, trying to find a way to use the evidence from Howard's house which sat in his drawer. The knife. Even more, eleven locks of hair.

It made sense that Howard was in it with Darden. It gave meaning to the blood on the merchant's coat and the changed testimony about him attending the cockfight at the Talbot. But try as he might he could find nothing to help him put them in court.

The next day he walked down Briggate to the cloth market before the bell rang. At home he'd picked up the stick, then replaced it against the wall, feeling stronger.

Howard and Darden were standing in the middle of the street, talking to some of the other merchants. The factor gave him a killing look, fists clenched, before turning back and trying to concentrate on the conversation. His face was pale, with dark smudges of sleeplessness under his eyes.

He knows, Nottingham thought. He'd looked in the chest and

now he was filled with fear. Perhaps it was time to make him panic a little. He returned to the jail, emptied the pouch of its contents and slid it into his pocket.

The market had started; Darden and Howard were making their way from trestle to trestle, fingers feeling the cloth and talking in soft whispers. There was a reverent hush over the street as business was conducted.

He strode up to the pair. In a voice that carried well, he said, 'Mr Howard, might I have a word, please.'

The factor turned quickly, a scowl on his face. Darden didn't look around.

'What do you want, Constable?' Howard hissed. 'More accusations and innuendo? You've been warned about that.'

'Nothing like that, sir,' Nottingham said with a genial smile. 'Someone found something close to your house. I was just wondering if you recognized it, that's all.'

'What is it?' he asked brusquely.

The Constable held the packet out on the palm of his hand, the pale light playing on the silk. He kept his eyes on Howard. 'Does this belong to you?'

The factor shook his head quickly. But not before desperation had flashed across his face. 'I've never seen it. Why would you imagine it's anything to do with me?'

'Then I thank you. I'm just trying to find the owner. This is costly material, I'm sure you'll agree.' He watched the man's face, a few beads of sweat forming on his forehead.

'Isn't there anything in it to tell you?'

Nottingham opened the pouch and heard Howard draw in a sharp breath. 'It's empty.'

'I can't help you,' Howard said. 'I have work to do here.'

'Of course. I apologize for dragging you from it.'

'You damned well should.' There was menace in the factor's voice.

The Constable walked away, resisting the impulse to glance over his shoulder and see what was happening. He'd done what he could. Something would happen now, he was certain.

By the middle of the morning he knew he'd made a mistake in not using the stick. His wound hurt, a low, nagging pain, and his leg ached more than it had in weeks. If he tried to continue, by the end of the day he might not be able to walk at all.

He limped slowly down Kirkgate, the cold air pulling at his face. By the time he reached Timble Bridge he was exhausted, stopping to lean on the parapet and catch his breath. He'd been foolish, too optimistic and hopeful.

The last few yards to the house passed slowly. It didn't matter; at home he could rest a few minutes before returning to work.

The front door was unlocked. That seemed strange until he recalled that Mary had planned to send Lucy to market; the girl didn't have a key to the house. He'd argued against it, but she'd said that cleaned up, in a better dress and cap no one would recognize the lass, and in the end he'd given in.

He pushed the door open and entered, reached for the stick and rested his weight on it. Immediately he felt better.

'It's me,' he said. There was no reply and he went through to the kitchen. In the doorway he had to stop, grab the jamb and steady himself.

NINETEEN

She lay on the floor in all her shattered beauty. A stream of blood on the flagstones glistened in the firelight. He knelt on the floor beside her, fingertips urgently touching her neck, seeking a pulse, or anything at all.

He stroked her hand and kissed her hair. Time passed. Moments or minutes, they didn't matter any more. She was dead. Murdered.

Silence seemed to fill the room, to press down on him. He wanted to speak, to scream, but there was no sound worth a thing now. His face was wet. At first he didn't understand why. Then he reached up to touch his skin and realized he was crying.

He looked around for something to cover her, so no one else would see her in the indignity of death. The tears wouldn't stop and he tried to wipe them away, pushing roughly at his face.

He stood, climbed the stairs, his heart so heavy he believed it would burst from his chest. He pulled the sheet off the bed, took it downstairs and draped it lovingly over her. The memories tumbled through his brain. Her face, the sound of her voice, the way she moved and laughed. Young and older.

Finally he heard the front door and the sharp, awkward sound of shoes on the floor.

'Don't come in here,' he said, his voice as raw as if he'd been shouting.

'What is it, sir?' Lucy asked. 'What's happened?'

He swallowed, trying to find something in himself. 'Go to the jail and fetch Mr Sedgwick. If he's not there, ask people, someone will know where to find him. Tell him to come here as soon as he can.'

'What's in there? Tell me.' She stood in the doorway.

He turned to look at her, the pain clear on his face. The girl understood. She'd seen death often enough.

'Please,' he said, 'just go now. Get him.'

She put down the basket and ran. He could hear the small echo of her footsteps down Marsh Lane and he turned back to Mary, taking her hand and trying to pray her back to life.

Suddenly, so quickly it seemed, the deputy was there, out of breath, Lucy just behind him.

'What's wrong, boss?' he asked. Then he saw the sheet, the shape of the body underneath. 'Oh Christ. No.' He looked at Nottingham in confusion. 'Who?'

The Constable never took his eyes off Mary. 'You know who, John. You know who it was as well as I do.' He was surprised that he sounded so ordinary, so matter-of-fact, that the pain inside didn't turn the words into shrieks.

'Boss, I . . .'

Nottingham shook his head slightly. He didn't need that. Not now. 'You know what to do. Get Brogden here, and a couple of men to take her to the jail.'

'I will.' He paused for a long moment. 'Emily can stay with us. You don't want her around this. I'll wake Rob and have him meet her.'

He hadn't even thought about Emily yet. 'Thank you,' he said.

'What about you?' Sedgwick asked. 'You can't stay here, either.'

'I'm going to, John.'

'I'll stay with him,' Lucy offered.

'Are you sure?' the Constable asked her.

'Yes.'

He pounded on the door until Rob answered, yawning and running a hand through his hair.

'Get yourself dressed,' the deputy ordered.

'What is it?'

'Someone's killed Mary Nottingham.'

'What?' He looked as if he hadn't believed what he'd heard.

'Someone came in their house and murdered her. The coroner's on his way over there now. I need you. Go and meet Emily. Tell her gently and take her to my house. Lizzie'll look after her. Don't let her go home, you understand? Then I want you at the jail. Wear your good suit.'

'Who'd do that?'

'I'm not sure, but the boss said it was Gabriel. And you know what that means.' His eyes were hard and his voice low with anger. 'Whoever it was, you and me are going to find them. Come on, get a move on, we have work to do.'

Sedgwick's next stop was the house on Lands Lane. Lizzie's face filled with sorrow as he told her.

'Bring the lass here,' she said, her eyes glistening. 'I like Mary. You remember how she came down here when James went missing. She never had any side on her. Bring Mr Nottingham, too. He's going to need someone around him who cares.'

'That new servant is going to stay with him.'

She sighed deeply. 'Well, if anyone knows about death, that girl will. You go and find who did it.'

'I'm going to,' he promised.

'You know who it is, don't you?'

'I have a very good idea.'

She looked up at him. 'Then do one thing, John Sedgwick. When you're sure and you find him, don't wait for him to swing on the gallows.'

'I hadn't planned on it.'

*　　*　　*

The coroner came and went, in the house less than a minute, lifting the sheet and seeing the eyes set in the fixed, stunned gaze of death. On his way out he said, 'I'm sorry,' but Nottingham barely heard the sound of his voice.

Lucy directed the men who came to remove the body, making them enter and leave through the back garden. The Constable sat in the parlour, staring at the hearth where the fire had died. After they'd gone he heard the girl working, scrubbing away at the stains on the stone. The blood would never go completely, he knew that. He'd see it every day. Worse than anything, he understood that one morning he'd see it and it would be nothing more than a mark on the flagstones.

'I'll start another fire,' the girl said as she raked out the ashes. 'It's perishing in here.'

In a few minutes the room was warmed, the flames licking at the air. He hadn't moved. Whatever was happening, it all seemed unimportant now.

'Do you want something to drink? To eat?'

He raised his eyes to her. Hers were red with crying, too, but she was doing her best. Nottingham shook his head slightly. He didn't have any appetite, any thirst. Outside, the day was ending, and she bustled around, closing the shutters and lighting candles. He heard her moving around upstairs and all he could think of was the way Mary walked, how familiar everything about her had been to him.

Lucy returned and sat on the small tied rug in front of the hearth. Its colours had faded and it was covered with small burns from jumping coals. He recalled Mary making it in the fifth year of their marriage, using scraps of fabric and part of an old sack.

'Do you remember when you were young and you lived out there?' the girl asked quietly.

'Yes,' he answered after a long silence.

'What did you do when someone died?'

'I don't know,' he answered. In truth he couldn't recall.

'We used to tell stories about them. No one else was ever going to remember them.'

'Not tonight,' he told her softly. 'I can't face that tonight.'

She nodded her head.

'I just need to be alone.'

For a few minutes she was busy, laying out her pallet in the kitchen. Then there was silence.

It was all his fault. If he hadn't goaded Howard with the silk pouch and made it clear that he knew the man was Gabriel, Mary would still be here, sitting in the other chair, sewing, reading, talking. But he'd been so confident about the taunt. And now sorrow and guilt wound tight around his heart. She'd paid the price for what he had done.

If he'd listened to her, if he'd retired after he'd been wounded, none of this would have happened. But he'd needed to show he was strong, to prove that he was still the man he'd once been, that he could do the job was well as ever. He had to be a proud man.

Now he was alone with his pride, and all its gold was tarnished.

He'd make them pay. But it would be a fleeting satisfaction. They'd taken something far greater from him. And from Emily. He knew he should be with her, comforting her, but he didn't have the strength right now. All he could do was feel the grief tighten all around him.

Tonight he needed her to himself, to gather the memories around himself and try to gain some warmth and solace from them. He had to breathe her in alone, to hear her voice in his ear from every corner of the house.

He knew no one would understand, least of all Emily. She'd want to be here, to have his arms around her, to share her tears with him. Tomorrow he'd do that, hold her and cherish her. Her mother was dead and she needed her father in a way she never had before. Part of him wanted to go and bring her home, but he couldn't. She'd hate him for it, he hated it in himself, but in his heart he knew he had no choice. One last time he wanted Mary with him.

If only. The words filled his mind. If only he hadn't shown Howard the pouch. If only . . . He knew the hours would trail and spin in front of him and the guilt would weigh heavier and heavier in his head. It would last a lifetime.

The afternoon had passed in a blur. The deputy had spoken to the undertaker. He'd pushed and bullied the curate at the Parish Church to arrange the burial for the next day. As twilight began, he turned from Kirkgate on to Briggate and climbed the stairs in the Moot Hall, the sound of his boots muted by the thick carpet.

Martin Cobb scribbled away at his papers, a circle of candle-light on his desk, glancing up as he heard someone approach.

'Mr Sedgwick. I haven't seen you since Mr Nottingham came back. How are you?'

'I want you to give the mayor a message.'

Cobb looked up at him curiously. 'What is it?'

'Tell him to be at the church at two tomorrow. In his robes.'

The clerk sat back and rubbed his chin. 'Why would Mr Fenton need to do that? He's a busy man.'

'Because someone murdered the Constable's wife this morning and we're going to bury her.'

'What?' Cobb asked, shocked.

But the deputy was already walking away.

He spent another two hours passing the word. He finished on the other side of the river, sitting in Joe Buck's parlour, feeling awkward in the dainty chair, sipping at a glass of ale. He wanted to be moving, to be doing something more.

Buck studied his face. 'You know who did it, don't you?'

'Gabriel,' Sedgwick answered. 'Solomon Howard. He's Jeremiah Darden's factor.'

'Powerful men,' Buck mused. 'What are you going to do about it?'

'Prove it. And then I'll kill them.'

The fence nodded. 'I'll be there tomorrow. And I'll have people start asking. Anything they find, it's yours. Mr Nottingham's always been fair with me.'

Back at the jail Mary's body was in the cold cell. He lit a candle and slowly unwrapped the sheet. It seem so strange to see her in death, her face still, her eyes empty. Alive, she'd been so gentle. At first he was reluctant to remove her clothes, to see her naked. She's was the boss's wife, a woman who'd shown his family kindness, whose voice he could hear in his head. He started then stopped. Finally he took a deep breath and tried to think of her as just another corpse.

She'd been knifed five times; all the cuts were the same size. There were the beginnings of bruises on her sides and legs, as if someone had kicked her. He ran his fingers lightly over her scalp and found a lump under her hair. Had that happened before or after she died, he wondered?

Tenderly, he covered her once more. Soon enough they'd come to remove her corpse. He knew he'd taken things into his own hands by arranging the funeral, but it was the right thing. The boss didn't need that on top of everything else.

He was sitting at the desk, thinking, when Rob arrived. He was wearing his good suit rather than his work clothes, his face closed and anxious.

'How is she?' the deputy asked.

'How do you think?' He poured a glass of ale and drank it down. 'She was crying and screaming. She wanted to go home.'

'You didn't let her?'

Rob shook his head.

'Lizzie'll look after her. The funeral's tomorrow at two.'

'Did the boss arrange it?' Lister asked in surprise.

'I did. It's one thing less for him to think about at the moment.' The deputy looked up. 'Right, here's what we're going to do. I'm going to talk to the clerks at Darden's when they finish work. You're going to see as many of the merchants as you can. You'll do better at that than I would. That's why I wanted you dressed up.'

'What do you want me to say?'

He'd thought about that during the afternoon. 'Tell them that someone murdered Mrs Nottingham and persuade them to come to the funeral. When you've done that, ask a few questions – can they think of anyone who might have done it. Then drop in something about Darden and Howard.'

'I will.'

'Leave everything else to the night men, I don't give a bugger what it is. You and I are going to work on this until we have them.'

'She was good to me,' Rob said emptily.

'Aye, and she cared about Lizzie, and James and Isabell. The world's lost a grand woman. The boss knows that more than anyone. But now she's in the cold cell. Someone stabbed her five times. Just keep thinking about that.'

TWENTY

He went from merchant to merchant, from home to warehouse. The news had passed already, the way it did in Leeds, and they all received him with serious faces and words of condolence. Without question they agreed to attend the funeral, but none had an idea who could have been responsible. And when he started his questions about Darden and the factor, their mouths shut and their eyes began to look elsewhere.

He found Tom Williamson at the new warehouse by the river. Men were preparing a shipment of cloth to leave for Hull the next morning. A small, fussy clerk checked against his list and pettishly directed Rob to the office.

The merchant was there, a brazier burning to give some heat to the room. His head was down, concentrating on a column of figures.

'Mr Williamson?'

He looked up, taking a moment to place Lister. 'Did Mr Nottingham send you?'

'You haven't heard the news?' He seemed to be the first who didn't know.

'What news? What's happened?'

'Someone killed the Constable's wife this morning. Stabbed her in her house.'

Williamson sat back, looking stunned. He ran his hands down his face. 'Richard . . .?'

'He found her,' Rob said.

'What can I do?'

'The funeral's tomorrow at two.'

'I'll be there, of course. I met her a few times. She always seemed a lovely woman.'

'She was,' he said with quiet feeling.

'You're James Lister's lad, aren't you?' the merchant asked thoughtfully. 'The one who's courting the Constable's daughter?'

Rob raised his head. 'I am.'

'How is she?'

Lister just stared at him.

'Please, tell them both how sorry I am for them.' He stayed silent for a short while, then asked, 'Do you know who did it?'

'Not yet,' Lister lied. 'Can you think of anyone?'

Williamson shook his head.

'What do you know about Mr Darden and his factor?'

'What?' he asked in astonishment. 'You think they're behind it?'

'No, nothing like that. We're just gathering information on them.'

'Richard had asked me about them, too. I told him what I knew.' He rubbed a hand across his chin. 'There's something going on, isn't there?'

'I'm just doing what I'm told,' Rob answered blandly, trying to keep all the expression off his face. Williamson stared at him, then sighed. 'There was something I was going to tell Mr Nottingham when I saw him. I'd forgotten all about it before; I was only a boy when it happened, but my father fumed about it for years.'

'What was it?'

'It must have been, what, twenty-five years ago now?' He counted off the years in his head. 'Close enough to that, anyway. Mr Darden lent the Corporation some money. I don't know how much it was and I'm sure it's long since been paid. But my father always said Darden received preferential treatment because of it.'

'What did he mean?'

'I don't know. It's probably nothing. I've never heard any more about it.'

'Thank you.' Rob stood.

'I'll be there tomorrow,' Williamson promised.

It was the only new thing he'd learned, an incident that happened a lifetime before. Still, he wondered why no one else had mentioned it. Memories were long, especially for anything that gave one merchant an advantage over the others.

He was walking back up Briggate, wrapped in his thoughts, wondering what he could do next, when a hand took his sleeve.

'I heard,' James Lister said. 'It's terrible. Do you have anyone yet?'

'No, Father.'

'Please, tell Mr Nottingham how saddened and shocked I am.'

'You can tell him yourself. The funeral's tomorrow at two.' He pulled away and continued up the street.

The deputy was waiting on the corner. The church bell had struck six and it was full dark when the three clerks emerged. They wore shabby clothes, the seats of their breeches shiny from being perched on stools all day.

'Evening, lads,' he said. They were all well into middle age, with grey hair and the worn-down look of men worked too hard for too little. 'I'm the deputy constable. I'd like a word.' He smiled. 'Can I buy you all a drink?'

The first jug of ale went quickly and he ordered a second. He listened to them complain, wittering like old women, ears pricked for any loose talk. As their words wound down, he asked, 'What did Mr Darden and Mr Howard do this morning?'

Ashton, the head clerk, the quietest and gravest of them, answered warily, 'Why do you need to know?'

'Knowing things is my business.'

'It's Tuesday. Mr Howard was at the cloth market. Mr Darden went with him.'

'Aye, I know that. And this morning someone killed the Constable's wife. Stabbed her five times.' He glanced around the faces. 'So you'll see why I'm asking.'

'They came to the warehouse after the market,' Ashton told him. 'They allus do that. Got to check the cloth the weavers bring and make sure they don't cheat us.'

'What about when that was done?'

'Looked at the orders we were sending out.'

'How long did that take?' Sedgwick asked.

'I wasn't listening to the church clock. Then they went out.'

'Where did they go?'

The clerk shrugged. 'They don't tell us, they just go.'

'When did they return?'

'Mr Howard came back about dinner time. Mr Darden didn't come back at all. Nowt strange in that. He's retired.'

'How did Howard seem?'

'*Mr* Howard was the same as ever.' The man emphasized the title. 'Wanted everything done yesterday. He must have been home, though.'

'Why's that?' the deputy asked sharply.

'He'd changed into an old coat and breeches. Spent part of the afternoon looking through cloth on the shelves.'

'Is that usual?'

'Mr Howard isn't a man to ruin a good suit.'

'Does he look through the cloth regularly?'

Ashton shrugged again. 'A few times a year.'

'Was he different in any way?'

'Not that I saw. But we were working.'

'He had a right short temper,' one of the other clerks said.

'What did he do?'

'Clouted one of the lads who moves the bales around. Not just once, quite a few times until the boy was crying.'

'Is he often like that?' Sedgwick watched them carefully, seeing the small, uncomfortable glances they exchanged.

'It happens,' Ashton said flatly.

'What else do you know?' the deputy pressed them.

'Nowt, really. I've worked for them for years and they've been good to me.' He paused. 'If you want them guilty of summat, I'll tell you now – they're not.'

Sedgwick stood and nodded his thanks. Outside the night felt raw; the chill clawed at his face as he made his way back to the jail. Rob was there, giving instructions to one of the night men. As soon as he'd gone, the deputy poured some ale and stood by the fire, feeling its heat.

'Well?' he asked.

Lister told him what he'd learned and Sedgwick recounted what the clerks had told him.

'What do you think?' he asked.

'They were gone part of the morning. They had the time, there's no doubt about that,' Rob answered. 'But there's nothing to show their guilt, is there?'

'Aye. We need to find out where they're supposed to have gone. I'd like to take a look at those clothes Howard wore during the morning, too.'

'What do we do next?'

'Nothing tonight, lad. I'm going home to rest. There'll be plenty of time for more tomorrow. And the funeral.'

'Will you tell Emily . . .?'

'Of course I will. Don't worry, we'll look after her.'

'What about the boss?'

'He'll do what he needs to do.'

He opened the door softly. Lizzie was sitting close to the hearth. She put a finger to her lips to hush him. He settled on the other chair, looking down to see Isabell sleeping peacefully in her crib, her illness now nothing more than a memory.

'I put Emily in our bed. I think the poor lass has cried herself to sleep for a while. That boy of hers didn't want to leave her.'

'I'll take her home in the morning. The funeral's at two.'

'Have you found anything yet?'

'Not any proof.' He was tired, the anger and frustration burning inside him.

'Find it, John,' she urged him.

'I will. Don't worry about that. If it's there we'll find it.'

'Have you seen Mr Nottingham?'

He shook his head. 'Better to let him be for now.'

'Mebbe.' She sighed deeply. 'I'll tell you something, that girl could have done with her father tonight. I did what I could but she needed more than me.'

'She'll have him tomorrow. And all the days after that, too. It'll just be the two of them now.'

'Not the same, though, is it?' He had no reply. She reached out and took his hand. 'I'll put out the candle. You look like you need your rest.'

He'd just woken when she came down the stairs. It was still dark and he heard her groping her way.

'Miss Emily,' he said quietly.

'I'm going home.' Her voice was nothing more than a hoarse whisper.

'I'll walk with you.'

'There's no need.'

'I need to see your father.'

Outside, in the half-light on the horizon, her face looked

ravaged. If she really had slept it had been for no more than a few minutes. As they passed the jail she glanced through the window, looking for Rob.

'He'll be out doing his last rounds,' the deputy told her. She tried to smile but it left as soon as it came, no heart behind it. He coughed and said, 'I talked to the undertaker and the church. They're going to have the funeral this afternoon.'

She looked at him sharply.

'I'm sorry,' he said. 'I thought it would be one thing less for you and the boss to have to think about.'

'I suppose it doesn't matter when we bury Mama,' she said emptily. She stayed quiet until they crossed Timble Bridge. 'Thank you. And thank Lizzie, too.' She looked up Marsh Lane at the house. 'Is Papa there?'

She picked up her pace, moving so briskly that the deputy had to rush to keep up with her. He followed as she burst through the door, seeing the Constable sitting and staring at the dead fire. As Nottingham turned his head, Emily began to hit him with her small fists, crying and howling out all her pain.

He sat there and took it all, the tears trickling down his cheeks. Once she'd exhausted herself he stood, leaning heavily on the stick at his side and wrapped his arms around her.

'I know, love, I know,' he said. 'I know.'

The deputy stayed by the door, feeling awkward, an intruder on this private grief.

The Constable kept whispering, words too low for anyone but her to hear. Emily cried against his coat, her arms tight around his neck, hair tumbling from her cap. Finally she nodded, wiping her face, and went upstairs.

'Boss . . .'

'Don't, John. Please.' His eyes were full of the dead, looking but not really seeing. 'Just tell me what's happening.'

Sedgwick summarized it all. Nottingham bowed his head and listened quietly.

'It's my fault,' he said finally. 'I had to brag to Howard. I emptied that pouch and asked if it was his. I said someone had found it near his house. He had his revenge.'

'Christ, boss.'

'If I hadn't . . .' He halted, searching for the words to flay himself. 'If I hadn't been so fucking arrogant, if I hadn't wanted to rub his nose in it, she'd still be alive.'

'You don't know that.'

The Constable looked at him. 'Of course I do,' he said dismissively. 'So do you, I can see it on your face. He knows I'm going to live with this every day from now on, that I'm going to feel it every time I walk through that door or sleep in my bed or wake in the morning.'

'We'll get him, boss.'

'I know. We will. But it's too late. He's killed Mary. He's killed me, he's killed Emily. He's killed all those children.' He slammed his hand against the wall.

'We'll find a way to hang him.'

'Thank you. And thank Lizzie for . . .' He raised his eyes.

He bought a pie from a seller at the bottom of Kirkgate and ate it as he walked. There were more people to see, questions to ask. The deputy knew that Hugh would never let him back into Howard's house now, no matter how much he threatened. That way was blocked.

At the Rose and Crown he strode through the yard to the stables, finding Hercules gently brushing dirt from a mare until her coat shone.

'Bad news about the Constable's wife,' the old man said without turning. 'What are you looking for?'

'Anything that can help me find her killer. You know Mr Darden and Mr Howard?'

Hercules bobbed his head, keeping a slow rhythm with the brush. 'Always a private parlour when they meet someone here. Or if they want to talk.'

'What do they talk about?'

The man frowned. 'They go quiet when anyone comes in. Are you sure it was them?'

'I believe it was Solomon Howard,' the deputy told him. 'And that he murdered the children, too. I just need to be able to prove it.'

'I'll keep my ears open.' The old man turned to face him. The hair was matted around his face, his beard long and uncombed. 'I'll promise thee that. When's the funeral?'

'Two o'clock.'

'Aye, that's what I heard. There'll be plenty of folk there. People have a high regard for Mr Nottingham in this city.'

Rob arrived at the house on Marsh Lane as the clock struck the half hour. Lucy answered the door, her face serious, a dark shawl around her thin shoulders. Emily sat in the chair that had been her mother's, small and slumped, her eyes red and her face pale. He took her hand, the flesh chilly against his, and he tried to smile for her.

The Constable said nothing, the pain buried deep behind his expression. Five minutes passed, then he stood and said, 'We'd best be going.'

They walked along, their steps slow and solemn. Nottingham used the stick, Emily holding on to his other arm, and Rob followed, Lucy at his side. Along the road one door opened, then another, and a third. Families emerged, dressed in their best, all crossing Timble Bridge to the Parish Church.

The Constable removed his hat as he entered, seeing the deputy standing near the font, James on one side and Lizzie on the other with Isabell in her arms, the baby's eyes wide to be in such a big building. He made his way down to a bench at the front and sat, his daughter beside him, Rob on her other side, then the servant girl.

The merchants and aldermen were alone in their private pews, looking uncomfortable, there under duty and sufferance. The mayor's pew stayed empty. But the back of the church was filled, folk standing, men, women, children.

Rob turned and saw faces he knew: Joe Buck and his servant, landlords from the White Swan, the Ship, the Turk's Head, even Mr Bell from the Talbot. All the Constable's men stood in a line, and behind them Morrison the chandler, Kirshaw the apothecary and too many others to see.

The coffin sat on trestles, plain, simple oak without decoration or polish. The congregation rose as the vicar emerged to face them, the Book of Common Prayer in one large hand.

'I am the resurrection and the life, saith the Lord; he that believeth in me, yea, though he were dead, yet shall he live. And whosoever liveth and believeth in me, shall not die forever.'

When all the priest's words were done and the bell began to toll, Rob moved forward, along with the deputy, Tom Williamson and the Constable himself to carry the coffin out to the grave.

It was next to Rose's, the soil piled to one side, dark and moist. The diggers stood apart, a jug of ale by their feet, hats off, heads bowed in respect.

Once they'd lowered the body into the earth, Nottingham knelt, picked up a clod of earth and crumbled it between his fingers. He held out his hand, letting the dirt drop, the sound of it hollow on the wood.

'Forasmuch as it hath pleased Almighty God of His great mercy to take unto Himself the soul of our dear sister here departed,' the vicar began. Nottingham stepped back and Emily took his place, tears coursing down her cheeks, and Rob stood by her side as she let the soil fall. 'We therefore commit her body to the ground, earth to earth, ashes to ashes, in sure and certain hope of resurrection to eternal life, through our Lord Jesus Christ, who shall change our vile body that it might he like to His glorious body, according to the mighty working, whereby He is able to subdue all things to Himself.'

Emily took hold of her father's hand and slowly led him away as the bell sounded its last dull note. Sedgwick put his arm around Lizzie's shoulders, holding her close, feeling her with him, alive, Isabell sucking on a damp rag soaked in sugar water.

He watched the Constable and his daughter go through the lych gate and then turn for home.

'I'd not want to be looking through their eyes today,' Lizzie said quietly.

'No.' The wind blew up and he pulled his coat closer.

'I'm going home. I still need to cook. Come on, James.'

He kissed her forehead. 'I love you, you know,' he whispered.

'Don't be so daft,' she told him, but she was smiling and her eyes were wet.

'What do we do now?' Rob was next to him, watching the man and girl cross Timble Bridge.

'You'd better go to her, lad. She's going to need you.' He looked over his shoulder, spotting Lucy standing by the church, lost and hopeless. 'Take that lass with you. Stay there as long as you need. The night men can look after things until tomorrow.'

The crowd of mourners thinned. Some would go up to the White Swan to drink and talk, others back to their work and homes. It was over; Mary Nottingham was buried. The grave-diggers were at work, bending their backs and filling the hole, the bell had gone silent, and all that remained were the sounds of the city.

He walked slowly back up Kirkgate to the jail, put more coal on the fire and waited for the heat to warm his bones. He sat at the desk, thinking how he could prove Howard's guilt.

Today was for grieving. Tomorrow he'd go out to Marsh Lane and question the people there, ask if they'd seen anything. Many worked in their cottages, the families all together in the weaving trade, the children combing and carding, the mother spinning and the father at the loom, trying to make a living between that work and a few animals grazing on what was left of the common land and food growing in the garden behind the kitchen. Maybe he'd be lucky and someone noticed a stranger.

He hadn't expected so many to turn out for the funeral. Not the rich, who had to be there from obligation, but all the others, the press of people who stood crowded together for the length of the service and in the churchyard. He knew them all and heard them mutter their anger at the killing, even men who'd rarely think twice about knifing another soul.

While they were still full of goodwill and their memories sharp he'd start to go round them, to see what they might know, what they might have spotted, anything that could be of use. He needed something that would help hang the bastards.

TWENTY-ONE

He unlocked the door and entered, feeling the dull silence in the house. He moved around the room, touching the chairs, the table, the candles, as if to assure himself they were real. Everything in this place held a memory of Mary.

He lifted his head and for a fleeting moment he believed he could hear her calling his name and the sound of her footsteps on the flagstones of the kitchen. But it passed in a breath and he knew that from now on the family would just be two of them.

'Papa?' Emily's voice drew him out of his thoughts. 'Would you like some ale?'

'Yes. Thank you.'

He understood that she felt as lost as he did, lost and probably even more alone. She couldn't comprehend why he couldn't have her here last night, why he couldn't have held her and offered her some comfort. Perhaps he'd never be able to explain it to her in a way she'd understand, but he'd needed the time with his guilt, the chance to ask Mary for her forgiveness.

He heard Emily in the kitchen, knowing he couldn't go to her in there. His gaze would fall to the floor, where no scrubbing would ever remove the mark. The door opened and Rob came in, Lucy behind him, her eyes fearful, standing in the corner, trying to keep herself small and unnoticed. If he didn't see her, he couldn't let her go. He knew what scared her, that he'd turn her back out to the streets, just when she'd found a home.

'She's through there, lad,' Nottingham said and Lister moved away quietly. There was a strange, unnatural hush in the house, every sound muted.

'Lucy.' He saw her flinch. 'I'm going to need someone to cook and clean and take care of everything here. I hope you'll want to stay.'

'Me?'

'You,' he assured her. 'Will you?'

'Yes.' She blurted the word out, then blushed and said, 'Yes, sir.'

'Good.' He gave her a wan smile. 'I'm glad.'

She scuttled through to the kitchen. He could hear Emily and Rob whispering in there, their voices urgent but too low for him to make out the words.

His world had changed. All the objects, all the surroundings were familiar, things he'd touched and known for years, but he felt as if he didn't know them at all.

'Boss?'

He looked and Rob was there, pushing a mug of ale into his hand. He tightened his fingers around it, the clay cold against his palm. Emily was on her knees by the hearth, piling kindling and coal for a fire, her movements an echo of her mother's. He drank, barely tasting the liquid.

'Mr Sedgwick said I didn't need to go to work tonight.'

The Constable nodded. 'Emily will need you this evening. She'll need us both.'

Lucy moved through the room, lighting candles from a taper, and the acrid smell of the tallow filled the air.

'There's only bread and cheese,' she told him apologetically. 'I haven't cooked.'

'It doesn't matter.'

'You didn't eat last night. You haven't eaten today.' Lucy looked up at him. 'You need to eat,' she insisted.

'Papa,' Emily said, her voice gentle and persuasive. 'We all miss her. We all loved her.' She smiled at him. 'Please.'

He swallowed the food on his plate but barely noticed it, refusing more when Lucy urged it on him. Finally they were done, a spare funeral feast for an empty death, he thought. The girl gathered the dishes and took them to the kitchen.

'Tomorrow,' Nottingham said.

'Boss?'

'I'll be back at work tomorrow.'

'Papa—' Emily began. He cut her off with a shake of his head.

'There's work to be done.' He poured more ale and drank. 'You're right, love, we miss her. We're always going to miss her. And we'll always love her.' He placed his hand over hers. 'But it's my job to catch whoever killed her, and I need to do that.'

'But Rob and Mr Sedgwick . . .'

'They can use another man to help them.' His face softened. 'I can't spend another day sitting here. You know what I mean.' She nodded her understanding. 'And you should go back to school. We have the rest of our lives for sorrow and memories. They'll be there forever.'

Later, after Rob had gone home and Emily was in her room, he settled in the bed and extinguished the candle, the weight of blame heavy on his heart. Even under blankets and a heavy coat he shivered. He reached out, knowing he'd never touch her again, but hoping for some ghost of shape. But there was nothing, no rhythm of her breathing, just the emptiness that would remain.

He knew he must have dozed, waking at times in the heavy

darkness. The night felt like an enemy, taunting him, offering him no real rest. Before first light he was up and dressed, moving quietly round the house then gathering up the silver-topped stick and slipping out into the cold.

Two of the night men were at the jail, warming themselves by the hearth. The fire crackled bright and the pitcher of ale was almost empty.

'Anything?' he asked.

'Nowt, boss,' one of them answered. 'Just a few who stopped by to say how sorry they were.'

He let them leave and sat to write the daily report, just two brief sentences to say there'd been no crime reported in Leeds the previous day. Dawn was close, and soon the city would be stirring all around him, servants lighting fires and preparing meals, labourers on their way to work, carters arriving and leaving with a trundle of wheels on the roads.

But there was only one thing he wanted now: to prove, beyond any doubt in court, beyond all that money could buy, that Howard had killed his wife and Darden had helped him. Once that was done, the future could do whatever it wanted; he'd no longer care.

By the time the deputy arrived the report was complete and sanded dry.

'Boss,' Sedgwick said.

'It was time to come back to work,' Nottingham said darkly. 'We have plenty to do.'

'Aye, we do.' He kept the surprise off his face.

'Anything more?'

'I went and talked to a few folk, but no one had anything helpful. I'll go out along Marsh Lane this morning and see if anyone saw Howard or Darden there yesterday morning.'

The Constable nodded. 'What do you think?' he asked.

'He's a clever bugger; we already know that. But if there's anything to find, we'll find it.'

'If.'

'There'll be something, boss. There always is.'

'Let's hope so.' He stared at the deputy. 'I want him soon.'

'We'll have him,' the deputy promised.

After Sedgwick had gone he walked over to the Moot Hall. Out in the open, a threat of rain in the heavy clouds, he felt the pain of missing Mary so intensely that he had to stop and breathe deeply. He looked around, realizing she'd never see any of this again. That she wouldn't be waiting when he returned in the evening.

Finally, he gathered himself, opened the heavy doors and climbed the stairs, treading gently on the Turkey carpet. Martin Cobb sat at his desk, his young face blushing as he saw the Constable.

'Mr Nottingham. I'm so sorry . . .'

'The daily report for the mayor.' He laid the paper between them.

'It must be terrible.'

He knew the man meant well, but he couldn't feel charitable. 'Then pray God it never happens to you.'

'The mayor didn't know when you'd return. He wants to see you.'

He knocked on the door and entered when he heard a voice inside. Fenton was hard at work, reading through a pile of papers on his desk. He was fresh-shaved, his cheeks pink and shiny, his expression pinched and irritable, as if he resented the intrusion.

'My condolences on your loss.'

The Constable nodded his acknowledgement.

'I'm sorry I couldn't come to the funeral. I had other obligations. I hear there were plenty there.'

'Yes.' He took a tighter grip on the head of the stick.

'Do you have any idea who killed your wife? And don't say Mr Darden and his factor.'

Nottingham stayed silent.

'I daresay you've made many enemies over the years,' the mayor continued. 'Maybe you'd do well to cast your net over some of them.'

'Is that an order?'

Fenton threw down his quill in frustration. 'If it needs to be. What you're doing is beginning to look like an obsession.'

'And if they're guilty? What then?'

'I've known Mr Darden for years. No one's more respected in Leeds.'

'Tell me, your Worship, when the city borrowed money from Mr Darden, was it ever repaid?'

The mayor brought his head up sharply. 'A long time ago. What he did then was a civic gesture.'

'Enough to buy gratitude and protection.'

'I'll put that statement down to your grief,' the mayor said coldly. He picked up the quill.

It was impossible not to look at the house as the deputy walked along Marsh Lane. The image of Mary Nottingham's blood was clear in his mind, and the loneliness and pain on the Constable's face. There was a sense of all the love gone from the place.

As he knocked at the first house beyond Timble Bridge he could hear the clack of a loom inside. The noise continued as a young girl opened the door.

'Hello, love,' he said with a smile. 'I need to talk to your mam or dad.'

The woman who appeared looked haggard. She was young enough but streaks of grey hair peeked from her cap.

'Help you, mister?' she asked, eyeing him suspiciously.

'I'm the deputy constable. We're trying to find who killed Mrs Nottingham.'

'Come in,' the woman told him without hesitation. Four children were working hard preparing the wool and a spinning wheel sat in the corner, yarn hanging from it. Along the wall stood a collection of painstakingly carved wooden animals – a cow, horse, sheep and more. 'Stop that,' she said to her husband, her voice loud over the incessant noise of the loom. 'Sit thisen down.'

She poured him ale and settled on her stool. 'She were a lovely woman. Always had time for a word, and to ask after the bairns.' She nodded at the children. 'Who'd do summat like that?' she asked.

'Aye, and why?' The man took a clay pipe from his waistcoat pocket and lit it.

'What we want to know is whether you saw anyone along here on Tuesday morning.'

'There's allus folk on the road going in and out of Leeds,' the man pointed out.

'Maybe you noticed someone in particular.'

The woman looked worried, pulling a small girl close and placing the child on her lap.

'We're working from daylight until dark, mister. Same as all the folk round here.'

'Give over.' The man blew out a plume of smoke. 'You're up and down and in and out and mithering round half the day.'

'Aye, and we'd never eat or have clean clothes if I wasn't.' She turned back to Sedgwick and blushed. 'I'm sorry, love. But he's right, people pass by all the time. Mostly we just hear them, there's no reason to look.'

It was the same wherever he asked. People had to scrape a living and work hard. At a few of the homes no one answered, off at their labours; he'd send Rob there after dark. With a falling heart he kept going. Finally, about fifty yards beyond the Nottingham house a young woman said, 'Aye, I saw a man at their door.' She held a sleeping baby close to her chest, gently stroking the back of its head and rocking back and forth on the balls of her feet. Over her shoulder he could see all the signs of poverty within, the room almost bare of furniture.

'What did he look like? Do you remember?' His throat was dry and he could feel the blood throbbing in his veins.

'I didn't pay him no mind.' Her eyes were wide with fear. 'Why? Was it him?'

'Most likely.'

'Really?' She frowned and hugged the child a little tighter. 'This one had been poorly. I was late emptying the chamber pot. That's the only reason I saw anyone.' She tilted her head towards the road. 'Mrs Nottingham had only been up the day before. She gave me some herbs she thought might help Anna here.'

'Did you know her well?'

'We've only been here a few month. But she had a good word and she was kind. Folk round about liked her.'

'What can you remember about the man you saw?' he asked urgently.

She thought for a long time, absently rubbing the baby's back. 'He had a dark coat and breeches,' she answered finally, her voice halting. 'And a wig.'

'What colour was his coat?'

'I wasn't paying attention. I'm sorry.'

'Did you see his face?'

She looked down the road to the Nottingham house. It stood too far away to see any detail. 'No. I'm sorry.'

'Was there anything else? Anything at all that you can recall?'

'I saw him knock and go in the house.'

'Did he come out again?' the deputy asked urgently.

'I'd emptied the pot so I went back in.' The girl hefted the baby higher on her shoulder. 'This one started crying again.'

'You didn't hear anything?'

'Mister, when our Anna starts crying you can't hear owt else.'

'Was there something else you might have seen?' he asked desperately. 'It's very important. It could help us find whoever killed her.'

'I did think I saw someone else . . .' she began.

'Where?'

She pointed at a tree in the distance. 'There.' She shook her head helplessly. 'I'm not sure. It was just something moving. It could have been a man. I'm sorry.' She looked up at him with wide eyes. 'He'll not be back, will he?'

'No,' he assured her. 'He won't.'

She had nothing more to give. He thanked her and moved on. The description only made him believe it was Howard, dressed as Gabriel. But the girl hadn't seen his face; she'd never be able to identify him. Why had Mary Nottingham let him in the house, he wondered? Had he forced his way in?

The deputy doubted they'd ever know the answers. And maybe they didn't matter. The important thing was finding the evidence to convict him.

He asked at the other houses but no one else had seen a man by the house. He even stopped carters and people walking along but there was nothing to aid him. One or two might have seen someone but they didn't remember who it could have been or how he was dressed.

All too often, that was the tale. There'd be something helpful but it wouldn't be enough. If he had his way, the merchant and his factor would simply disappear and no one would ever see them again.

Instead of returning to the jail he went to the Talbot. Only a few drinkers huddled over their ale on benches far from the windows. Bell the landlord was checking the barrels, a new cask standing by, ready to be changed. He stood quickly when Sedgwick rapped on the counter.

'Good to see you at the funeral yesterday,' the deputy said brightly.

'Aye, well . . .' The man shrugged his large shoulders.

'Show willing, eh?'

Bell said nothing, ready to turn back to his work.

'I want a word.'

'What about?' The landlord bunched his fists then opened them again.

'In the back,' Sedgwick told him.

'I need to keep an eye on that lot.' He gestured at the customers. 'They'll drink me dry otherwise.'

'Call one of the girls to do it.'

Bell stared at him for a moment, then yelled, 'Essie!' He pulled at a ring of keys on the belt under his leather apron and unlocked the door to the cock pit. Faint light came through the high windows. The room smelt strongly of blood and death. The landlord settled himself on a bench, crossing his arms over his belly.

'Right,' he said. 'We're alone now, Mr Sedgwick. What did you want to talk about?'

'Truth and lies.'

'Oh aye?' Bell smirked. 'And what about them?'

'As long as I've known you, you've been very good at the lies.'

'Why would you think that?'

'Funny how you remembered that Mr Darden had been at the cockfight not long after you said he hadn't.'

'I'd forgotten he was here,' the landlord answered blandly.

'The jingle of money's always good for the memory, eh?' The deputy smiled.

'You think what you like.'

'Oh, I will. And would you like to know what I think, Mr Bell?'

'If you like.'

'I think I've had enough lies from you.'

The landlord shook his head slowly. 'I've been threatened by better men than you.'

'Happen you have,' the deputy told him. 'But I daresay it won't be too good for trade to have a Constable's man standing outside all the time, will it, or if we keep taking in your girls for whoring?' Bell sat quietly, sucking on his teeth. 'You ought to know by now that I don't threaten,' Sedgwick continued. 'Consider that a promise, Mr Bell.' He paused for a moment. 'And it'll be the first of many.' He slapped his palm against the wood surround of the pit. 'I'd give it three months before you're out of business. Maybe you want to think on that.' He began to walk away. 'I'll be back to see about some truth.'

Nottingham opened the desk drawer and took out the silk pouch, feeling it slide between his fingers. He closed his fist around it, the sorrow rising in his chest. If he hadn't been so arrogant . . .

He breathed deeply and put the pouch away. The design, the texture, were fixed in his mind. He stood, took hold of the stick and left the jail, walking down Briggate towards the bridge. People stopped him to offer their condolences. They were kindly meant, but each time it only brought Mary's face into his head and he had to turn away in case they saw his tears ready to fall.

Tom Williamson's warehouse lay on the riverbank, downstream from the bridge. It was still new, the stonework clean and sharp, not yet worn down by weather and winters. In the clerks' office the brazier burned and beyond men worked busily, preparing a shipment for somewhere.

The Constable spotted Williamson, an apron over his coat and breeches, pulling at a heavy cloth on the shelf. The man next to him said something and the merchant turned, then came forward, his hand extended.

'Richard,' he said, his voice filled with sadness. 'I'm so sorry.'

'Thank you.' Nottingham shook his hand. 'And for yesterday, too, for coming forward to carry the coffin.'

'I was honoured,' Williamson said, and the Constable believed him. 'Come on, let's go outside. I need some fresh air after all the dust in this place.'

The cold wind swept down along the river and the men walked with their backs to it.

'You didn't come here just to thank me.'

'No,' Nottingham admitted. 'You told one of my men something interesting.'

'Lister's boy, you mean? He seems sharp enough.'

'He is. You talked about Mr Darden lending money to the city.'

Williamson sighed and pushed a hand through his hair. 'I said it was a long time ago. I was just a boy then. All I really know is that it angered my father.'

'He thought it put Darden in a special position.'

The merchant nodded then gave a wry grin. 'He believed a lot of strange things. To be honest, I think he just wished he'd had the money himself, so he could have lent it.'

'Who'd know more about it?'

Williamson stopped and looked at the Constable. 'You'd better tell me what's going on, Richard. I heard that the mayor had warned you away from Darden. Then your man was asking about him and his factor.'

'Fenton did warn me, yes. And Howard brought his lawyer to see me.'

'Then why?' His eyes were curious.

'I'm as sure as I can be that Solomon Howard murdered Mary, and that Darden has been in it with him. I believe they killed those children. Eleven of them.'

Williamson stayed silent for a long time.

'If you know all that . . .'

'My proof won't stand in court,' Nottingham said flatly. 'I'm looking for something that will. That's the reason I'm looking at everything. It doesn't matter how small it is or how long ago it happened. I want anything I might be able to use.'

'Charles Trueman,' the merchant said. 'Go and talk to him. He was privy to things for decades. If anyone knows the full story, he will.'

The Constable nodded. He'd never met Trueman but he'd heard the name often enough over the years. He had to be eighty if he was a day, but he worked all his life for the city, rising until he became head clerk of the corporation. 'Where does he live, do you know?'

'A little way along the Newcastle road, I think. It should be easy enough to find his direction.'

'Thank you again.'

'Richard.' There was a note of warning in the man's voice. 'If they're guilty I want them to hang as much as anyone. Please, take care trying to prove it.'

'Part of me's well beyond care now,' he answered.

TWENTY-TWO

I t was the work of a minute to discover exactly where Trueman lived, close enough to stay in touch with the city, but still enough distance away to be separate from it. The Constable crossed over the Head Row, passing the grand houses and the grammar school at Town End before Leeds vanished into countryside.

The fields were dark and moist where they'd been pulled over by the plough. Sheep grazed on the hillsides. They were what gave Leeds its wealth, a fortune in their fleeces. He strode out, hands pushed into the pockets of his greatcoat, the stick clicking out a rhythm on the road.

The house was out beyond Sheepscar, past the few houses there that were barely a hamlet. The garden was small but well-tended, the building itself in good repair, more than a cottage but certainly nothing grand. He knocked at the door and waited until the servant answered.

She was a young girl, modest, but with lively blue eyes and an intelligent face.

'I'm Richard Nottingham, the Constable of Leeds,' he said. 'I'd like to see Mr Trueman.'

She bobbed a quick curtsey and invited him into the hallway. 'It's right parky out there,' she said. 'Come in and get yourself warm.' She vanished through another door. He heard a quiet exchange of voices, then she came and led him through.

Trueman still had a full head of white hair, side whiskers extending almost to his chin. He was seated in front of a roaring fire, neatly dressed in an expensive coat and breeches, the stock tied at his throat. He looked at the Constable with perceptive eyes covered by a cloud of rheum.

'Mr Nottingham. I've heard plenty about you, but we've never met.' He had the voice of a younger man, sonorous and regal.

'No. Thank you for seeing me.'

The man gave a short nod. 'My condolences to you, sir. I lost my wife ten years back. I know what it's like to find yourself alone.' He steepled his hands under his chin, the spots of age all across his flesh. 'But I do wonder what brings you all the way out here.' He raised his bushy eyebrows. 'Something from the past, perhaps? I can't imagine why else you'd need to talk to me.'

The Constable smiled. 'It is.'

'Then sit yourself down. I don't want a crick in my neck from looking at you. Some ale, a glass of wine? You've had a fair walk out here.'

'I'll be fine.' He sat on the other chair in the room.

Trueman picked a small glass from the table and sipped. 'Cordial,' he explained. 'Keeps my throat moist. Now, what do you want to know?'

'I've heard that quite a few years ago Jeremiah Darden lent the Corporation some money.'

The old man mulled over the question. 'He did, yes.'

'What was it for?' Nottingham asked.

Trueman smiled. 'There were some purchases of land the Corporation wanted to make, down by the bridge. Mr Darden offered the money so everything could be conducted speedily.'

'Why did it need to be done so quickly?'

'It didn't, I suppose. But it simplified things. We didn't have the money at the time, so we'd have been forced to wait until revenues came in. This way was much easier and made sure we obtained the land, rather than someone else buying it and selling to us at a profit.' The surprise must have shown on Nottingham's face. 'Yes, that has happened before. I won't say who or where.'

'How much money was involved?'

'Not as much as many people have claimed, I can assure you of that. I've heard all manner of wild figures. It was four hundred pounds. That's still a handsome sum, I think you'll agree with me on that.'

'That's true.' It was as much as many good merchants took in profit during a year, enough to live on without caring or ever having to count costs.

'You know how these things are,' Trueman continued. 'They become exaggerated. I've heard he lent a round thousand, but I know that's wrong. I was there and I helped draw up the papers.'

'He was repaid?'

'Of course,' the old man said with an emphatic nod. 'And within three months.'

'Was he paid interest?'

'No. That was part of the agreement. It was civic spirit on his part; he was a member of the Corporation. All he received was the amount he lent and a vote of thanks.'

'But he never became mayor.'

'Now you're digging deeper,' Trueman told him with a smile. 'And you're doubtless wondering why he resigned from the Corporation.'

'I've heard stories.'

'I'm sure you have – I've heard more than a few myself.'

'What's the truth?' Nottingham asked him.

The old man hesitated before answering. 'Sordid and crude,' he said. 'Mr Darden tupped a servant.'

'There's nothing unusual about that.'

'Of course not.' Trueman's smile became wolfish. 'But not his own servant. And not a girl. This was a boy who'd just begun working for another member of the Corporation. He hadn't just enjoyed him, he'd beaten him hard, too.'

The Constable was silent for a long time. 'How did people find out?'

'The boy collapsed the next day. When he came to, he told them what Mr Darden had done.'

'What happened to the lad?'

'He died,' Trueman said flatly, then stared at Nottingham. 'You can understand why Mr Darden was asked to resign. We couldn't have someone like that running the city. But neither could we have the truth come out, of course.'

'The tales I heard were about a girl.'

The man waved an old hand, the skin wrinkled and pale. 'Vague fancies. People could build on them as they wished. And better they believed it was a girl than a lad.'

'But the city and the merchants still protect him.'

'They always will, Constable. He's paid for his crime. He gave up his seat on the Corporation, he lost the chance to be mayor. He's been punished. Underneath all that he's still one of them. He helped them when he needed it. Surely you understand that?'

He nodded sadly. He understood it all too well.

'Besides,' Trueman added, 'imagine the damage it would cause if the real story ever came out. Not just to Mr Darden, but to the city. I'll ask you to think about that. I've told you all this in confidence. I'm trusting you have enough respect for Leeds that you'll never make it public knowledge.'

'Should I have?'

'Would you care for one more story from the past?' He took another sip of the cordial and leaned back in his chair. 'Did it ever surprise you when Constable Arkwright first took you on?'

The question took him aback. It had been over twenty years ago, when he worked the jobs he could, none of them steady, none paying much. He'd survived living on the streets of the city. He believed that Arkwright had seen something in him, something that would make him a good Constable's man, and he'd been grateful for the steady employment.

'Should it?' he answered warily.

'There were folk on the Corporation who thought your father had treated your mother very shabbily. He flaunted his sins, his gambling and philandering. Then he put the two of you out because he'd discovered her affair.'

'And you'll know she died,' Nottingham said bitterly.

'I do,' he acknowledged. 'A few people thought that perhaps you deserved a little better. After all, none of it was your fault.' Trueman sighed. 'Eventually someone had a quiet word with Mr Arkwright. Without that you wouldn't be sitting here today.'

'Thank you for being so honest with me.' The Constable stood, pushing himself slowly upright with the stick and groaning at the pain in his legs.

'You're going to have more of that as you grow older,' Trueman told him with a sympathetic nod. 'I'm sorry for your loss, I truly am.'

The trees were bare, branches stark against the sky. The bitter November wind suited his mood as he walked back into Leeds. So now he knew exactly why Darden had left public life. No one had cared that the boy had died. A lie or two and a few pounds to his parents would have covered that. He doubted if any of those in power had remembered the lad's name. And still they protected the merchant to hide all the secrets and shame of the past.

And now he knew another ugly truth. There'd been no special promise for the old Constable to spot. It was simply a sop, a way of relieving a little guilt, but long after his mother had died with nothing, all she owned legally stolen from her by her husband. Telling him had been the price Trueman exacted for his secrets, and the words had stung.

But only for a moment. Nothing anyone said could really hurt him now. He was already overflowing with pain. It was so heavy that he felt he could touch it, that it stood between him and the rest of the world. And he knew he'd been good at his job, good enough to become deputy and then Constable. He'd earned his position.

He waited outside the dame school, huddled in his greatcoat, a heavy coat and breeches beneath it, with thick hose and sturdy boots. Still he felt the cold through to his bones. It could be another long winter, he thought.

There was no gaiety or life in her face when she came out. Mrs Rains had a brief word with her, then Emily gave a quick reply and she was beside him, her small fingers warm in his hand. She closed her eyes.

'Take me home,' she said. 'Please.'

Rob smiled at her and she tried to return it. But there were dark smudges under her eyes and her face seemed pinched with sadness. He knew she'd find no relief in the house. Her mother's ghost would fill the place; it would always be there.

'Do you know what I wish?' Emily said.

'What?'

'That we could just walk away from here and never come back.'

'But we can't.'

'I know.' She sighed deeply. 'I miss her. It hurts. I want her to be there when I open the door and she won't be.'

It would fade, he knew that. It would always gnaw at her, but other joys, other treasures of memory would fill the hole that consumed her. But telling her wouldn't help. At the moment she wouldn't even understand. He stopped and pulled her close to him, stroking away the tears that started to fall down her cheeks.

'Come on,' he said, putting his arm around her shoulder. 'Let's get you home.'

They walked in silence. At the house he could see her hand shaking as she slid the key into the lock. Inside, he heard Lucy moving in the kitchen, then she came through with two mugs of ale.

'Thank you.' Emily took the cup.

The girl curtseyed, looking serious. She moved away then halted in the doorway. 'I know you wish it was your mam doing that and not me.'

'No,' Emily said, taken by surprise.

'I can see it in your face,' Lucy told her quietly. 'I'm sorry.'

He sat at the jail, considering what Trueman had told him about Jeremiah Darden. Was there anything he could use, some scrap to help him convict the man? After all these years it had become nothing more than rumour scattered on the wind. The merchant could laugh it off and deny it all. Even passing it as gossip wouldn't damage him; it had all happened too long ago.

Outside, darkness had fallen quickly. Through the window he could glimpse candlelight flickering through shutters on the other side of Kirkgate. The fire was burning low in the grate. He knew he should go home but was reluctant to leave. All that waited for him was more sorrow.

The door opened and the deputy entered, rubbing his hands together. 'It's going to freeze out there tonight. Won't be much work for Rob, they'll all be round their firesides.'

'Did you find anything worthwhile?'

Sedgwick held his arms out to the weak blaze. 'Not really. I had another word at the Talbot and threatened Bell a little. There might be something tomorrow.'

The Constable explained what Trueman had told him about Darden.

'And nothing happened?'

'He left the Corporation.'

'He's in it with Howard. He has to be,' Sedgwick said. 'Some
of those dead children were boys.'

'I know.' Nottingham shook his head. 'Have I done all of this
wrong, John?'

'What do you mean, boss?'

'We're no closer to putting them on the gibbet, are we?'

'No,' the deputy admitted.

'Could I have done it differently?'

'Not that I can see. You mean the pouch, don't you?'

'Yes.' It was the question he'd never stop asking himself.

'I'd have done the same.' Sedgwick shook his head. 'I doubt
that's much comfort, though.'

'No.'

'Go home, boss. There's nothing more you can do here. I'm
off myself soon. Tomorrow we'll come up with something.'

Lucy's pottage was flavourless. After a few spoonfuls he pushed
the bowl away, seeing the disappointment on the girl's face. 'I'm
just not hungry,' he said.

Even Emily, with her appetite, couldn't finish.

Head bowed, Lucy cleared the table. She was trying hard, he
knew that, and it was difficult for her, working in this house full
of heartbreak.

'Papa?' Emily's voice pulled him out of his thoughts. 'What
are we going to do?'

He understood. She was lost, flailing. All the hope had gone
from her face.

'We'll do what we have to do,' he told her. 'We'll carry on.'

'But . . .'

'I know.' He reached across the table and placed his hand
lightly over hers. 'We survived when Rose died.'

'Mama was with us then.' Her eyes were glistening.

'She's still here,' he said quietly. 'She's always going to be
here.'

'It hurts.'

'It does,' he agreed.

'Was it like this when Grandmama died?'

Had it? His mother had been ill for so long that he was
the only thing keeping her alive. They existed in rooms where the

runnels of damp came down the walls and he stole and begged food that she could barely eat. When her breath stopped he'd felt relief first of all; she didn't have to struggle any more. The pain took longer. It was still there, buried deep, and it would never vanish.

'No,' he answered finally. 'But I wish she was still here. She'd have been very proud of you. Mama was, too. So am I.'

She smiled and the tears began. Better that she let them out, he thought.

They sat by the firelight and talked, sharing their memories. He told her tales that brought laughter, and he learned things about Mary as a mother that he'd never known. Eventually he stood.

'We both need our beds,' he said.

'Thank you, Papa.' She hugged him, still sniffling a little.

'As long as we're here, she'll never go away,' he reminded her.

'I know.'

TWENTY-THREE

'Do either of you have any ideas how we can put Darden and Howard in the dock?'

They'd gathered in the jail, Rob yawning behind his hand, the deputy looking dishevelled, his old hose filled with rips. Nottingham looked from one face to the other.

'That Lucy of yours can identify Howard,' Sedgwick said.

'His lawyer would tear her apart in court. Especially since she came to work for me.'

The deputy grunted. 'Couldn't they just disappear?'

'No. I want them to go to trial and I want to see them hang for what they've done. I want everyone to know.' His voice was hard and determined.

'Yes, boss.'

'We'd better keep digging. The longer it goes on, the harder it'll be for us to find anything.'

He watched them leave, finished the daily report and walked it over to the Moot Hall. A heavy frost had fallen overnight, leaving the flagstones and cobbles white and slick. Martin Cobb was at his desk, head bent over his work; he looked up as the Constable approached.

'The mayor wants to see you,' he warned.

'Is he in?'

'Arrived five minutes ago.'

He knocked and entered. Fenton was at his desk. The fire blazed in the hearth, making the room luxuriously warm.

'Sit down, Nottingham.'

He settled awkwardly on the delicate chair and waited. The mayor looked harried, in need of a shave, white bristles sprouting on his chin. He read through a paper, dipped the quill in a small jar of ink and scribbled his signature across the bottom before pushing it aside.

'People have been talking to me,' he said.

'Oh?'

'It seems you're still asking questions about Mr Darden and his factor.'

'I am,' the Constable admitted.

'Why? I told you to stop.'

'My job is to find who killed those children.' He looked directly at Fenton. 'And my wife,' he added.

'When we put up the reward, people came forward. Have you looked at them?'

'Of course. All it did was waste good time,' Nottingham told him flatly.

'You'd already made up your mind.'

'It was them.'

The mayor sighed. 'You're grieving. Your thinking is muddled.'

'Is it?'

'That's what I'll tell Darden's lawyer when he complains. But if you keep it up I'm going to talk to the Corporation and we'll start looking for a new Constable. I'm sorry about your wife but you've been nothing but trouble since you came back to work. I'll not tolerate you defaming Jeremiah Darden. Do I make myself clear?'

'Very.' He stood. 'But you'd better think about what you're

going to say when it comes out that they killed those children.
I know about Darden and that boy.'

'You know nothing,' Fenton replied firmly. 'You've got an
idea fixed in your head and it's the wrong one. I've given you
the last warning; there won't be another.'

Once he was outside all the rage of the last few days welled up
in him. His wound hurt and his legs ached, but he forced himself
to walk out along the Head Row, beyond Burley Bar and into the
countryside beyond. The road to Woodhouse snaked off into
the distance and he followed it along the hill, all the way to the
common land where people still grazed their cows in the summer.
The beasts were all away in their byres now and the ground was
empty; most folk were too sensible to be out in the cold.

The wind tore at him, harsh enough to take his breath away
for a moment. He opened his greatcoat, letting everything buffet
him. Slowly he knelt, the dampness of the earth soaking straight
through his breeches. Alone, he could cry, letting the tears fall
and the sobs shake his body. He shouted out for her, for himself,
for everything that was lost. He put his hands on the grass, feeling
it damp against his fingers, and tore up tufts of it, anything that
could ease the pain inside.

When he'd finished he pushed himself slowly back to his feet.
His throat was raw, and a thin drizzle hid the tears. He breathed
deeply and walked slowly back to the city.

The clock had struck eleven by the time the deputy entered the
Talbot. He could smell a stew cooking somewhere, but he'd
have put money on the meat being tainted, bought cheap, the
taste hidden with spices. Soon enough folk would be in for their
dinner, some spending the rest of the day here, meeting and
making their bargains behind tankards of ale. None of them
would stay if they saw him.

Bell the landlord was wiping down the trestle with a wet, dirty
cloth. He looked up as Sedgwick approached.

'I said I'd give you a day.'

'Aye, I remember.'

'Have you done some thinking?'

'Mebbe,' Bell replied. He poured himself a mug of ale from
the barrel and tasted it.

'It's your choice. I've a man with nothing better to do than spend his day outside the door.'

'What do you want to know?'

'Was Darden here from that cockfight?'

'No,' the landlord admitted grudgingly.

'First he wasn't here, then he was, and now he wasn't. Which is it to be, Mr Bell?' He kept his voice low and pleasant, enjoying the man's torment.

'He was never here.' There was hatred in Bell's eyes.

'So why did you lie?'

'I was offered money.'

'Who by?'

'Hugh Smithson. He works for Mr Howard.'

'I know who he is. He told you to say Mr Darden had been here and paid you for that?'

'Aye, if anyone asked, that was what I was to tell them. I had to say I'd forgotten he'd been here.'

'You'd better be prepared to swear to that in court,' the deputy told him.

'You never said owt about court,' Bell said sharply.

'Didn't I?' Sedgwick asked blandly.

'I can't do that.' The landlord shook his head slowly. 'I'll tell you, but that's it.' He raised his head defiantly. 'I don't give a bugger what you do.'

'Are you sure about that?'

'Aye,' he said. 'I am. Leave a man here all the time if you want.'

The deputy stared at him for a moment then nodded and left. He wouldn't be able to push Bell further. He had something now, though, even if he couldn't use it in court. It might be worth going to Solomon Howard's house to talk to Smithson once more.

But the man who answered the door wasn't familiar. He was heavily muscled, starting to run to fat, with dark hair cropped short against his skull and a thick, fleshy neck.

'I'm looking for Hugh Smithson,' Sedgwick began.

'Gone,' the man answered bluntly and began to close the door. The deputy wedged a foot on the step.

'Gone?'

'Mr Howard wasn't happy with his work.'

'When did that happen?'

'Two days back.' Tuesday, the deputy thought. The day the boss showed Howard the pouch. The day Mary Nottingham was killed.

'Where's he gone?'

'Buggered if I care.' The man pushed harder and Sedgwick gave way. The door slammed closed in his face.

'Tell your men to keep their eyes open for someone called Hugh Smithson,' the deputy told Rob. Outside the jail it was full dark, the night bitter.

'Who's he?'

'He was Howard's servant until Tuesday. Sacked. He's the one who let me in the house. The older men will remember him. He has a bit of a past, does Hugh.'

'What do you want me to do if I find him?'

'Bring him in. He'll likely welcome a bed for the night, anyway.'

'What's he done?'

'If he's been out of work for two days and doesn't have any money, he'll have done something,' Sedgwick promised.

'I can't sleep,' Sedgwick whispered to Lizzie. They were in bed, both James and Isabell asleep, the night quiet around them.

'Work?' He was holding her close, enjoying the warmth of her body. His greatcoat and her cape were piled on the bed, on top of the thin blanket.

'Aye,' he answered slowly. 'We're trying to find evidence on the bastard who killed Mary Nottingham and those children. It just feels like we're chasing him and he keeps moving another step ahead.'

'You'll prove it, love,' she said lazily, curling around him. 'Just settle down and rest. You need it.'

He sighed and closed his eyes. Images and ideas roiled through his mind. He let them pass, breathing quietly until they passed and everything faded away.

There was a sharp frost on the ground, the grass edged with white, the ground iron-hard under the worn soles of his boots. Away in the bare trees birds were beginning to sing. Soon enough there'd be snow and ice covering it all and the year would be dead.

The deputy was already at the jail, standing close to the fire. The skin was tight over his face, his eyes filled with weariness.

'Anything, John?'

Sedgwick explained what he'd learned, then said, 'He's not in the cells,' and shrugged.

'If we can find him . . .' the Constable mused.

'Aye. If.'

The door opened and Rob entered, his cheeks red from the cold.

'Did you find out about Hugh?' the deputy asked.

Lister shrugged off his heavy coat and came close to the fire before answering.

'There's no sign of him.'

'What do you mean, no sign?'

Rob poured a little ale into a mug and drank. 'Two of the men remembered him. They asked around. Smithson was out drinking Tuesday night.'

'The Talbot?' Sedgwick interrupted.

Lister nodded. 'He said he'd been dismissed and he was leaving Leeds. But he had money, he was buying flagons most of the evening.'

'Did he say where he was going?' Nottingham asked.

'No, boss.'

'Fuck!' the deputy shouted in exasperation and began to pace round the room. 'Howard's just making fools of us. He's paid Smithson off and sent him away so we can't question him.'

'It sounds that way,' the Constable agreed calmly.

'Well, what are we going to do?'

'We're still going to find a way to catch Mr Howard.'

'How?' Sedgwick raged.

'I don't know yet, John,' Nottingham admitted. 'But we'll do it.'

The deputy grabbed his greatcoat and left, the door closing loudly behind him.

'You leave, too, lad. I'm sure Emily could use some company on the walk to school.'

'Yes, boss.' Rob smiled.

'Just be kind to her. She's going to need a lot of tenderness. It was bad enough when Rose died, but this . . .'

'I will.' He hesitated, then asked, 'What about you, boss?'

'I'll survive,' he replied grimly.

Martin Cobb was at his desk, a wary smile on his face. The Constable dropped the daily report on to the man's desk.

'Does he want me again?' he asked, nodding at the mayor's office.

'Not today, Mr Nottingham.' He gave a small cough. 'Do you have your accounts ready for the year?'

'My accounts?' For a moment he wasn't sure he'd heard properly.

At least Cobb had the goodness to blush. 'Mr Fenton wants you to meet the treasurer for the Corporation on Tuesday and go through the accounts for the jail.'

'We're trying to catch a murderer. Before that I was off for months after being stabbed, as his Worship well knows.' He barely managed to keep his voice under control. 'Of course the accounts aren't up to date, and they won't be by Tuesday.'

'I'm sorry,' the clerk said, the flush rising on his face. 'That's what he said to tell you. He wants you there with the accounts for the jail.'

The Constable sighed and nodded slowly. 'Oh, I'll be there,' he agreed.

He understood perfectly well what the mayor was doing. There would be discrepancies in the accounts, just as there always were, and the treasurer would find them. That would be enough to dismiss him as Constable. It wouldn't be the deputy who took over this time, either, but someone more deferential to authority.

Back at the jail he sat at his desk, pulling papers from drawers, items dating back to the start of the year. He started to place them in order, then put them aside. No matter what he did, the mayor was determined to find some excuse to replace him.

He sat back, tired to exhaustion in his soul. It seeped through his bones and into his heart. Mary was gone and nothing mattered any more. He took out the silk pouch and let the eleven locks of hair fall to the desk. They were painful to see, but even they couldn't stir his anger the way they had before she was killed.

He wanted Howard and Darden in court, wanted to walk up to Chapeltown Moor and see them hang, but the numbness in him was growing. They'd killed part of him, too, the best part, taken away so much of his love. So little seemed important any more. The weight was too heavy on his shoulders.

He picked up the stick and slowly made his way down Kirkgate, his greatcoat still on a hook at the jail. Thin sleet had begun to fall; people hurried down the street with heads bowed, trying to stay dry. Nottingham turned at the lych gate and walked through the mud of the churchyard to the graves.

Lichen was beginning to grow on Rose's headstone, starting to eat away at the sharp cuts of the words. He knelt and scraped it away with his fingernail. She'd be nothing but bone now, the flesh all eaten away.

Next to her the earth was mounded dark over Mary. He could find a spade and dig it all away, pull the nails from the coffin lid and see her again before nature took her. He remembered kneeling by her body in the kitchen, his fingers smoothing her hair, the texture of it in his hands. He'd kissed her cheek, his face beside hers to draw in the scent of her for the final time.

He could still conjure up her voice calling his name, the love she put into a simple word even when he exasperated her.

'Boss?' The word made him turn to face the deputy, dragged back to the pain of the present.

'You've been here for over an hour,' Sedgwick told him gently. 'Someone came to fetch me. You're soaked through.' He smiled. 'Come on, let's get you in the warm.'

The Constable followed him meekly to the jail. Sedgwick talked of anything and everything, how James was at school, the way Isabell was growing, almost ready to crawl, words to fill the space between them, to keep Nottingham's mind in the here and now.

The Constable sat on his chair, surrounded by all the papers. He put more coal on the fire and watched as the flames licked upwards. The deputy poured some ale, put it in his hand and stared until he drank it down.

'I should start on all this,' Nottingham said finally. 'The treasurer wants to see the accounts on Tuesday.'

'Why?'

The Constable raised his eyes and brushed the fringe off his forehead. 'The mayor wants me out,' he answered emptily. 'He refuses to believe that Darden and Howard could be guilty. He'll have you out, too, and Rob.'

'Then we'd better show him he's wrong.' He smiled. 'Have the lad work on the sums, he has the mind for it. If this weather keeps up there'll be little enough for him to do at night, anyway.'

Nottingham nodded. Rob would make sense of all the figures with ease.

TWENTY-FOUR

The deputy buttoned his heavy coat and pulled up the collar. The sleet was still falling, icy puddles forming on the roads. His boots and hose were soaked, his feet chilled. He'd considered telling the Constable to go home, but what was there for him there? Just more memories to hurt him.

The man he'd talked to by the graves this morning wasn't the one he'd known for years. This one was broken, lost, looking for something he was never going to find, more like a helpless child than a grown man.

He could only imagine how he'd feel if Lizzie died, and they'd barely been together for a heartbeat. If someone killed her . . . then he'd commit murder of his own. The older you grew, the more you had to lose, and the more life could hurt you.

He didn't even know where he was going. He'd put out the word about Smithson. The man had probably left Leeds, paid off by Howard, but if he'd decided to linger the deputy wanted him. Landlord Bell at the Talbot had made it plain that he wouldn't testify.

They had nothing. Short of a miracle they'd never arrest Howard and Darden. It was as if their lives were charmed, that guilt could never touch them. But he was damned if he'd let them look at the world with scorn and take whatever they wanted. He pushed the old tricorn hat more firmly on his head. All he could do now was follow wherever his feet took him, and ask questions.

There was hardly a soul on Vicar Lane, and the carters making their way up and down the Head Row were few and far between. Finally he ducked through an opening off Briggate and into the Ship. The place was bustling, the fire crackling loudly. He looked around as he waited for his ale, spotting familiar faces among the crowd.

The landlord waved away his money. 'Tha knows better than that, Mr Sedgwick.'

He smiled his thanks and squeezed through to the hearth. Joe Buck the fence and his servant, Henry, had a small table to themselves. Some might stare at Henry's colour but they knew to leave the pair alone.

'Joe,' the deputy said. 'Henry.'

Buck moved along the bench. 'I've been hearing some strange things about the Constable,' he said with concern.

'Oh aye?' Sedgwick took a long drink.

'Standing in the rain at the churchyard today, out near Woodhouse in that weather yesterday.'

The deputy shrugged. 'He's just lost his wife, Joe. He's not himself.'

'Little birds have been talking to me, Mr Sedgwick.' Buck frowned. 'They say the mayor wants rid of Mr Nottingham.'

Sedgwick smiled. 'How long have you lived in this city, Joe?'

'All my life.'

'Then you know not to believe everything people say here.'

'The person who told me was well-placed,' the fence said.

'Aye, they always are, Joe. And how often are they right?' He shook his head. 'Come on, you know the answer as well as I do.'

Henry was staring at the mug in front of him, the light shining on his shaved, dark skull.

'But what happens to you if someone else becomes Constable?' Buck asked. 'A new man might have other ideas for a deputy.'

'Happen so.'

'Tha dun't sound too worried,' Henry told him.

'I already said it's not going to happen. So why worry about it?'

'But if it did,' Buck began slowly, 'you'd still need to earn money. You've got that family to feed.'

'Going to offer me something, are you, Joe?'

'Always good to have something up your sleeve, Mr Sedgwick.'

'Except the boss won't be going anywhere.'

Buck nodded. 'Tell me something. You already know full well who was responsible, don't you?'

The deputy nodded.

'Then why's he still alive?'

'You know why. The boss wants them to hang.'

'Bugger that.' He looked around cautiously and began to speak in a quick, low voice. 'I know folk who'd take care of the problem for nowt. They'd be gone by tomorrow.'

'That's not how Mr Nottingham does things, Joe.'

'Not even when they murdered his own wife?'

'Not even then.' He gave the man a warning look. 'And don't you go getting ideas, either.'

'We need rid of scum like that.'

'Don't,' the deputy repeated. 'And that's not advice, either. You try it and I'll be coming for you.' He held Buck's gaze until the man nodded.

'Right, I've had a warm and a wet. I'd best get back to work.' He put the battered hat back on his head. 'Good to see you again, Joe. Henry.'

Outside, he took a deep breath, strode through the narrow ginnel and back on to Briggate. The sleet was still coming down. Any colder and it would turn to snow, he thought. But not yet, not yet. He wasn't ready for another winter.

But he'd learned something interesting from the encounter – Joe Buck was paying someone at the Moot Hall for information and he had a good idea who. It could be worth paying Martin Cobb a visit sometime.

Darden and Howard had money and influence to protect them. Somewhere, though, there had to be the evidence to put the pair of them in the dock. And he was going to find it.

At the jail the Constable was putting the documents for the accounts in order, small piles of them scattered across the desk.

'Boss, how closely have you questioned Lucy about Gabriel?' Sedgwick asked.

Nottingham looked up thoughtfully. 'I've asked her about him, about when he came after the children. Why?'

'Have you asked her *about* him? Anything that might have stayed in her memory.'

'No,' he admitted slowly. 'I was going to give the girl time to settle, then . . .'

'Let's go and talk to her. She might know something we can use.' He gave a deep sigh of frustration. 'Christ only knows we need some help.'

The Constable was already rising and putting on his greatcoat. 'She trusts me, John. I'll do it.'

'Do you want me to come with you?'

'No. It'll be better if it's just me and her.'

He walked purposefully, glancing over at the graves in the churchyard, picking two of them out immediately and feeling the yearning that had been there that morning and would still exist tomorrow and all the days that followed. The sleet stuck the hair to his scalp and a thin, cold trickle of water ran down the back of his neck.

His boots clattered on the boards of Timble Bridge and he turned on to Marsh Lane. The house was barely two hundred yards away, every stone and window familiar. He didn't feel any joy at the sight, but it was still home, where the past had soaked into the walls, where he'd made notches in the door frames to mark how the girls grew each year, where Mary's touch was there in every little thing.

He unlocked the door and entered, slipping off the coat and hanging it on the nail. When he turned, Lucy was there, standing at the entrance to the kitchen, a long knife in her hand. He understood.

'I didn't know who it was. I thought he'd come back . . .'

'He won't return,' Nottingham assured her gently. 'He did what he meant to do here. Come and sit down.'

She perched on the edge of the chair, as if she wasn't sure she should really be there, and looked at him questioningly.

'Are you letting me go?'

'No, nothing like that.' He smiled and her mouth twitched nervously. 'I told you, you have a position here. I need you more than before, now that . . . my wife's gone.'

'Have I done summat wrong? Just tell me and it won't happen again. I promise it won't.'

'You've been doing a grand job.' He looked at her. 'I want to ask you about Gabriel.'

'I told you before.'

'You saw him,' he told her. 'You talked to him.'

Lucy was silent.

'What was he like? Was he gentle?'

'Aye.' She bit her lower lip. 'It was like he could tell which were the weak ones. He'd make them promises until their eyes were shining.'

'What kind of promises?' The Constable sat forward, hands on his knees, listening intently.

'You know,' the girl answered. 'Food. Somewhere to live. Somewhere warm.' Lucy glanced at him. 'When you lived out there, weren't you allus cold?'

He nodded, remembering for the first time in years the way the weather gnawed at him back then, prickling his skin and burrowing into his marrow.

'Yes,' he said. 'I was.'

'I heard him talking to the young ones sometimes. It was like hearing someone tell a story about this lovely place where you want to go.'

'Did he prefer younger children?'

'He gave them little sugar things. They liked that. And they'd listen to him.'

'Didn't anyone try to stop him? To chase him away?'

'What do you think? But we couldn't watch the little ones all the time. He'd find them when we weren't around. We'd warn them, but some of them would still believe him,' Lucy said sadly.

'What did he do when he talked to them?'

'You mean did he touch them or owt like that?'

'Yes.'

'He'd just talk to them. But that was enough. You know?'

He knew all too well. When all you had from adults was shouts and threats, kind words and attention were like honey. Of course they'd listen.

'He'd make it sound like they were going to get all these things. Food, clothes, somewhere warm to live.' She paused. 'He has a tongue made of sweetness. I'm just glad I didn't meet him when I was little.'

'You're safe now,' he told her.

'Aye.' She gave a small, sad smile. 'I am. But what about them still out there? And the ones still to come?'

'We'll catch him.'

She raised her eyes and stared at him. 'You've not done a good job of it so far, have you?'

'No,' he admitted.

'Why don't you just kill him? You know he killed all of them. You know he killed the mistress.'

'Because that's the law,' he told her. 'Both of them will die, but they'll do it properly when a judge has pronounced sentence.'

'And what if that doesn't happen?' she asked him.

'I don't know.' Fury bristled inside him at the thought.

'Then happen you'd better find an answer,' she said sharply. 'I don't know how you can sit there and just talk about it.' She blushed. 'I'm sorry.'

'What do you think?' he asked quietly. 'That I'm not hurting? That I don't miss Mary? That I don't feel responsible for what happened to her?'

'I said I'm sorry.'

'I'm the Constable. I have to keep to the law. If I don't, why should anyone else?'

'I know, but—'

'There can't be any buts. And you know the hardest part? They know that. They're laughing at me.'

'Because they have money.'

'That's part of it.'

She stood. 'I need to start cooking.' In the doorway she turned and said, 'If you want justice, give me a knife and two minutes with them.'

He heard her moving around, the dull, metallic clack of pans as she started work. He curled his right hand into a fist then opened it again. He hadn't told her what he really wanted to do to the men. He couldn't speak about it to anyone. Once the words and the feelings came out he could never put them away again.

He was caught, bound by the law, stretched between what he wanted and what he had to do. A few would understand the truth, but he knew that most people would be like Lucy and see him doing nothing.

He felt hollow inside. They'd taken everything good in his

soul. Doing anything at all took all his strength. He stood at the bottom of the stairs, wishing he could hear her footsteps above. Then he went back into the cold, bitter rain.

Rob stood in the doorway; it kept some of the sleet away. But by the time Emily came out of school his hat was soaked and his shoes sodden.

'I didn't know if you'd come out in this,' she said, putting her arm through his.

'Of course you knew,' he said with a smile. There'd been no colour in her face since her mother died, he thought, and no joy or life in her words. They walked quickly, trying to avoid the horse dung that lay smeared and slimy on the street, not saying anything more until they were by the road that led from Kirkgate to the White Cloth Hall. He glanced across, seeing the bell pits neatly filled in, circles of dark earth on the grass.

'Why did they do it?' she asked, her voice lost and far away, and he wondered what he could tell her that might have any kind of reason to it. 'She didn't hurt them. She never hurt anyone.' Emily turned to him, her face wet. 'Why couldn't Papa save her?'

'He would have if he could,' he said quietly. 'You know that.'

'And then he didn't even want me to come home and be with him.' He heard the desperate confusion and anger in her voice. 'He wouldn't let me see her.'

'He was trying to protect you.'

'I'm not a child,' she said defiantly. 'I saw my sister die. After that we were all together. Mama was there.'

They moved aside as a cart rushed up the street, one wheel dipping through a puddle and sending a small wave over the cobbles. The hem of her dress was already wet and dark, but she didn't seem to notice it.

'Maybe he just doesn't know what to do,' Rob suggested.

'But he has to,' she pleaded helplessly. 'He has to know what to do.' She clutched his arm tighter. 'He has to.'

There was nothing he could say to give her the comfort she needed. All he could do was put his hand over hers and be at her side.

*   *   *

The sleet passed during the night as the wind shifted to the east.
On Saturday morning the skies were clear, the air cold, frost
clinging to the grass. The puddles had a thin coat of ice that
cracked under his feet as he walked up Kirkgate, the stick tapping
on the ground.

In the cells three men were sleeping off a night of drinking.
One of them had a bloody face, his nose mashed to one side;
another had pissed himself on the bench. The Constable put coal
on the fire and poured a mug of ale.

Soon enough Rob returned from his final rounds. The cold and
rain had made things quiet enough; he'd had time to start work on
the accounts, putting them into the kind of order a clerk would value.

'You've done more than I could,' Nottingham told him.

'I'll have them finished for Tuesday, boss. They won't find
any fault.'

'Good. You get yourself off to your bed. You deserve it after
that.'

'Boss?'

There was something in his tone; the Constable looked closely
at the lad as he struggled for the right words.

'It's Emily. She . . .' He ran a hand through his hair, leaving
it even wilder. 'She's scared.'

'Scared?' The words took him by surprise.

'I don't think she knows what to do. She needs to have you
there.'

He nodded. He knew he hadn't done the best by her. He'd put
himself, his grief, his guilt ahead of her. But it was all he could
manage. He remembered when Rose had died, how all the words
had vanished from the house, how they'd been too fearful to say
anything, retreating from each other, too scared to love properly
in case another of them died.

He walked Briggate with the deputy, the weavers bundled into their
heavy coats against the bitter wind, their faces set and stubborn as
they laid out cloth on the trestles. The men chewed at the hot beef
of their Brigg-End Shot breakfasts, swilling the food down with a
mug of ale as they worked.

The merchants sheltered in the lee of a building, all gathered
together in a group, dressed in rich wool and polished leather.

Nottingham kept his eye on Darden and Howard, their faces half-hidden by hats, then passed on down the street.

'What do you reckon they're thinking, boss?'

'I wish I knew, John,' he answered, shaking his head. 'I'd hope they're praying we don't find the evidence to send them to the hangman.' He gave a grim smile. 'But I'll give you odds the bastards are smirking at us instead.'

'Did Lucy have much to say?'

'Plenty, but none of it anything to help us.'

They continued in silence all the way to Leeds Bridge.

'Lizzie thinks we should just kill them.'

'You think I don't want to?' The Constable gazed out at the river. The water was high, dark and dangerous. 'I want to make it so there's pain in every breath they take and they beg me to finish it.'

'But?'

Nottingham shook his head. 'You know as well as I do. We'll prove it, John. We'll get them in court. And when we do, the mayor and all the rest of their friends will desert them.'

'You hope.'

'They will. They'll leave them to die alone, then they'll peck over the carcasses like crows. You just wait and see. Let's go back up. It's bloody freezing out here.'

The market bell rang as they were part way up the street, the merchants moving quickly among the clothiers, examining a length and moving on or making their bargain before someone else could offer more.

And elsewhere in the city, the Constable thought, folk wouldn't give a thought to all this and the money it made. They'd be at their work, the servants and clerks, the shopkeepers and apprentices. They'd count their pay at day's end and struggle on into another week.

The deputy left to follow word of a burglary, a piece of silver plate and some lace gone missing from a house. Nottingham walked up to the market cross at the top of Briggate, the traders all setting up their stalls for the Saturday market. Farmers brought eggs and butter, their chickens squawking in their wooden cages, a Sunday dinner for those who could afford it. The tinker had his brazier lit, ready to mend pots and pans later; for now, others crowded round its warmth.

'Grand to see, isn't it?' He turned towards the voice, seeing Joe Buck's face, Henry two paces behind him, oblivious to the stares people gave.

'People make money, people spend money. Same as every-where. But that's a business you know well, Joe.'

'That's as maybe,' the fence said with a smile. 'You found the evidence to hang your Gabriel yet?'

'What do you think?'

'Best have a word with yon clothes seller, then.' Buck nodded in the direction of a stall further down the street. 'He has something that might interest you.'

'What?'

'You'll have to go and see for yourself.' He touched the brim of his tricorn hat. 'I'll bid you good day.'

TWENTY-FIVE

The man was still laying out his goods. Not too long ago it had been Isaac the Jew who'd done all this, selling dresses and coats and linen that had seen better days. But he was gone, another murdered soul, and someone else had drifted in, hoping to make a little money.

The man was in his middle years, gaunt, with cheerless eyes, helped by a boy with the same thinness in his face, straining as he carried bundles from a cart.

'We're not ready yet,' he said, fussing with the garments. 'Market bell hasn't rung, anyway.'

'I'm the Constable,' Nottingham said.

'Oh aye?' The man was suddenly interested, standing straight and pulling at the sleeves of his greatcoat. 'I'm Charles Johnson. Looking for summat to wear, maybe?'

'Not for me.' He kept the friendly tone in his voice and scanned the piles of clothes, some little better than tatters, a few garments almost new. 'What have you bought lately?'

'Not so much. Weather like this, folk are buying not selling.'
The man rummaged deftly in one of the piles. 'But there's this.'
He pulled out a shirt, the white almost yellow with age. 'Good
quality, last for years.'

The Constable shook his head and Johnson gave him a steady
look.

'I tell you what. I bought this on Tuesday. Beautiful, it is.' He
opened up a chest under the trestle and carefully unfolded a grey
coat. 'What about that?'

'Can I see it?'

The cloth and weave were exquisite and expensive, far better
than anything else the man was offering. But that wasn't what
he noticed. The grey coat was spattered with dark stains, the
colour of rust. Some were tiny, almost lost, others larger, a couple
almost the size of his thumb.

'Where did you get this?' he asked.

'Like I said, I bought it on Tuesday.' The man looked
worried, eyes shifting around uncomfortably. 'What is it? What's
wrong?'

'Who did you buy it from?'

Johnson shrugged. 'A man came up and asked if I wanted to
buy it.'

'When on Tuesday?'

'Afternoon. Why? I was enjoying some ale at t' Rose and
Crown and he came up to my lad. He sent him on to me.'

'Did the man give his name?'

'I never asked him. It was a coat and it were cheap and quality.
Have I done summat wrong, mister? Did he steal them?'

'No, I don't think he did,' the Constable assured him. 'What
did he look like?'

'A big bugger.' He held his arms apart. 'Shoulders like that
on him. I knew it couldn't be his coat, but he said his master
had given it him. He was wearing the breeches that went with
it. Tight on him, they were, too.'

'Did he have anything else to sell?'

'Aye. A pair of shoes and some hose.'

'What did you do with them?'

'Kept them for mesen. There's good leather on them shoes
and nice shiny buckles.'

Those buckles would certainly be shiny enough, Nottingham thought. Most likely silver.

'I'm going to need the coat and the shoes,' he said, watching Johnson frown.

'I should have known it were too good to be true. What's he done?'

'You know what these are?' the Constable asked, rubbing the stains with his fingertips.

'No. But I reckoned that was why he'd been given the clothes to sell.'

'It's blood. The man who owned this suit killed people.'

He watched all the colour leave the man's face. 'Christ.'

'The man who sold you the clothes, did he say anything else?'

Johnson shook his head. 'Just wanted his money and then he left. Didn't take no more than five minutes.'

'Did he bargain with you?'

'Took the first offer I made.' He nodded at the coat. 'Got that at a good price, thought I'd make a pretty penny off it. You're going to take it, aren't you?' he asked sadly.

'I am,' Nottingham answered. 'You'll have to bring the shoes to the jail. I'm sorry.'

'Aye.' The man sighed. 'My mam always used to say that if summat seems too good to be true, it probably is.' He looked up with a wan smile and a small, world-weary chuckle. 'She were right an' all, weren't she?'

'I'm afraid so, Mr Johnson. And if you see the man again, send your lad to find me.'

'I'll do that.'

He rolled the coat and put it under his arm. Gabriel's grey coat. Solomon Howard's coat. Either the factor had told Smithson to get rid of it, one last task, or the servant had stolen it before he left. However it happened, they needed to find Hugh Smithson. He was the one with evidence to put Howard on the gallows. And the Constable would make sure that Darden stood beside him.

He spread it out on the desk, stroking the blood stains. Some of them would be Mary's, the last drops of her life. Finally, after gazing at it for a minute, he put the coat into a deep drawer of the desk.

He knew the deputy was hunting for Smithson. Now he'd put the word out, too. If the man was still in Leeds, they'd find him. The servant would peach on his employer quickly enough; it was better than death. They just had to hope he was still in Leeds, or someone knew where he'd gone.

For the rest of the day he trailed across the city, from the Calls to the Head Row, from London Road to the Ley Lands, asking the same questions over and over. Did they know Smithson? When had they seen him last? Had he said where he was going? Who knew him well?

By the shank of the afternoon he was exhausted, his throat raw from so much talking. High clouds had begun to settle in, others following and filling the horizon. There'd be rain during the night. Any colder and it could be snow.

He finished the day at the White Swan, taking his time over a mug of ale. The inn was loud, folk coming in to spend their wages and find some brief joy in their lives. He settled at the end of a bench, lost in his thoughts until Sedgwick sat across from him.

'Found him yet?' Nottingham asked before telling him about the coat.

'So far I've had him telling people he was going to York, Wakefield and London.'

'I've had all of those, and America to start a new life.'

The deputy snorted. 'Wherever he's gone the bastard doesn't want anyone to know.'

'Unless he's still here and hiding.'

Sedgwick shook his head. 'He's gone, boss. The last anyone saw of him was Tuesday night. If he was in Leeds someone would have spotted him. He could be anywhere by now.'

'Probably,' the Constable agreed. 'Let's keep looking, just in case.'

'What else do you want me to do?'

'Didn't you say Solomon Howard had a cook?'

'Aye.'

'Find a way to talk to her and see what you can discover.'

The deputy nodded and Nottingham drained his cup. 'I'm off to my home.'

*   *   *

Emily was there, sitting in her chair with a book on her lap. But she'd barely turned three or four pages and her face was full of memories and sorrow.

'It's not right, is it?' he said as he stood in front of the hearth.

'What, Papa?'

'This house without your mother in it.'

'No,' she answered.

'Do you remember where we used to live, before I became Constable and we were given this place?'

She shook her head.

'You were still very small. There was you and your sister and me and your mother all in one room. That was all we could afford on what the city paid me. But your mother made it into a home. Coming home every night was a joy.'

'What was it like?' she asked.

'Clean and dry,' he said after a while, calling the picture into his mind. 'That's the best anyone could say about it. The whole place wasn't much bigger than this room. You were just a baby and we were always scared you'd end up crawling into the fire. Your sister almost did that when she was little. You mother managed to pull her away in time.'

'How was it when we moved out here?' Emily asked him, and he knew he had her interest. 'How old was I?'

'How old?' He pushed the fringe off his forehead as he thought. 'Two, maybe three? We thought we'd moved into a palace.' He smiled at the recollection. 'You can't imagine it, going from one room to all this space. We didn't know what to do with it all. I brought everything we owned out here in a handcart while your mama carried you and Rose walked next to her.'

'She loved this place, didn't she?' The girl moved, curling her legs under herself and smoothing down the dress.

'From the first moment she saw it.' He could still see it as if it had just happened the day before. 'She said it felt like home as soon as she walked in. Her eyes kept growing wider and wider as she looked around.' He laughed. 'And then you went out in the garden and fell over in the mud. She cleaned you off in the kitchen and said we'd be happy here. She was right, too.'

Lucy bustled through, carrying bowls of stew, the smell of meat quickly filling the room. The mood vanished like mist.

'I hope I did it right,' the servant said apologetically. Her skin was flushed from the heat of cooking, Mary's old apron tied tight around her. 'I've never made this before.'

They ate in silence. It was better than her pottage, he thought; there was some taste to the mutton and the gravy was thick. He emptied his bowl, poured ale and sat back to drink.

'Very good, lass,' he told her and saw her face light up as she smiled.

'The mistress told me how she did it. I just tried to remember what she said.'

'You've done very well.'

The candles cast long shadows as they settled back in front of the fire. He poured on more coal and watched the flames dance up the chimney.

'What are you and Rob going to do?' he asked finally.

'Do, Papa?' He could hear the caution in her tone.

'Do,' he said again. 'You love each other. The whole of Leeds can see that.' She lowered her head so he couldn't see her expression. 'You're not going to marry him, are you?'

She shook her head, the hair shaking over her shoulders. 'You know I'm not. And I'm not going to change just because Mama's dead.'

'I don't want you to, love,' he told her gently. He took a deep breath. 'I've been thinking about what's important.'

Emily looked up quickly. 'Important?'

He nodded. 'What matters in life. If you love Rob, you should be with him. Do what your heart tells you. And I don't mean you have to marry him.'

'But—'

'I know what I've said before. It was your mother who always told me to let you be yourself. She was right. You don't know how long you'll have any happiness. You need to grab at it. You've got a good lad there. Just make sure you love him with all your heart.' He reached over and squeezed her hand lightly. 'I was thinking we could ask him to lodge here, if you wanted that.'

'But where would he sleep? There's no extra bedroom.'

'Aye, I know.' He smiled at her. 'But it would all look above board if he was a lodger.'

'People would still talk. There'd be a scandal,' she objected. 'Mrs Rains would let me go.'

'I don't think folk would even notice. Plenty of folk have lodgers. And if Mrs Rains is outraged, open your own school. There are plenty in Leeds who have nothing, who'd like a little learning for their daughters.'

She was lost in thought for a moment, daydreaming, he thought.

'How could I afford it?'

'You have the money Amos Worthy left for you. There's more than enough for that.'

'You said you want me to refuse that. You told me it was tainted. And you were right.'

'I know,' he agreed with a short nod. 'And I know better than you how he filled his coffers. But it's done with. The money's there. Maybe doing something good with it would be right. Educate the poor girls who'd never have a chance otherwise.' He smiled. 'Your mother would be proud of that.'

Emily sat and stared at the fire.

'Believe me,' Nottingham said, 'life's too short to end up with any regrets. I've learned that in the last few days. I want to see you happy, and I don't give a bugger what anyone else thinks. It's up to you, though. Would you like Rob here?'

'Yes,' she answered, giving the first smile he'd seen since Mary's death. 'But what about your position? What will people say?'

'Nothing, most like. As long as it looks right, no one will take much notice. And if they do, he's the lodger. I've been thinking about a lot of things since . . .' He swallowed and forced himself to say the words. 'Since your mother died. If you don't make the most of your life no one else will. Love that boy of yours. Be happy. Christ only knows there's nothing else worthwhile.'

'Thank you, Papa.' She stood in a smooth movement and hugged him, her head against his chest. He put his arms around her, pulling her close, her hair against his face. The scent of her was just the same as it had been when she was a little girl, and the images of those years tumbled through his mind. Of Emily, Rose, Mary. Of himself, younger, healthier and happier. Back when he could taste the future and grabbed for it. God knew he missed his wife, but perhaps he and his daughter could forge some kind of life.

*   *   *

He didn't want to leave his bed. When he opened his eyes he could feel the pounding in his head. The landlord of the Ship had given him a flagon of strong twice-brewed ale, and he and Lizzie had drunk it all once Isabell and James were asleep.

Her arm was thrown across her chest and he could feel her furred breath close to his ear. They'd talked and laughed their way through the evening, carefree and careless, the drinking turning to touching and kissing before they tumbled between the sheets, feeling alive and loving.

Through the gap between the shutters he saw the sky lightening. He knew he should get up and go to the jail, but the warmth was so lulling and comforting, and he could guess how he'd feel when he moved.

Finally, though, he had to stir and use the chamber pot. The sounds of movement woke Isabell. Before she could begin to cry, he picked her out of her crib and placed her next to her mother. Lizzie stirred with a small groan and drew the baby to her nipple.

The deputy dressed quickly, before the heat of the bed vanished. Down in the kitchen he took a quick drink from the dregs of the ale, swilling it around in his mouth. He felt rough, no doubt about it. It was his own fault; the landlord had winked and warned him it was strong.

His breath clouded the air as he walked down Lands Lane, the cold pulling at his face, his head hammering with every footfall. The ground was soaked from the rain that had lasted most of the night. But the thought of Lizzie the evening before made him smile. She hadn't been like that in a long time; he'd forgotten how much he missed it.

Rob was at the jail, head down as he checked a column of figures.

'Keeping out of mischief?' He poured some beer, letting it take away the dryness in his throat.

'More than you, by the look of you.' Rob chuckled. 'Good night?'

'Grand. How about you? Much here?'

'They must have all stayed indoors. Saturday night and only three arrests. They're all sleeping in the cells.'

Sedgwick sat and stretched out his legs. 'Wish I could do that myself.'

'You'll live.'

'I daresay.' He covered his eyes with a hand. 'Right now it doesn't sound like a good idea, though. You almost finished the accounts?'

'Close enough. They'll be ready for the boss to give to the treasurer on Tuesday.' Rob stood and reached for his greatcoat. 'I'm going home.' He glanced at the deputy. 'God help Leeds if anything happens this morning.'

'Bugger off.'

Lister left, laughing. The deputy could hear the city stirring, a few folk off to early services. He drank a little more. It helped. He'd be spending most of the day outside, standing and waiting in the bitter weather.

Sedgwick stood far enough away, hidden from sight, and watched Solomon Howard leave for church, his new servant right behind him. Five minutes later the cook emerged, wearing her good dress, a heavy shawl pulled tight around her shoulders. She started up the Head Row, and his long legs soon brought him up beside her.

'Morning, love,' he said, tipping the brim of his old hat. She turned to look at him, taking in the bloodshot eyes, the old clothes and worn boots.

'Morning,' she said cautiously.

'You work for Mr Howard, don't you?'

The woman frowned. 'What about it?' she asked. 'Who are you, anyway?'

'I'm John Sedgwick, I'm the deputy Constable.'

'Then you can get yourself gone,' she said coldly. 'I'll have nowt to do with you.'

'I just want to ask you some questions.'

'You'll get no answers from me. You're hounding him, you and the Constable, and he's done nowt wrong.'

'Are you sure of that?'

She stopped, brought up her hand and slapped him hard on the face. 'Of course I bloody am. Now leave me alone.' She walked on, leaving him to rub his face, the skin stinging in the chill.

He kept an eye on her until she crossed the road and vanished along Town End towards the church. She'd tell her employer, he had no doubt about that, and the man would be at the jail with his lawyer.

There was nothing to be done. He'd tried. It was time to make his rounds and see if he could walk off his throbbing head.

The Constable walked down Marsh Lane, Emily's arm threaded through his, Lucy on the other side. He'd slept badly, dreams tugging darkly at him and waking him several times. His leg ached and the knife wound on his belly felt hot.

At the churchyard they stood by the graves for a few minutes, saying nothing, lost in their own thoughts. He saw Emily wipe away tears, and put his arm around her shoulders. There was space beyond Mary where he'd lie when his own time came.

The service was as long as ever, the vicar's voice droning through his sermon. He closed his eyes, hoping to rest a little, but all that came to him were pictures of Mary decaying in her coffin, jerking his eyes back open and leaving his heart pounding in his chest. Eventually it was over, the final blessing given, and they made their way outside, taking condolences and making greetings. Mayor Fenton passed with a curt nod, glowering at him.

A few raindrops began to fall as they walked back over Timble Bridge. Last Sunday he'd enjoyed an afternoon with his wife. This week she was under the soil and he didn't know how long he had left to find evidence against the man who killed her. If the mayor had his way, Tuesday could be the end of his time as Constable.

At home he changed into his old coat and breeches, the warm hose that had been darned so many times over the years, and his good, thick boots. He cut bread and cheese, put the food in his pockets, then headed back to the jail.

'Did you see the cook?' he asked Sedgwick.

'She gave me a good slap for my trouble,' the deputy answered ruefully.

'Not the first you've had, anyway.'

'Aye, probably not the last, either.' The smile left his face. 'So what now, boss?'

'I don't know, John. Is there anywhere we haven't looked?'

'Joe Buck gave you the nod towards that coat. He might know more.'

The Constable shook his head. 'If he did he'd have said something.' He sighed. 'Just go around the people you know. See if there's something they've forgotten. Ask if any of them have seen Smithson. I'll do the same. If we don't have them by Tuesday . . .'

The deputy understood perfectly. If the mayor brought in a new man as Constable he'd likely lose his job too. And then what would he do? He didn't have an education like Rob; finding work would be difficult, and he'd made any number of enemies, men who'd love to take advantage of his misfortune. He wanted to see the men who killed the children and Mary Nottingham swing, and he also wanted to keep this position.

The door opened and both men turned their heads.

'What are you doing here, lad?' Nottingham asked.

'I've come to help,' Rob said. 'There must be something more I can do.'

The Constable weighed his words before answering. The boy could be with Emily where he was needed. 'Thank you.'

'I'll finish the accounts tonight. They'll be in order for you.' Nottingham dipped his head in appreciation. 'But I want to do some real work this afternoon.'

'Then get back out there and talk to everyone you know,' the Constable advised. 'It's what we're all going to do. We've run out of other choices.' He saw the looks of determination on their faces. 'Someone out there knows something. We just have to find them. We still have a day and a half.'

'Yes, boss,' Rob said.

The inns were closed, but the dram shops and alehouses kept their doors quietly open. Everyone knew, a few complained, and business carried on as usual. Men always needed somewhere to drink and blunt the pain of living. Sunday saw them busy, small rooms crowded, the serving girls rushing from table to packed table, slapping at groping hands.

The Constable and Rob slipped from place to place, talking to men hunched over the benches. Most knew nothing and simply shook their heads. Others had a few words, enough to make them press on somewhere else, searching for another face.

Sedgwick bantered with the whores, out on Briggate in all weathers, goose flesh on their cleavage, faces always hopeful of making a few coins. They sheltered in the small openings to courts and yards, trying to duck away from the frigid wind. He found two who'd been with Solomon Howard and shuddered at the memory. Another claimed Darden had used her so hard when she was young that it had taken a week for the bruises to heal, and showed off a small scar on her back.

The stars were brilliant up in the clear sky and frost was already forming on the grass when they returned to the jail. The deputy's face was set grimly as he drained a mug of ale.

'Any luck, boss?'

Nottingham shook his head. 'Rob?'

'Nothing. But we're talking to ordinary folk. If we want to find out about Darden and Howard we should be talking to the merchants again. They're the ones who'd know.'

'Those ordinary folk see plenty,' Sedgwick told him. 'And half the time the rich don't even notice them.'

'The merchants and the Corporation aren't going to give up their own,' the Constable said. 'Not when the mayor's on their side.'

'Do we have anything to lose?' Rob asked.

'No,' Nottingham admitted. 'We'll do it tomorrow. There might be one or two who have no love for Darden; I'll ask Tom Williamson.'

The church bells began to ring for evening service. The Constable stood. 'We can't do anything more today. Are you coming for your supper, Rob? Emily would like to see you.'

'Yes, boss.'

'Thank you both for your work today. I appreciate it.'

'Long day?' Lizzie asked as Sedgwick stretched before sitting at the table. He pulled Isabell on to his lap, tickling under her arms to watch her giggle.

'They all are lately.'

'Was your head as bad as mine this morning?'

'Worse, mebbe. I spent most of the morning suffering. What did you three do today?'

'Mama took us out,' James said excitedly. 'She showed me what different plants are for.'

'Did she?' He smiled at his son. 'And do you remember what they do?'

'Dock leaves take away nettle stings,' he began, 'and she showed me the trees where you shouldn't eat berries.'

Isabell wriggled on his lap and he let her down slowly. For a moment she stood, before collapsing on to all fours.

'She'll be walking soon.'

'And then she'll be trouble,' Lizzie said with a grin.

'Just like her mam.'

'Better be careful, John Sedgwick.' Her eyes were lively. 'At least if you want to keep eating here.'

He held up his hands in surrender.

'Have you found anything yet?' Lizzie's voice became serious.

'No.'

'I still say you should just kill the bastards.'

'The boss wouldn't allow it.'

'You know they're guilty.'

'That's true.' He thought of the silk pouch and the locks of hair.

'And you're sure he killed Mary Nottingham.'

'As sure as we can be. But—'

'No buts, John,' she said, staring at him with hard eyes. 'Or I'll bloody do it meself.'

TWENTY-SIX

'They won't be able to find any fault with that, boss.' Rob patted the neat pile of paper. 'Everything tallies, all the money's accounted for.'

'Thank you.' He was grateful; he knew he couldn't have faced the task himself. Now the accounts were ready, prepared in a neat hand, for when he met the treasurer. In the end it would probably make no difference. The mayor was determined to dismiss him, and it wouldn't be hard for him to find some other pretext. The aldermen would do whatever Fenton demanded. But he was damned if he'd go quietly. If it was there, he'd find the evidence against Howard and Darden. He'd have his revenge for Mary.

'Boss?' Rob asked.

'What is it?' The word had dragged him back from his thoughts.

'Emily told me what you said to her,' he began nervously. 'Did you mean it? About lodging with you, I mean.'

'I meant every word, lad,' he answered with a smile. 'Life's too short. If you don't grab it, it'll be over before it begins. I don't want that for her. Or for you. But it's up to the pair of you, if that's what you both want.'

Rob nodded, unconvinced. He'd learn, the Constable thought.

'You get yourself on home, lad. You've earned your sleep.'

'I'll work on, boss. Maybe I can help with the merchants,' he said hopefully.

Nottingham nodded. The lad would be able to talk to them, and he could use the help.

'Come along and talk to Tom Williamson with me, then. If he can come up with some names, we'll divide them.'

The deputy had already been and gone, quiet and preoccupied. He was off looking for anything, for anyone, useful. He'd be worried about the future, the Constable imagined. If Nottingham lost his job the mayor would get rid of Sedgwick, and Rob, too. Out with the old and the tainted, in with the new. Lister was educated, he knew folk in the city, he'd find good work whatever happened. The deputy, though . . .

'Right,' he said finally. 'Let's go.'

Williamson was at the warehouse, examining the invoices and making notes on a piece of paper.

'Richard,' he said in surprise, putting down the quill and flexing his fingers. 'And Mr Lister again.' He smiled. 'More business about Mr Darden and Mr Howard?'

'Very serious business,' Nottingham said.

The merchant cocked his head curiously. 'You'd better sit down, then.' He gestured to a pair of battered chairs and poured three mugs of ale. 'Now, what is it?'

'Do you know anyone who doesn't like Jeremiah Darden?'

Williamson leaned back, clasping his hands behind his head. His long waistcoat was pale blue silk, the shape of flowers – forget-me-nots, cornflowers and others – skilfully picked out in darker colours.

'I can think of three,' he replied after a while. As the Constable sat forward expectantly, he added, 'But I don't see how they'll be able to help you. They'll only know about his business, not his life.'

Nottingham shook his head. 'I'm clutching at anything, Tom.' The image of Mary lying on the kitchen floor flickered in his head. 'I know what Darden and Howard have done and I want them for it. All of it. I'll talk to anyone who might be able to help.'

'Then you'd better see George Lamb. There's no love lost between him and Darden. Nicholas Dunsley and Harold Hammond have never cared much for him, either, but Lamb truly hates him.'

'Thank you, Tom.'

The merchant stood and extended his hand. 'Good luck to you, Richard. Remember, you still have some friends on the Corporation.'

'Give them my gratitude.'

'Do you know any of them?' he asked Rob when they were back outside in the cold. A chilly, misting rain had begun to fall, the clouds thick and low.

'I know Dunsley's son. He works with his father.'

'You go there, then. We'll meet at the Swan later.'

'Yes, boss.'

He trudged up Briggate, stopping at a house close to the Moot Hall, just below the Shambles. Lamb still conducted business in the old way, from his home; he wouldn't be spending his money on building a warehouse by the river, Nottingham knew. The gates through to a cobbled yard were open, the gap just wide enough for a cart. The warehouse stood at the back, made from thick stone, with no windows. Lamb was there, inspecting cloth and giving orders.

He was sixty if he was a day, dressed in good, plain clothes, his stock neatly tied at the throat, a covering of white bristles on his cheeks, most of the hair gone from his head, leaving just a few grey wisps over his ears.

'I'd not expected to see you here,' he said after a clerk had shown the Constable through. He smiled. 'Have I broken the law?'

'I'm hoping you can help me.'

Lamb raised his eyebrows. 'Help you?'

'About Jeremiah Darden and his factor.'

The man frowned. 'Let's go somewhere more private.'

The house was old, opening directly on to the street, its timbers twisted and black, the limewash in need of a fresh coat. Inside the wood was dark and carefully polished. Small windows let thin light into the parlour.

Lamb settled into a worn chair, crossed his legs and poured himself a glass of wine from a decanter on a side table. He picked up a clay pipe and lit it, the acrid fug of tobacco filling the room.

'What do you want to know about Mr Darden and Mr Howard?'

'I believe they're responsible for the murder of my wife and of at least eleven children.'

The merchant sipped slowly from the glass. 'Those are very dangerous accusations, Mr Nottingham. But I'm sure you've already been told that.'

'Several times.'

'I was saddened to hear about your wife.'

The Constable said nothing.

'I assume you're here because you know that Mr Darden and I don't enjoy . . . good relations,' Lamb continued.

'That's right.'

'However, that's in business,' he said carefully. 'I don't like the way the man deals with people, but that doesn't make him a murderer and a . . .' He didn't need to speak the word.

'I understand that. And I'm sure you know that if I could prove it they'd already be in the cells.'

The merchant nodded. 'So what do you want from me?'

'Anything you have. Anything you can offer,' Nottingham answered candidly. The room was warm, a fire burning high in the grate. He could feel dampness on the palms of his hands.

'I wish I could help you,' Lamb said with a restless sigh. 'As I said, my dealings with the two of them are business. Nothing more than that. You're aware of Mr Darden's past, that cloud over him?'

'I am.'

'You might not know that I was the one who pressed for his resignation back then. But no one was going to let him end up in court over a servant.' He looked up. 'Not when it would affect the reputation of the city. I have no idea if he's guilty of anything in all this you're talking about, but even if he is it'll be exactly the same thing. He'll never see the gallows over it. He won't even see the inside of a courtroom.'

'Not if I have my way.'

'You won't,' Lamb told him firmly. 'They might let you have the factor as a sop, but never Darden. Not when it can hurt the reputation of Leeds.'

'What about you?' Nottingham asked. 'Do you want him in court?'

'I'd like him bankrupt and begging,' the merchant answered with a wolfish grin. 'But that's business, and wishing it certainly doesn't mean it'll happen. Whatever you've come here for, I can't give it to you. I'm sorry.'

'What about justice?'

'How long has justice ever mattered?' Lamb dismissed the idea. 'You've been Constable here long enough to know better than that.'

'That doesn't mean I have to accept it.'

Lamb stood. He was as tall as Nottingham, and his gaze was even and bemused. 'I'm not sure you'll have a choice.'

The warehouse for Dunsley and Sons lay a little way along the riverbank from Williamson's. They'd been one of the first to build, with a prime spot, part of the creeping growth of Leeds. Although it was no more than a few years old, the stone of the building was already blackening from the soot in the air.

Inside, things were bustling. Labourers were shifting lengths of cloth to be loaded on to a barge bound for Hull. A pair of clerks wrote quickly, hunched over their desks. He spotted Luke, standing to the side and supervising, giving brisk orders.

They'd gone to the Grammar School up in Town End together for a while, until Dunsley had withdrawn his son to start him on his apprenticeship in the business. The two of them met from time to time, sharing some ale or a dinner in one of the inns. Luke had seen the Low Countries and Spain, Rob knew that much; quite probably other places by now. He seemed to be someone with a purpose in life, wearing fine clothes, moving with the confidence and grace of money.

'Luke,' he said.

The young man turned, frowning as his concentration was broken, then his expression bloomed into a smile. 'Rob. What brings you here?' He laughed. 'Looking for another job already?'

'I'm looking for your father.'

'Try out on the dock. He'll be making sure nothing goes wrong with the shipment.' He indicated an open double door that let in bitter air. 'He'll be finished in a few minutes. Are you still courting?'

'I am.'

Luke grinned. 'God help her. If you're the best she can do, the girl must be out of her senses, that's all I can say.'

'How's business?'

'We're making money,' he said cautiously. 'A few more orders from America. If that keeps on it could be a good market for us.' He stopped to yell an instruction to one of the men. 'What do you want with my father?'

'It's to do with Mr Darden.'

Luke rolled his eyes. 'You'll have his attention, then. He can't stand the man.' He watched a length of cloth being carried out. 'That's the last one. Go on out, if you want, he'll have time.'

Nicholas Dunsley was a small man with dark, questioning eyes and a hooked nose too big for his face. The thick woollen coat seemed to overwhelm him; it was beautifully cut but he almost disappeared inside it; a tricorn hat covered his thinning hair. He turned at the sound of footsteps on the flagstones.

'Robert Lister,' he said, then glanced back to check that the final bale was loaded properly. 'I'd not have thought to see you here. Your father well?'

'Same as ever, the last time I saw him.'

'Good, good.' He continued to watch as the hatch was lowered and secured. 'Now, what is it?'

'Jeremiah Darden.'

Dunsley, hawked, turned his head and spat in the river. 'If you're out to find him guilty of something, good luck to you.'

'What do you know about him?' Rob asked.

'Other than the fact he's a conniving bastard? He's cheated me out of three good accounts over the years.'

'What about his factor?'

'Howard?' He shook his head. 'He's a strange one. Does his master's bidding. But there's always been something dark about him.'

'We believe he murdered those children and the Constable's wife.'

'Howard did?' he asked in astonishment. 'I don't like the man but I'd never seen him as a killer. What about Darden?'

'Both of them,' Rob answered.

'And you're looking for evidence against them?'

'Yes.'

'Well, you'll not get it from me, lad. If I knew anything, I'd gladly tell you, just to see the two of them done down. But I don't. I'm sorry.'

Rob bobbed his head in acknowledgement and began to leave.

'I'll tell you something,' Dunsley said quietly. 'It won't matter if you find all the proof you need. Darden will never hang in Leeds.'

'We'll see.'

The Constable had only met Hammond a few times, but he'd heard plenty of rumours about the man. He had a good brain for business, people said, but he kept himself to himself. His warehouse, a cramped place in the yard behind his house near the bottom of Briggate, was full, every shelf packed with cloth.

The merchant had skin as wrinkled as last year's apples and blue eyes that seemed filmed by rheum. He was likely close to seventy, Nottingham imagined, old enough to have seen the wool trade here grow until it was the biggest in the kingdom.

'I don't think I've ever had the Constable in here before,' Hammond said with a grin that made his face look youthful. 'I suppose there's a good reason for it.' He hesitated for a moment. 'I was so sorry about your wife. I lost mine a while back. It leaves a house empty and loveless.'

'Thank you.' He paused. 'I'm told you don't care for Jeremiah Darden.' This place was his last hope to find something; he had nothing to lose by being blunt.

'You heard right,' the man answered carefully. 'Why does it matter?'

'Do you know his factor?'

Hammond nodded. 'Little worm of a man.'

'I think he murdered my wife, and the children who were found. He and Darden were in it together.'

The merchant rubbed his chin, the scratching of bristles loud in the room. 'From the sound of it you don't have the evidence, do you?'

'Not evidence that I can use, no,' Nottingham admitted.

'So you're wondering who knows what.' He turned his cloudy eyes on the Constable. 'That right?'

'More or less.'

'I know what Darden did to that boy. Years ago, now. Perverted. And I know what his punishment was. I daresay you do, too. A man can't change what's in his heart, and his is as black as the devil. I can well believe he did what you say.'

'But?'

'But I don't know anything that can help you.' He smiled sadly. 'Even if I did it wouldn't make a jot of difference. You know the Corporation's not going to accept a scandal, not with a merchant like him. Business is too important to be tainted.'

'And you'll understand it's my job to try.' He tried to keep his voice under control.

'I'd think less of you if you didn't. But you'll have no joy from it. From what I hear, Mayor Fenton's against you now, too.'

He smiled. There were few secrets in Leeds.

'You've heard the truth.'

'Then you'll have another battle there. He'll have the aldermen lined up behind him. He's a canny sod. I wish you well.'

'I just want to see some justice before I go,' the Constable told him.

'You won't,' Hammond said simply.

'I will if I can.'

'Then good luck to you, Constable.' Hammond turned his back and began counting the lengths of cloth on one of the shelves, pointing with a white, bony finger. Nottingham left, pushing the door to lightly, his heels sharp on the cobbles of the yard.

The cold, misty rain was still falling as he made his way to the White Swan. Rob was already there, halfway through a large piece of pie, crumbs scattered on the table.

'What did Dunsley have to say?' He signalled to the pot boy for ale and food.

'That the Corporation would never allow Darden to be convicted.'

'Do you believe him?'

'Yes. Do you?'

'I do. It's the same thing I've just been told twice.'

The deputy slid on to the bench next to Rob.

'Did you find anything, John?'

'Bugger all.' The mug of ale arrived and he poured himself a cup. 'No luck with the merchants?'

'No.' Nottingham looked down at the scratched wood.

'So what do we do, boss?'

The Constable sighed. He felt that he'd failed her. They'd won, and her death had been for nothing at all. But they were always going to win in a place like this.

'I don't know,' he answered.

'You can't give up,' Sedgwick protested.

'We're never going to put them in the dock.'

'Then fuck the law,' the deputy hissed. 'They've killed too many already. They killed your Mary.'

Nottingham's eyes were glistening when he looked up.

'I remember that every single minute, John.'

'I'm sorry, boss.'

'But as long as I'm the Constable I'm going to do things legally.' He stared at the pair of them. 'We all are. That's why we're in this job.'

'What about the ones who don't care?' Sedgwick asked. 'Them as run this place?'

'We keep to the law,' he insisted. 'If we don't, who will?'

'Boss . . .' Rob began.

'What?'

'I don't understand how you can say that when you know Solomon Howard killed Mrs Nottingham.'

'Because it's the only thing I *can* say while I'm Constable. And I'm that until tomorrow, at least.' He drained the ale. 'If you're done with that pie, you'd better show me what I need to know about the accounts. I don't want to look like a fool tomorrow.' He looked at the deputy. 'Anything you can find, John. Anything at all.'

During the afternoon a messenger came from the Moot Hall; the mayor wanted to see the Constable. He'd been expecting the summons. It would give Fenton one more chance to harangue him before he had to present the figures.

He walked over slowly, happy to take his time, to make his Worship wait a few minutes. A few folk came to offer their condolences. Then he climbed the steps and walked along the corridor with the thick Turkey carpet, past Martin Cobb, and knocked on the door.

'Come in.'

Fenton was leaning back in his chair, smoking a clay pipe with a long stem. 'Sit down.'

He perched carefully on the chair, his hands folded over the silver head of the stick.

'You don't like the wealthy, do you, Nottingham?'

'Don't I?'

'You've got it in your head that Mr Darden and Mr Howard are responsible for crimes they'd never have committed. I've heard about you over the years, going after men with money.'

'The law's for everyone,' the Constable replied calmly. 'There's not one for the rich and another for everyone else. And I'm paid to make sure people keep to the law.'

'For now. It'll be different after tomorrow.'

He shrugged. 'If it is, it is.' He'd discovered that he didn't really care any more. The person that kept him going more than any other had gone. Emily had the money Worthy had left her; she wouldn't want for a roof over her head, or for something to eat. What happened to him was no longer important. 'But the truth will come out sooner or later. And if you back those two you're going to look like a bloody fool.'

'Get them out of your head,' Fenton shouted, slapping the desk. 'They're not guilty. I've been talking to the aldermen and enough of them will back me to replace you.'

'Do what you will.'

'I intend to,' they mayor told him with a wolfish grin. 'You think your power is greater than anyone's here, that you're the only one who cares about justice. You went too far, Nottingham. Your comeuppance is long overdue.'

The Constable just smiled, letting the words wash over him and away again.

'I'll be interested to hear what your accounts show. I daresay there'll be enough discrepancies to warrant your dismissal.'

Nottingham stood. 'Was that all, Mr Fenton? I have pressing work to do. If there's nothing more I'll take my leave.'

'Go. This might be your last time here as Constable.'

He returned to the jail to go through the rest of the figures with Rob. By the time they finished it was close to full dark. Emily would have walked home alone. Nottingham pushed the papers into a neat pile.

'You've done a good job there.'

'Thank you, boss.' In the candlelight he could see the lad flush with pride.

'Come on home and have some supper before you start for the night. She'll be happy to see you.'

The thin, bitter mist of rain was still falling as they went down Kirkgate. As they passed the Crown and Fleece the door opened and the landlord came bustling out.

'Mr Nottingham,' he said loudly, his face beaming, his words starting to slur. 'Mr Lister. I was hoping to see you.'

The Constable gave him a gentle smile. 'What can we do for you?'

'There's something I want to show you.' His mouth closed suddenly. 'I'm sorry, I should have remembered. My condolences to you.'

'Thank you.'

'But please, I'd like you to look at this.'

Nottingham glanced at Rob and raised his eyebrows. Lister shrugged. They followed the man into the yard, where a torch lit everything.

'There,' he said proudly and pointed. One of the stones in the stable wall had been removed and replaced with another, artfully cut so a pair of skulls protruded. 'They kept coming to me, they wouldn't leave me alone, dying like that with no one to care. So I talked to the mason and had him do that. Cost a pretty penny, too. We put it in place this morning. What do you think?'

'I think it's a fine tribute,' the Constable told him. 'People will remember them.'

'They can rest now,' Rob said.

'Aye, they can,' the landlord agreed. 'Will you come in and drink a mug? We've been celebrating.'

'Not tonight, thank you. Perhaps we can toast them another time.'

'Whenever you want,' the man offered. 'Whenever you want.'

They walked on. At the churchyard he glanced over, seeing the dark earth of Mary's grave and the small memorial to Rose next to it, feeling sorrow like a weight around his heart.

'You know, lad, Mary and I used to talk about the things we were going to do together. All hopes for the future. Now we won't have the chance to do them. You and Emily, though, you have time.'

'But—'

'There isn't a but,' he answered quickly. 'You're happy together. Make the most of it. I mean it.'

'What about the money? She was going to refuse it.'

'I know. I was the one who suggested it. But there's no point, really, is there?'

'Isn't there, boss? What do you mean?'

'If she turns it down, it'll just end up in some lawyer's pocket. Emily might as well use it. She can do whatever she wants. Open a school. She can be a writer – she used to want to do that.'

'She still does.'

Nottingham nodded. 'You're young enough to have plenty of

dreams. When Amos Worthy left her that money he told me he was giving her freedom.'

'Was he? It seems more like a burden.'

'When he said it I didn't believe him, either. I thought it was bad money, made on the backs of his whores. Now I wonder if he wasn't right.'

'Why did he leave it to her? I still don't really understand it.'

They crossed Timble Bridge, boot heels muted on the soaked wood.

'It's a long story, lad.' His mother's face came into his head, the woman Worthy loved for so long and lost. 'I used to think he did it to spite me. Maybe he saw more than I did.'

The house was warm. Emily was seated close to the fire, a small pile of books on the floor beside her, the smell of damp wool filling the air. He could hear Lucy moving around in the kitchen, humming softly to herself, a tune he didn't recognize that drifted in and out of hearing.

Nottingham walked through, leaving the lovers alone for a few minutes. He kept his gaze level, unable to look down, scared of what might remain on the floor, and of the pictures in his head. Lucy stood by the fire, stirring the pottage as it simmered over the flame. She turned and smiled at him, her face guileless, hair hanging over her shoulders.

'Another half hour and it'll be ready.' She wiped her hands on her apron. When he didn't say anything or move, she asked, 'Is owt wrong?'

'No,' he answered slowly. 'Just thinking. Remembering.'

'She loved you, you know.' Lucy gave a small grin.

'I know.'

'You had a long time together.'

'Never enough.'

'When she was showing me what to do, she asked me about mesen. She was the first one to do that. Like she really cared. Like it mattered.'

'It did,' he told her. 'It does.'

She took him by surprise. 'If you ever want me to leave, just tell me.'

'Why would I want that? I need someone to look after the house.'

'But how much longer will you be here?' He began to reply but she continued, 'I've got ears and a brain. I've heard you talking.'

'I don't know,' he said. 'But wherever we go, you'll have a job. I promised you that.'

'I've had promises off men before. I can look after meself.' Her face hardened for a second and he could see the strong woman she'd become in time.

'I know that.'

She nodded, willing to accept his word, not needing to say anything more. He left her to finish cooking, and saw Rob and Emily by the window, looking out into the night. He had his arm lightly around her waist and she leaned into him. The little girl who'd once told her father that she wanted to marry him when she grew up had given her heart completely to someone else now.

He ate the meal approvingly; Lucy had seasoned the pottage well enough to give it taste, and he wiped up the last of it from the bowl with a heel of bread.

'That was excellent,' he said truthfully, and the girl smiled wide as if he'd given her the greatest praise in the world.

As she cleared the bowls away, Rob stood. 'I should go to work.'

'I'll see you in the morning, lad.'

The door closed on Emily and her young man. She'd be out there for five minutes, saying her loving goodbye, then watching him walk away, picking his shape out of the darkness until he reached Timble Bridge.

She came back in, sat in the chair and picked up the books she'd been studying earlier.

'Rob tells me you still write.'

'Yes,' Emily said, puzzlement crossing her face.

'Did you show it to Mama?'

'Sometimes.'

'Would you be willing to let me see it?'

Her eyes widened in surprise. 'Are you sure, Papa? I know you don't really like to read.'

'I'm certain.'

'Then yes, of course I will.'

He smiled. 'Thank you.'

They sat in silence. She worked and Nottingham gazed into the fire. He closed his eyes and for a few minutes he could imagine it was Mary next to him, turning the pages as she read. Always *The Pilgrim's Progress* before winter put its cold breath on the world, and poetry to welcome spring. He could tell the passing of the seasons by the book in her hand. For a fleeting moment he felt her in the room, as if she'd come to warm her cold bones at the fire.

The bed was large as a country, the other side too far to reach. He felt empty of God's grace, lost, tired and alone. Sleep hadn't been a willing visitor since Mary had died. He stared at the darkness, the sheets cold against his body.

Tomorrow . . . He'd gambled that he could find the evidence against Darden and Howard and he'd lost. The accounts were in order but that wouldn't matter to the mayor. He'd find some reason to appoint a new Constable.

It was humiliation, disgrace, and some day he'd feel it deeply. For now there was too much pain in his heart to absorb more. It was as if it was happening to someone else and he was no more than a spectator, watching it all play out.

He'd failed Mary and now he'd failed Sedgwick and Rob. They'd believed him, trusted him to discover the proof. He had no doubt that Fenton would dismiss them, too. The man likely already had other candidates prepared for the post, pliable men more eager to please than serve justice. Darden and his factor would continue to walk free.

He drifted in and out of rest, buffeted by dreams that dragged him back to wakefulness, a clammy sweat on his skin. Before dawn he was up, dressed and locking the door behind him. The drizzle had stopped, the stars were clear in the sky, the ground hard under his boots, a sheen of frost on the grass.

Smoke was beginning to climb from a few chimneys as he walked up Kirkgate; servants were already at work, preparing food, cleaning the house before their masters and mistresses rose. The warmth of the fire at the jail was welcoming; Rob was preparing the nightly report, exhaustion showing on his face.

'Anything?' Nottingham asked.

'A burglary up on the Head Row. Took two pieces of plate and some lace.'

'We had one like that last week in Turk's Head Yard,' the Constable said thoughtfully. 'How did they get in?'

'A window left unlocked.'

'Mr Sedgwick can look into it. You take yourself off home. You've put in too many hours lately.'

'Yes, boss.' Rob didn't put up any argument, just gave a weak smile as he stood.

Alone, he prepared the daily report for the mayor, keeping it curt, a summation of events. He placed the paper on top of the accounts and poured a mug of ale. The door opened and the deputy entered, shrugging off his greatcoat and standing close to the hearth.

'Another burglary,' Nottingham said.

'Where?'

'Up on the Head Row. Someone left a window open.'

'Very similar to that other one, isn't it?' Sedgwick said thoughtfully.

'I'll leave it with you.' He gathered up the report and the accounts, brushed off his coat and straightened his stock. His stick clicked hard on the cobbles as he made his way to the Moot Hall. Martin Cobb took the report without a word. The Constable took a deep breath and knocked on the door of the treasurer's office. In the distance he heard the bell signalling the start of the cloth market.

Rob felt the ache of tiredness all through his body. He'd eaten some bread and cheese and washed it down with a few gulps of ale. He knew he should go and escort Emily to school, to grab at a few more minutes with her, but he needed sleep. He'd stripped down to his shirt when the knocking came at his door.

'Get your coat, lad,' the deputy told him. 'And bring your knife. We have work to do.'

'What?'

'Some justice. For those little ones and for Mrs Nottingham.'

He stared at Sedgwick, his mouth open.

'Well, are you in or do I have to do it myself? This is the best chance we'll ever have. The boss is with the treasurer, I'm with Joe Buck and you're sleeping.'

'Mr Nottingham will know.'

'Aye. And however much it might go against the grain he'll never say a word. There's too much honour in him to do it himself, but inside he'll thank us.'

'Do you think we can get away with it?'

'I know we can, lad. I've been planning this.' The deputy grinned. 'Trust me. Now, are you coming? We don't have much time.'

It was late afternoon when the Constable returned to the jail. The treasurer had queried every item in the accounts, wanting justification for each expenditure, asking questions about every tiny detail. But in the end he'd been able to find no fault; Rob had done his work thoroughly. Nottingham felt some small satisfaction in that.

It was the start of the end, he knew that, and the rest would come quickly. A note from the mayor in the morning. If he was lucky he might keep the job for another few days. More likely it would all be over in a few hours.

Sedgwick was pacing the floor, a piece of paper in his hand. He stopped as the Constable entered.

'They've gone. Darden and Howard.'

'Gone? Where?' He felt as if he'd walked into a dream. The deputy held out the paper.

'A boy brought this an hour or so back.'

It was no more than a few words. *We have left. Ask the Constable why. He knows the truth. Jeremiah Darden. Solomon Howard.*

He looked again. The signatures seemed real enough, shaky and nervous. For the rest, even disguised, he could make out Rob's hand.

'What have you done, John?' he asked.

'Me?' Sedgwick asked blandly. 'I went to that burglary, then I've spent the rest of the day with Joe Buck. I thought it was time to put a little pressure on him. Ask him if you like.'

'And Rob?'

The deputy shrugged. 'Sleeping, I expect.' He stared at the

Constable. 'I thought you'd be happy, boss. This just proves you were right all along. Who knows, maybe the guilt was too much for them.'

'How did you get them to sign?'

'Sign?' Sedgwick asked innocently. 'All I know is what's on that paper.'

'And a boy brought it?'

'That's right. Come on, boss, this is the best news we could have had.'

'I know. I'm just tired. It's been a long day.'

'What about the note?'

He looked into the deputy's eyes, seeing the hope there. 'I'll take it over to the mayor's office, and then I'm going home.' As he passed he put his hand on the other man's shoulder, then halted at the door, looking out at the street. 'Thank you, John,' he said quietly.

At the Moot Hall he handed the paper to Martin Cobb.

'You best see that the mayor reads this as soon as possible,' he announced, then added, 'I daresay it'll all be in the next edition of the *Mercury*.'

TWENTY-SEVEN

The snow came and went before Christmas, leaving the ground muddy, the grass a sharp green against the brown of the fields and bare trees. He made his way down Marsh Lane towards the Parish Church, picking his way carefully between the puddles. Lucy had sponged his good suit and breeches clean, his stock was bright white, his hair wetted down and combed.

Emily and Rob walked arm in arm behind him, Lucy trailing after in a thick shawl, wearing the blue mantua that Mary had loved so much. She and Emily had altered it to fit, working long evenings with awkward, fumbling fingers. Whenever he saw it a stab of pain pierced his heart. But he'd said nothing; Lucy was so proud of it.

The bell was ringing, drawing in the faithful to celebrate the nativity. But there was no charity in his soul, no love for his fellow man, no sense of the season. He went because it was expected of him, no more, no less.

The mayor had taken the news about Darden and Howard with bad grace. He summoned the Constable, ranting and shouting and demanding an explanation, accusing him of murder. But Nottingham had been with the treasurer, Joe Buck backed up all Sedgwick said, and Rob's landlady had seen him enter his rooms in the morning.

He'd let Fenton run on until he had no more to say.

'You've read it. They've admitted their guilt,' the Constable told him. 'That should be enough for you. For anyone on the Corporation.'

'Get out, Nottingham.'

He'd won. As soon as word of the confession spread, his position was safe. But he felt no joy in the victory, no success. No one had seen or heard of the men. No bodies had been found. Their disappearance would remain a mystery that would fade. It had already begun to slip from the tongues and minds in the city. He'd spoken no more about it to Rob or the deputy. They'd put it aside; there was enough to keep them all busy with burglaries, a cutpurse causing havoc until they caught him, fights and killings that punctuated the weeks of Advent.

He did his job, then spent his evenings sitting by the fire, lost in thoughts and memories. Sometimes, in the restless dark, he could believe he felt Mary lying beside him, the comfort of her body and gentle breathing, with night for her gown. Then he'd wake and the mist of dreams would clear.

He felt apart from the world, as if it couldn't quite touch him any more, cut off by the sorrow that surrounded him. He said less and kept his thoughts inside, where they were safe.

They passed under the lych gate. Nottingham turned and said to the others, 'You go in. I'll join you shortly.'

He walked over to the graves, Rose and Mary side by side, preparing words for them both in his head.

AFTERWORD

The story of Skull and Stones Yard, as it became known, is a real Leeds tale. The stone with the two skulls stood in the yard of the Crown and Fleece for many years, then vanished when the stable was pulled down. It was rediscovered in the 1970s as part of the wall of a warehouse on Buslingthorpe Lane. Quite how or why it ended up there, no one seems to know. But it remains a link to a long gone Leeds.

Rather than a tale, the bell pits are very much Leeds history. Excavations under Briggate have found evidence of them, and they were dotted around Leeds. They date from medieval times (and can be found in other areas, such as South Yorkshire and Derbyshire). The pits were dug by hand, a shaft that descended vertically, after which people would dig outward at the bottom, continuing until the pit was in danger of collapse. The miners descended by ladder and the coal would be raised in a bucket. It was small-scale mining before any industrialisation, mining on a very human scale. Generally, pits would be filled in before they fill in, to eliminate danger.

As always, I'm grateful to Kate Lyall Grant and everyone at Crème de la Crime for believing in this book and in Richard Nottingham, to Lynne Patrick, the best editor a writer could ask to have, and to Thom Atkinson, whose insightful critiques improve everything I write. Penny, as ever, shows remarkable patience and incredible support for which I'm constantly thankful. A bow, too, in the direction of Leeds Libraries and Leeds Book Club.

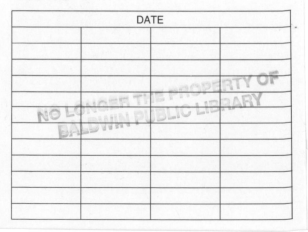

DATE		

NO LONGER THE PROPERTY OF
BALDWIN PUBLIC LIBRARY